RUST

RUST

JULIE MARS

THE PERMANENT PRESS
Sag Harbor, NY 11963

Copyright © 2012 by Julie Mars

All rights reserved. No part of this publication, or parts thereof, may be reproduced in any form, except for the inclusion of brief quotes in a review, without the written permission of the publisher.

For information, address:
The Permanent Press
4170 Noyac Road
Sag Harbor, NY 11963
www.thepermanentpress.com

Library of Congress Cataloging-in-Publication Data

Mars, Julie–
    Rust / Julie Mars.
        pages cm
    ISBN 978-1-57962-226-8
        1. Women artists—Fiction. 2. Welders (Persons)—Fiction.
    3. Fathers and daughters—Fiction. 4. Reunions—Fiction. 5. Self
    realization—Fiction. 6. New Mexico—Fiction. I. Title.

PS3613.A7695R87 2012
813'.6—dc23   2011048266

Printed in the United States of America.

Dedicated, with gratitude, to Joan Schweighardt

ACKNOWLEDGEMENTS

THANK YOU so much to Marty and Judy Shepard of The Permanent Press for supporting this book, of course, but also for thirty-three years of providing a very independent voice in the publishing world. Special thanks to Joan Schweighardt and Whitney Woodward, my writing partners, and to Ryan Henel for welding tips. My deep gratitude to the writers who helped me and the friends who keep me vertical: Robert Farris, Marietta Benevento, L'aura Bodmer, Kathy Brown, Starr Goode, Minrose Gwin, Jennifer Hix, Basia Irland, Marsha Keener, Jami Porter Lara, Michele Meyers, Chris Newbill, Julie Reichert, Laura Robbins, Julie Shigekuni, Mary Starling, Alexcia Trujillo, Ana and Robert Wauneka, and Maggie.

SHE ARRIVED in a nineteen-year-old Dodge Colt Vista, a beater with New York plates, in which the air conditioning was shot and the backseat was wedged up with a two-by-four. She came with a dog, a German shepherd who—she claimed—was a retired drug-sniffer from the NYPD. It was a story she had invented just a few nights before when a motel owner in Amarillo hadn't wanted to let her into a room with such a big dog. She'd looked right into his bloodshot eyes and, as if possessed or perhaps inspired, said, "That's a retired police dog. She's not about to cause any problems." The motel proprietor had glanced out the office door toward the car, where Magpie sat, alert and huge in the driver's seat, laughed, and said, "Okay. Thirty-nine bucks for a single." In the room, which stunk of cigarettes, Margaret had scratched Magpie's ears and encouraged her to sleep on the bed. When she drove on the next morning, the story already seemed plausible. Perhaps it was the emptiness of the landscape. She wanted to fill it with something interesting, and even a lie would suffice.

So, just days later, it was automatic, even natural, for Margaret to say no when the neighborhood children asked to pet her big scary dog. "Not unless I'm right here," she warned. "Never come into this yard unless you see me outside first. Tell your parents." Margaret knew the value of such a myth in such a *barrio*, and she smiled to herself as the children ran off, past skinny shotgun houses with bars on the windows, past dogs chained at the neck to trees, past old people who sat outside their front doors on folding chairs, drinking and smoking and waiting for the evening desert breeze to find its way through the iron security doors into their houses to cool them off.

She stood out, she knew, a skinny Anglo woman, all alone in a *vecino* where all she heard was Spanish. The young girls pushing strollers along the dirt strip at the edge of the street smiled shyly at her, though, and she smiled back as she unloaded three canvas suitcases, a box of oil paints, some kitchenware, two milk crates of books, and not much else. She carried these items one by one into a small adobe house with a big yard shaded by Chinese elm trees and filled with ants, the kind that pack a bad bite, the kind of bite that has you wondering, if you're not local, if you should run fast to the hospital emergency room.

Margaret was an artist, a woman whose high hopes had flattened out on the pavement of New York, where, despite her formidable talent, she couldn't even get a show in an unimportant gallery, where her bartending job had gotten old, and her commute into Manhattan had gotten longer and longer the farther out she moved, one step ahead of the rent hikes. Plus, her interest had evolved from painting, which was manageable in her tiny studio apartments, to sculpture, which wasn't. And not just any form of sculpture. Margaret wanted to weld. She dreamed of acetylene torches and sparks flying in arcs onto some nonflammable flooring.

She saved money, tucking dollar bills, fives, and tens, into books, drawers, and old coffee tins all over her apartment in Far Rockaway. Fresh from work, she stretched out on her old upholstered couch at four-thirty in the morning and perfected a wish list for the next place, her personal paradise on this earth, and the first thing on it was "good junkyards," for Margaret had fallen in love with rust, with old metal that slowly transforms itself to dust after going through a long redheaded phase. It began one winter morning when, walking Magpie along the beach just after dawn, she had found an ancient lock washed up from the sea. It was thick with rust and Margaret immediately imagined the wooden locker that had rotted away around it, setting it free to tumble in the surf for a hundred years. She had peered intensely into the grey waves, thanking them for the gift. When she turned around, the lock cradled in her woolen mitten, fog had formed, and it seemed as if the whole city, which had always been her home, had abruptly disappeared. There is nothing left for me here, she admitted to herself, and she gripped the rusty lock tighter. It was no longer bearable, all the loss, and she decided then and there, as if the deep fog had provided a moment of paradoxical clarity, to move away, to find a new place and start over, fresh. She carried the rusty lock home and placed it on her bedside table. It was the first thing she put in the car on the day she left.

She picked Albuquerque on the spur of the moment when she read in a travel magazine that coyotes still run along the riverbanks right in the middle of the city. Margaret had closed her eyes then, imagining a streak, skinny and yellow-eyed, shooting toward the muddy water of the Rio Grande, as, in the background, downtown buildings pulsated in waves of desert heat. When her lease expired, she collected her dog, her car, and her eight thousand dusty dollars, saved over three long years, and took off. Speeding along the highway at eighty miles per hour in a pack of wild eighteen-wheelers, she noticed a few tendrils of hope starting to sprout, and then a ribbon of fear, and she turned the radio up louder and pressed down harder on the gas.

She had found the tumbledown adobe house near the zoo by accident—turned her head at precisely the right moment to see a small "for rent" sign in the window on a street she happened to turn down while cruising the greenbelt along the river looking for coyotes. From a pay phone in a nearby Diamond Shamrock gas station, she called the landlord, and while she waited for him to arrive, she walked Magpie up one side of the street and down the other. The neighborhood seemed lawless, with beat-up cars on blocks in dusty yards, ranchero music spilling from open doors, and the air weighted with the frenetic speech of seals and monkeys, and the infrequent roar of a bored or angry lion. But next to the house was a cement pad big enough for a one-car garage to have fallen down around it and been carted away. And, just staring in through the gate at a chain-link slider that would keep Magpie in if she remembered to lock it, Margaret imagined a welding tank and torches lined up along the edge of that cement pad. She could build a little shade structure and work out there all spring, summer, and fall. She could fill the dirt in the yard with shapes, all made of rust, and keep on making more. She could fill the whole city if they'd let her.

The house was three times the size of her ex-apartment, and she felt deep relief the moment she opened the door. The walls inside were a foot thick and rippled, like pillows; they had *nichos* carved out where she placed her rusty lock and her shell collection. She shined up the old *saltillo* tile floors with Mop & Glow, whispering "Viva Mexico" as she worked. Without knowing why, she understood the rhythms of this house, this city. She quickly learned to step around black widow spiders in the yard, and, mercilessly, she yanked up the sprawling green ground ferns with their pretty yellow flowers before they produced thorns, called goats' heads, that got embedded in Magpie's feet. Without effort, she remembered to draw the curtains tightly closed as the first rays of blazing western sun slanted into her living room, just after the monkeys in the zoo began to howl and the stray dogs disappeared off the street into unknown shady places for the long, hot afternoon.

When the man from the phone company finally arrived to install her phone, he brought the Yellow Pages, and she pored through the junkyard listings until she spotted an ad for Coronado Wrecking. The very next day she drove there, straight down Broadway into the throbbing sun. She made a left onto a dirt road that led her toward twenty-seven acres of junk piled into the sand dunes along the interstate highway, and she thought, Yes. Immediately, she made a three-point turn and sped to Home Depot where she bought four sturdy five-gallon buckets, and from then on she spent her days at Coronado Wrecking. Alone among mountains of junked engines, obsolete machinery, and esoteric construction equipment, she used her pliers and screwdrivers to pry off rusty parts, loading her buckets until she could barely lift them to the scale in the office, and paying pennies a pound.

She carried the buckets back to her cement pad, spilling them out with a sense of destiny. Then she laid out the pieces, a fine film of dust—rust-colored—settling into her hair, which was long and black, just like every other woman's in this *barrio*. She forgot about looking for a job or finding a kitchen table. She forgot to unpack her pots and pans. She forgot about everything, except walking her dog, a habit she had had for eight years, every day, three times a day, no matter what.

Which is precisely what she was doing when she rounded the corner onto Barelas Road and happened to catch a bolt of blue-tipped lightning in her peripheral vision. From inside the dark cavern of Garcia's Automotive Repair Shop on the corner, just three blocks from her house, she saw shooting sparks and she floated toward them, a woman in a serious trance. A car, a low rider painted green and gold, was up on the lift, and a man, strong armed and tattooed, stood beneath it and worked a torch, lifting the flame up and into the underbelly of that car. Margaret stood at the door, her toes crossing the line where the bright sun and the inside shade met, and a great, overwhelming lust formed in her. She wanted her fingertips to extend, to incorporate fire in them. She wanted heat, melting molten metal. She wanted to sever what was and reconstruct it into something vivid and original.

The man wore green mechanic's coveralls with the sleeves cut off at the shoulders and a nametag embroidered with "Rico" on the pocket. He had a ponytail with a streak of silver woven through it, and the muscles in his arms had such fine definition, so many curves and shadows, that they looked like they'd been pasted onto him from some younger man. He turned toward her, aware through some ghetto-inspired psychic sense, of a strange presence too close. When he saw her outline, a small white woman with hair like pitch and a face that rivers of weariness had flooded through, her and her big dog outlined in the sunbeams so a halo was created, he thought for a moment she was the Virgin of Guadalupe come to Garcia's Automotive Repair for a personal visitation—maybe to punish him for the "In Guad We Trust" bumper sticker he had on his truck as a little joke to himself, for Rico never trusted anything or anyone. But now he wanted to fling his welding torch into the corner and get down on his knees in front of this woman. Her lust hit him like a fist. It had been a long time since a woman looked at him with such desire. It made him straighten his shoulders and turn his hips to face her, head on.

PERHAPS YOU could say Rico's hips, turned like that toward a woman, had grown rusty. They no longer moved with the rhythm that wrapped itself around a man and a woman like rodeo rope and mercilessly yanked them off their feet. His wife, Rosalita, had turned away from him four years before, slowly frozen over until all he could do in bed was stare at her back, or rather at the prim nightgown that covered it, and listen to her breathe. He was not a man to push himself on her when she said no. And the no had grown impenetrable, like cement, and finally he turned away himself. He was still in shock, knocked down flat even, by the way things change over time.

They had brought three daughters into this world, and before the youngest had even purchased her first lace bra, Rosalita had ebbed away from him, like the sea when it sucks itself out to create a killer wave. And for Rico, having a cold wife, a wife who still looked good, who still moved in those enticing ways that made her bottom jiggle, this was the wave that kept him drowning, over and over, for four years now, never having enough air in his lungs to decide what to do next.

And the *vecino* was changing, too. Anglo people arrived with their purebred dogs on leashes and water bottles hooked onto their waistbands in specially made holders. They walked along the banks of the Rio, where, two decades before, he himself had dug up the *terrones* for his house and brought them home by wheelbarrow. The sons and daughters of the *viejos*, his neighbors, sold out to white people the minute their parents died, moving like sheep to subdivisions on the West Mesa, where the houses were new and came equipped with dishwashers and microwave ovens, where streets did not flood during the monsoon season and crowing roosters were not allowed.

There he was, forty-three years old, traveling two miles to his shop and two miles home six days a week. The shop had been his father's, a corner garage with two work bays and a little office in which, over time, he accumulated a mini-fridge, a hot plate, a desk with four drawers, an office chair on wheels, and two folding chairs. His mother had signed it over to him two weeks after his father was laid to rest, dead at fifty-six of a blood clot that hit his brain like an atom bomb.

Rico was a man who felt caged up, like a murderer serving a life sentence in a bad jail, the kind they have in Mexico where you pray to die. Many times he looked at his body, where the skin was so tight—even now that he felt old—that the veins were like road maps; and he could almost, but not quite, see what it was underneath it that wanted to break out and make a run for it but couldn't. It was another man completely, one who never fell for the lie that wives and babies and places by the river were worth a goddamn. It was a man who turned his back on that two mile stretch from his *casa* to his shop, who had the balls to take off in his youth, maybe join the navy or find some war to fight in, maybe disappear into the dry hills of Mexico and take peyote morning, noon, and night. He felt this strongly, but he told no one, not even Rosalita, even after all these years. Long ago, when he and Rosalita were young, they spent every weekend night dancing in Enrique's bar on Isleta and then thrashed around the bedroom like two demons from hell. Now, she was a ghost, floating through the kitchen in her long nightgown. What was the use of talking to a woman who sucked herself so far inward that she never even thought to glance in his direction?

One night, three years before, the day his middle daughter, Ana, had graduated from Rio Grande High, the first in the family line who ever finished, Rico had come home from the ceremony all shook up. His shirt had wet circles under the armpits, and he felt the blood in his neck like a snake about to strike. In the dark, he ran through the *bosque*, ran along the riverbank like a coyote, until he fell into the dirt and cried like a baby. He could still feel the loss of everything, the nothingness of his life, in the bones of his wrists and hands when they held the torch. But when he came home that night, his boots caked with mud and his new shirt ruined by the red clay of the riverbank, Rico had made a decision, and he had stuck to it ever since. He would keep order in his life, despite this part inside, this madman, who wanted to get out and tear up everything. In his shop, his tools were clean and oiled. They each had a specific place, and they were in it, always. The corners were swept, the weeds that grew up through the cracks in the sidewalk out front were pulled, and even his desk was organized, with slots prepared for receipt books, pencils, pens, and phone numbers. At home it was the same. Even Rosalita teased him about the way he hung up his shirts, always buttoning the top button so they looked alive on the hanger. For years now, Rico had just moved along, from one thing he had to do to the next, like a train across the mesa.

So he was taken by surprise by what stormed over him when he saw that woman in the doorway of his shop. In that moment, seeing her in the arc of light, he felt his life caving in, an old mine shaft that intended to collapse no matter how many miners were still inside. But in another way, he felt it open up.

"CAN YOU teach me to weld?" she asked, her voice not much more than an echo.

"I can teach you anything you want to learn," he replied, and the power in these words centered itself right in his balls, and he felt like a king.

"I want to learn to weld," she said. "I already have the parts laid out in my yard."

"What kind of metal?" Rico knew women. He knew they couldn't tell the difference between a piece of steel and a piece of aluminum, that they thought all the metals in the world would melt before the torch. He knew that women lived in a dream world, that they never saw the truth of the simplest thing, like what metals will bond together and which ones won't, or how to tell what was hot enough and what wasn't.

"Iron," she said. "I think."

"I better take a look," Rico said. It sounded casual, as if the words were skidding across the ice that once in a great while formed on the river, pretending there was no dirty water underneath.

"Could you?" she asked, and, as if she owned the place, she quickly moved to his desk, and wrote down her address on his notepad. The whole time, that big dog watched Rico, her eyes communicating in the way only a big dog's can. They said, *Stay back, old man. Stay back.*

"Does that dog bite?" he asked.

"Only when I tell her to. She's very well trained, an ex-police dog." She said this over her shoulder so automatically that he almost believed it. But that would probably make this woman an ex-policewoman, and Rico could tell from the curve of her hips that that was not true. He could tell by the way she didn't look around, never swept her eyes toward the bays or the closed door to the bathroom behind her.

"Can you come by today? Later? After work?" she asked, and her voice was breathless, as if she wanted to burn in the fire between them.

"Yeah. About six," he said.

15

"Great. I'll wait for you."

I'll bet you will, he thought. I'll bet you've been waiting for me for your whole life. This thought arrived like an avalanche. It carried him away, tumbled him head first into the desire she was not able to hide. He looked at the slip of paper she'd left behind. Her name was Margaret. Rico moved to the doorway to watch her walk to the corner and turn left.

All afternoon, he worked his torch with the precision and focus of an assassin. He imagined Margaret on fire beneath him, reminding him how passion burned, how it scorched the human body from the inside out and left it wanting more. At the end of the day, he didn't wash up. He didn't change out of his coveralls. He didn't call Rosalita to tell her he'd be late. He went straight to Margaret, dirty.

When he pulled up in front of her house, she was on her hands and knees on the cement pad, her rear end aimed toward the driveway, and he felt himself get hard. He climbed out of his truck not caring if she or anybody else saw the bulge in the front of his coveralls, and he walked toward her. There she was, surrounded by a hundred old rusty parts, things he knew she had no idea how to use. Carburetors and condensation pumps, tie bolts and butterfly nuts, oil pans and heavy duty towing chain. Her face was the color of apricots when they first appear on the trees in May, but her eyes, which were green, blazed at him, like the eyes of a cornered animal.

She sat back on her heels. "What? No torch?" she said and she smiled a little, like they had a big secret between them already.

"I got it right here for you, mama," he said, though he didn't mean to. They were words he had heard his older brother, Fernando, use on girls a long, long time ago, magic words that melted the girls from the *vecino*, causing them to lower their eyes in a way that drew Fernando toward them. But they were not his words. Truthfully, though, standing not ten feet from her, it had crossed his mind that, with her squatting down like that, she was at just the right height to blow him to kingdom come, and he had to resist the urge to reach for the zipper of his coveralls.

Rico saw it when the words hit her, the way they knocked her speechless and disgusted her, and in that moment if he could have moved fast enough, he would have made a joke of himself, given her his most devilish smile, and saved everything. But he was too slow, always had been, his whole life, and he saw the moment pass, on its way to rust, just like everything else.

"Sorry, buddy," she said at last, her voice instantly drained of any color. "I just want to learn to weld."

And here was another opening, another place to step in and resurrect the moment, but now his face burned with shame and foolishness. "I'm sorry, too," he said, and he meant it, but it came out of his mouth with a macho edge, like words he wanted to cut into her with a knife. So he turned and left before it got any worse, and the last thing he saw was an old tractor fender in the shape of a rusty crescent moon, which she seemed, because of the angle at which it rested against the cement pad, to be squatting in, just waiting to stand up and be counted.

1974

H_E WAKES up to the roar of one thousand men, murmuring, chanting, talking, yelling. Walled in.

This is a nightmare, he thinks. Please.

But the way his shoulder aches, pressed as it is into the dirt, and his shirt, which had bunched up around his neck like a noose when he'd finally collapsed and rolled to the edge of this room, these things tell him it is real. He had arrived in the back of a truck, fifty men packed in like animals. They were chained to one another at the ankles. Only a few were able to shove their way to the long benches that lined either side of the truck bed to sit. It had been a long ride. Dusty. He had kept his head lowered, refusing to look through the open sides of the truck at the city, then its edges, and then the green countryside.

Finally, they had spilled out. They were pushed through a gate.

Into this room. A pen, really. One word above the door was in English: "Processing."

He has not slept for three days. When he closes his eyes at last, not caring what happens to him anymore, no matter what it is, everything stops and the world goes black. He does not know how many hours have passed when he opens his eyes again.

He faces the concrete wall, a whitewashed wall that has turned dark grey. The sun, beating down from overhead, cuts a dividing line across the dirt floor. The heat feels like a hot iron pressed against his back. He pulls his shirt down and sits up. Two feet away from him, a filthy man in rags squats to shit in the dirt. The smell sickens him.

I cannot do this, he thinks.

MARGARET COULD feel Rico's heat, how it switched from steam to burning shame in an instant, how out of control he was, as if a flash fire had ignited inside him and was burning him to the ground, right at the edge of her concrete pad with all those rusty parts strewn far and near. She felt herself detach, her calmness moving inward while a more engaged self suddenly floated upward, far above the scene, coming to rest in one of the highest branches of the Chinese elms, the one that shaded her work area and had the "No Trespassing" sign nailed to it. She had all the time she needed in that one split second to evaluate the words he had said, and she could have chosen to reach out to him with a kind, soothing remark, or even a witticism that dispersed his comment into little remnants, like fireworks on their way to nothingness. Or she could have chosen to stare at the ground, as if she were digging a hole with her eyes and burying the moment in it. She was a bartender, after all, adept at sidestepping arrows and darts of sexuality, letting them fly past her no matter how excellent the aim.

But something had shifted deep inside of Margaret as she tore out of the east, slipped silently through the factory towns of Ohio, crossed the Mississippi with hardly a glance to the right or left, and then stampeded over the plains, the engine of her Dodge Colt Vista straining like a horse forced to run too far too fast. So focused was she on the highway ahead, and then the center line disappearing in one long stripe behind her, that she hardly noticed the fine mist that rose from her pores like a tiny rainstorm in reverse. Perhaps she mistook it for sweat, because the car was hot, hot as hell, so hot she wore two bandanas to catch the drips, one around her neck and one around her hairline, which also helped keep her long black ponytail from blowing into her eyes. Yet she never passed a wrist across her forehead, never wiped her palms on her summer drawstring pants. What seeped upward from deep inside through her skin, or perhaps was sucked out of her body by the high speed, the heat, and the intensity of the highway, were tears she never shed. These tears, frozen inside her for so long, melted in the heat, and washed away her willingness to give even one more inch.

Margaret had given inches and feet, yards and miles, for thirteen years behind the bar. And the night she cashed out for the last time and then dumped out her tip jar on the wooden tabletop in the back booth of the Stereophonic Lounge and counted up the quarters and dollar bills, it had hit her like a sledgehammer, how much she had given. She had never allowed herself to acknowledge it before, what it cost her every night to smile, banter, pretend that every man who sidled up to the bar was magnetic, defer to every woman, play the game of bartender. She'd had her last drink—a margarita made from freshly squeezed limes—served to her with fanfare by Mitch, the owner of the Lounge and a good friend in a casual way, feeling as if she were in a slow motion car wreck, a feeling that persisted on the drive home and made her wary of changing lanes or taking the curves of the BQE at high speed.

There she was at thirty-seven, five years past the last defensible moment, in her own opinion, that a woman should be a bartender, and what did she have to show for it? Her small savings, some good bar stories, a few intimate moments or months with musicians who had gone on to become great and sometimes famous, who, she was certain, hadn't thought of her in years. She had a storage bin in Queens packed with paintings and drawings, some of which she knew were garbage and some of which she thought were worthy of a wall in the Whitney, a whole show perhaps, though she knew she'd never get one. They documented the underworld she lived in, had always lived in, ever since she was a child, shuffled off at five years old to live with her grandfather while her parents backpacked for a year through India. They never came home. Even the cards, letters, and little gifts—like tiny elephants carved from onyx and gauze shirts with mirrors embroidered into the edges—stopped arriving in the mailbox.

Her grandfather, Donny, a bartender himself at an Irish joint called the Bit O' Blarney on the waterfront in lower Manhattan, enlisted the help of the State Department to find them, but the trail went cold in Goa, and after a few years he gave up. "They probably got into drugs, honey. Vincent was a big hash head, and, really, your mother was, too, after she got wrapped up with him," he told her, years later, when she suddenly, at age sixteen, expressed a burning desire to know the truth. "Over there, you get into something like that, there's no telling what could happen. We'll just never know. That's how it is."

So she was used to important things disappearing: her mother, with her raven hair and restless energy; her father, who, she remembered vaguely, was a painter like her, hanging canvas after canvas on the brick walls of some loft with grimy windows near Chinatown where they'd all lived long ago; Donny, who died of a heart attack, keeled over on the job, before she'd even turned nineteen. Radical change seemed normal to her. Lives combusted, singeing the edges, even of memories.

Which, perhaps, was part of the reason why Margaret often described herself, when someone would seriously ask, as a person who'd spent her whole life sitting on a hot stove, trying to get off. She also felt her skin was too tight. And she was one of those rare people who sensed, very genuinely, that she had somehow gotten in her own way just by being born. No matter how hard she tried, she could never sidestep herself and get free. All this was normal for Margaret. She lived with it like other people live with emphysema or rheumatoid arthritis. There was no point in asking, Why me?

She watched Rico as he turned and crossed her yard, his ponytail picking up the rays of sun and turning it shades of blue and purple along the black strands. He hurried, as if he were running away from something terrible. His back, in his mechanic's coveralls, was straight to the point of stiffness, and she knew without looking that his hands were clenched by his sides, that they had to pry themselves open to reach for the door handle on his truck or insert the key into the ignition. The engine turned over. It was quiet, perfectly tuned. He pulled away slowly, as if caution were his middle name.

"So much for that," she said to Magpie, who was sprawled out on her side nearby. Magpie's eyes drifted toward the street, where Rico's truck had just disappeared. They paused there, as if they could see something more than just thin air.

RICO DROVE to the corner, where there was a stop sign, which he didn't need to see to feel like stopping. He wanted to stop everything. Sometimes, when he was working on a car, brazing a rusty exhaust pipe or welding a lift kit bracket onto the frame of a '92 Bronco, a sensation would come over him, like the shade that creeps over a man taking a nap in a hammock when a cloud passes overhead and blocks the sun. There was darkness to it, and a change in temperature. The change was subtle, but for the colder. Whenever this would happen, he would stop what he was doing because he knew this sensation, whatever it was, dulled his concentration and made him sloppy.

Rico looked both ways, carefully, and then crossed the intersection and pulled to the curb. He had both hands on the steering wheel, his eyes peering through the windshield as if he were gunning it along I-40 with the whole desert spread out before him. In his peripheral vision, he saw an old woman raking up last year's leaves in her tiny front yard. She worked slowly, as if it was fine to take all day to finish the job. She never glanced up from the work at hand.

What had just happened? Rico wanted to take some time to backtrack. He had a need to get the events of the day into some form of order, make some kind of accurate map of them, so he could think clearly. It was better for him to nail it all down. If he didn't do it now, it would only get harder. She had come into his shop. She had asked him to teach her to weld. He had made a mistake, thinking it was him she wanted. It was the fire, the torch, the skill it takes to wield the fire and the torch that she was after. She had been clear, but he had not seen it.

He dropped his hands off the wheel into his lap. It was a mistake, no more, no less. Still, if he had been right, if he had shown up in her yard and she had led him inside, taken him into her arms, and acted out every one of those fantasies he'd been having all afternoon, he would have stayed with her forever, poured his heart and soul into making her happy, fucked her till neither of them could see straight. This was something he had no idea he was ready for. In all the years since he and Rosalita had fused together, he had never, not once, been with another woman. He'd had chances, but he'd turned away, which he thought was the right thing to do. But now, something had shifted. He hadn't even known there was a shift, but it had already happened and he had proof, how he had rushed from work directly to Margaret's house, got a hard-on just looking at her, made a comment that no decent woman could overlook.

She had responded in a way he could best describe as neutral. "Sorry buddy, I just want to learn to weld," she had said, and there was no mockery in it, no accusation, no judgment, and no mercy. And he had said, "I'm sorry too," which was a perfectly respectable thing to say, the only right thing to say, but it had come out all wrong, and he saw, in that moment, his whole big plan, his whole cock-of-the-walk fantasy, crack and shatter, and all he could do was turn around and walk away.

Nothing terrible had happened, and yet he felt terrible, parked on the street, too shaken up to drive, as if he had just run over a dog and was trying to bring himself to get out of the truck and face the carnage. He glanced up. The mountains in the east formed a jagged line—up down up down—across the horizon, and the sky that dipped down to meet them was so blue it looked thick, the way a five-gallon bucket of paint looks when you first pry off the lid. He had lived here, in Albuquerque, his whole life, seen those mountains glow pink at sunset, pink like the watermelon they were named for, every day. He was used to skies like paint and mountains bursting with colors and mesas so flat they looked man-made, and the dirty Rio, and the dull brown dirt and smoky green sage of the high desert, stretched in all directions. He was used to the smell of the chiles roasting in late August and, in the winter, the piñon smoke from the chimneys of the fireplaces and kivas all around the city. He was used to work, and routine, and the way it felt to raise three daughters and live with a cold wife, but today he had learned something new about himself. Put an opportunity in front of him, even one he made up himself out of misunderstood signals, and he would go for it, tackle it, throw everything away for just one chance to change it all.

"You're a volcano, Rico, *mi hijo*," his mother, Elena, had teased him when he was a little boy. "*Todo por dentro*, everything under. Calm and quiet on the top, maybe a little rumbling now and then, but underneath, *el fuego*." It had made him proud to be compared to a volcano, capable of erupting and spewing boulders, burning lava, ashes, and smoke into the atmosphere. Now it worried him. His mother lived in a little *casita* he had built for her on the three-quarter acre he owned on Riverside Drive. She was sixty-eight years old now, skinny, and almost blind from diabetes that went undiagnosed and untreated for way too long. Elena lived a small life, inside her *casita* and the yard. She seemed much older than her years. She didn't complain. She prayed the rosary twice a day, and waited for her dead husband to come and get her.

Now, sitting alone in his truck, Rico wanted to talk to her. Since her eyes had clouded over, it had become easier and easier to tell his mother the truth of his life, something he had kept from her, even the everyday, routine problems, for two decades. But when the chill had come over Rosalita, he first waited for it to pass, then tried for one long year to warm her up, and only when he gave up did he let himself out of his *casa* to pick his way through the sagebrush and deadly nightshade to his mother's door. She was sitting in a stream of morning sunlight at her kitchen table having a cup of mint tea.

"Elena, *mi madre*," he had said, his way of addressing her for years now, as he came in, and she had turned in the direction of his voice and answered intently, "What's wrong, *mi hijo?*"

"Rosalita . . . she doesn't want me anymore. In bed I'm talking about," Rico had said, just like that. This from a man who had never even mentioned when he came close to losing the house during a rocky spell in his garage; who never told her, or anyone else, how his heart shattered when his oldest daughter, Lucy, got pregnant at sixteen, just like Rosalita had; who hand-built Elena's little *casita* and moved her in there over the protests of his own wife who didn't want a mother-in-law, even a good one, in the family compound.

Rico had stood in the doorway, not even taking a step into the kitchen. He thought he might cry, but no tears came. And he knew he wouldn't pound the walls and scare his mother.

"Come in, *siéntate*," she said. "Sit with me for a while."

Rico dropped into the chair next to her, and she reached over and placed her hand on his forearm. That's when the tears rushed in, like a violent storm. He had collapsed over his folded arms, wedging his mother's fingers in, and while he sobbed and sobbed, mostly silently, he felt the warmth of her touch like an electrical current, pulsing into him in a steady way that after a long while calmed him down.

"Wait a little while," she finally said. "Women go through things. Just wait a little while and see what happens."

That was three years ago. Nothing had happened since. Until today.

Rico reached for the ignition key and turned it. He checked his rearview mirror. He could still see the corner of Margaret's house, her mailbox, and one of those big trees in her yard, as he pulled out into the street.

1974

NOTHING. THAT'S what the days and nights are filled with. A thick, airless nothing that makes him afraid to move too much. An idea has developed in his mind: to preserve his sanity, if such a thing is even possible, he needs to stay completely still, his back pressed hard into the grey concrete wall. So hard that he might leave a permanent imprint in the shape of his upper body.

He draws his knees up, folds his arms on top of them, and rests his head there, where he can stare down into the dirt. After a while, it begins to swim before his eyes. He watches intently.

Molecules of brown dirt, helpless and trapped.

Everything helpless and everything trapped.

THE NEXT morning, Margaret and Magpie took a long walk by the river, and they saw their first coyote. They had gotten an early start, maybe six-thirty, plenty of time to get in three brisk miles and still have an hour, before the sun got too hot, for Margaret to collect sticks and stones and assemble them into a spontaneous sculpture on the riverbank, a pastime she had fallen into on their very first walk in the *bosque*. Magpie tended to find a shady spot under some giant cottonwood and sprawl as Margaret worked. Despite her size and her ferocious look, Magpie was a gentle dog—Buddha Dog, Margaret sometimes called her—and perhaps a little lazy. If there was ever an opportunity to stretch out and snooze, she took it. So when Margaret happened to glance in her direction and saw her sitting up, alert, her ears moving like radar to tune into some sound in the brush, she took note.

The *bosque* all along the river was designated as open space, forever wild, by the state of New Mexico. Margaret, who grew up in the city parks of New York, was astonished that the stretch of it by her little house was often empty in the early morning, no joggers swerving around her, no yuppies pushing high-tech strollers, no bums sleeping it off. She unhooked Magpie's leash and they strolled along feeling like people may have felt when the world was less crowded and therefore less violent. But she had her years of wariness behind her, and she stopped what she was doing and followed Magpie's gaze, reaching into her pocket for her keys, lacing them through her fingers like a weapon which she would use if it came to that.

But instead of a man, bent on causing trouble, she saw the coyote, or rather its head barely visible through the leaves and the splashing sunshine. Come out, let me see you, she thought, though she didn't say a word. Instinctively, she knew that to try to make a friend of a coyote was wrong. Coyotes needed their distance from all humans. To learn to trust even one was a mistake. But she dropped to the ground, just sat there, her gaze focused just beyond the coyote so even eye contact was not an issue. Magpie remained alert, and Margaret noticed that there in that little triangle—her dog, herself, and a wild creature—she felt happier than she had in years, so alive in this moment, so sure that she was exactly where she needed to be, doing just the right thing.

The coyote moved forward into a small open space, gave them one more disinterested look, and took off downriver at a fast trot. Magpie's head swiveled to follow, and after a few seconds, she dropped back down to the earth and sighed, as if the whole interlude had been a distraction from her nap and she was glad that it was over. Margaret closed her eyes and breathed it in, that final image of the scrawny untamed yellow dog, the way he fit into this landscape, matched it in color and even vibration so closely that he simply vanished. She felt a little fire had been lit in her heart, and it was warming her blood.

She added a long dry stick, twisted and gray, and a few black seedpods she didn't recognize to her sculpture, and wrapped part of it in reeds from the river until it felt finished. Then she and Magpie walked home before the traffic heading over the bridge toward Avenida César Chávez had even revved up. When she got in, Margaret made a pot of strong coffee, and while it was brewing she was suddenly seized with a desire to hang up the paintings she had shipped from New York. The wooden crate, which had arrived three days ago, left in the yard while she had been at Coronado Wrecking, still remained in the same place—too bulky and heavy to move inside by herself. She went outside and dug through the tools she had stashed under the front seat of her Dodge, finally wrapping her fingers around the crowbar she had packed for just this purpose. She pried the lid off the crate and carried the paintings inside, one by one. Having no success at driving a nail into the adobe, she leaned them up against the walls in the places where they would later hang. She sat in the middle of the living room floor and looked around the perimeter of the room. So much of her life was suggested in the colors and textures, the images and backgrounds. She could get very lost in them.

On impulse, Margaret picked up the phone and dialed Nicolas Brandao, her first painting teacher at the School of Visual Arts, where she had studied for seven years. He'd been a part-timer then, barely out of art school himself, though now he was a full professor—and respected in the art world of New York too, which was no easy thing. His machine picked up on the second ring.

"Nick? It's Margaret Shaw. I'm actually calling from—"

"Margaret, hello." His voice sounded sleepy, though it was close to eleven in New York. "Calling from where?"

"New Mexico. Albuquerque. I moved here."

"Really." It sounded like a statement, not a question or a verification of fact.

"Really." A few seconds of silence passed, fairly comfortably. "When? What brought this on?"

"A couple weeks ago. And I don't know. It was an impulse."

"Shit, I wish you'd called me before you left. I would've tried to talk you out of it."

"I know. But that didn't happen."

They both laughed, and Nick said, "Just one more of the many things that didn't happen between us." Margaret heard him inhale sharply and knew he had just lit a cigarette. She could picture him settled into his old leather reclining chair, positioned so he could see a small section of the Manhattan Bridge and a patch of the East River through the buildings outside his window. "So how's it going?"

"Good. Different. I feel inspired. I want to learn to weld."

"And your painting?"

"Back burner for the moment, I think."

"Margaret . . ."

"Don't start, Nick."

"You have so much talent. When are you going to give yourself a chance?"

"That's what I'm doing in New Mexico. Taking my chances. I'm okay, Nick. Be happy for me."

"Well . . . if I must." He took another long, audible drag on his cigarette.

They had never slept together, not once in the nineteen years since they first met. Both had wanted to, but never at the same time. They were circling close in the early days, but then Donny died, and Margaret had gone into a lengthy tailspin that seriously scared Nick. Just as she was recovering, Nick fell in love and got married, a mistake it took him nine years to undo. Margaret had refused all advances during that time, a matter of principle. Meanwhile, his art star had begun to ascend, along with his ego, and Margaret, with her blue collar mistrust of sudden success, found him pretentious and phony. By the time he snapped back to reality, she was involved with a saxophone player. And so it went.

Once, long ago, he had introduced her to a gallery owner, a woman famous for jump-starting art careers. This woman had encouraged her, talked seriously with her for a whole hour, but ultimately said no, which crushed Margaret. It made no difference when Nick reprimanded her. "You know how many galleries rejected me before I got a show. Thirty-one! In three cities! So stop acting like you're the only artist who ever got knocked down. Get up."

But Margaret couldn't.

It had been hard labor for her to put herself forward, collect her slides, and present herself at a gallery so revered by painters she barely felt she had the right to enter it. The owner, a woman in her late forties, wore a Dutch boy haircut and a pair of delicate Italian boots that obviously cost more than Margaret made in a whole month of full-time bartending. She had led Margaret into her office, where a projector was permanently set up. An assistant had come in to pour two glasses of sparkling water and drop Margaret's slides into the tray. The gallery owner dimmed the lights using a switch built into her desktop. Margaret felt actual physical pain, a deep ache shaped like doubt, press into her throat as the first slide came up.

"Very Brice Marden," said the woman. But all Margaret saw projected on the wall was her breath and blood.

"I have my influences, like any painter," Margaret replied, her fingers closing into little fists in her lap.

"I see that," said the gallery owner as she clicked through three more slides. "These are somewhat derivative, Margaret." She stopped to sip her water. "Are they early work?"

Margaret forced herself to remain calm. She held her ground, knowing that art was all she had, and she could not let this businesswoman, not an artist herself after all, take it, or make it shrink and fade. But when she'd left the gallery, she'd had to lean against a nearby building for balance. The streets felt mushy and the faces of the trendy passersby were mocking. All she had to hold onto was the handle of her black leather portfolio, an expensive gift from Nick. Margaret was a person who needed—desperately—a yes, not a no. Her whole life was a wall of no: no mother, no father, no brothers, no sisters, no husband, no children, no Donny, no money to speak of, no sense of direction, no degree, no surprises, no sense of belonging, no belief in herself, no idea of the point, no power, no air in her lungs. And now, no art show, either.

It was too much for her, that's all. And, given her reaction to that very polite rejection, she had to add fragile and weak to the rest of her list of problems, and that slim chance of a yes somewhere in the future wasn't worth it. Yet she stayed in touch with Nick, and he stayed in touch with her, for years— just in case. Just in case so many things.

They talked for twenty minutes, Margaret sprawled on her couch with her leg flung over the back and the sun streaming in, before she was distracted by a knock on the door. She looked out the kitchen window, and there was Rico.

ON THE way home from the incident at Margaret's the night before, Rico had stopped at Modelo's Take Out on Second Street and bought a whole bagful of tamales. He enjoyed being the provider of these little treats that made everyone happy and kept Rosalita out of the kitchen after a long day on her feet at Albuquerque High, where she worked in food prep in the school cafeteria. The aroma of green chile filled the cab of his truck with a certain type of security. It kept his mind off the trouble he felt brewing inside him, despite his efforts to make sense of it all and thereby make it disappear.

The silver lace and the scarlet trumpet vines on the chain-link fences along Riverside Drive had filled out, but not yet reached the point of spilling over. Rico liked that moment, the last days before the long spurt of chaotic growth inspired by the summer monsoons turned everything ragged at the edges. He slowed down and waved as his neighbor's son, Wilfredo, a lively boy of eleven who reminded Rico of himself at that age, trotted by on the old nag that had lived on this block just one year less than Rico. Wilfredo rode that horse bareback along the river every evening, winter or summer. He was a boy with a big imagination who probably thought Negrita was a black stallion instead of a prime candidate for the glue factory.

Rico drove through his gate, noting that both Rosalita's and his daughter Maribel's cars were parked under the *ramada* he had built for shade. He pulled in next to them and turned off the engine. Sometimes living surrounded by women—his wife, three daughters, a granddaughter, and his mother—Rico felt comforted; other days he felt smothered. Such loveliness came with a high price. For every time he received an unexpected kiss on the cheek, a door was closed along the hallway and behind it was a daughter sobbing over something inconsequential. For every time they sat at the dinner table, all together, and he looked from one pretty face to the next— four generations represented right there in his kitchen—the bathroom door was closed while somebody primped behind it, for hours it seemed, sending him outside to do his business in an old outhouse on the far corner of his property, attached to an ancient one-horse barn-shed that, thank God, he had not knocked down when he bought the place. Sometimes he felt that marriage and family were nothing more than a long row of closed doors, blocking him from something far more interesting. When those moods came upon him, he found some work to do outside and just sweated it out.

"*Tamales para todos*," he called out, as he maneuvered himself around a tricycle that his granddaughter, Jessica, had abandoned next to the front door. "*Vámonos. Let's eat.*" This produced a flurry of activity: Rosalita quickly setting out silverware and plates, Maribel heading out the back door to collect her *abuelita*, Lucy rounding up Jessica and putting her in a high chair, and Ana closing up the big nursing textbook she was studying on the couch and slowly making her way toward the kitchen. Rico washed his hands in the kitchen sink, and dropped into his chair at the head of the table as all the women in his life settled like dust around him.

But his mind was elsewhere.

It kept drifting back to the moment when Margaret had appeared in the doorway of his shop, how the sun had conspired to place a halo around her; and he had felt, though he didn't articulate it, that his destiny had finally found him. And later, the way she looked, so cute in the middle of all those useless engine parts laid out like precious gems. Her hair was black, her skin was pale with a few freckles even, and her eyes were as green as the leaves on the Chinese elm trees above her. He thought she was beautiful. So what if she looked half worn-out. Lots of women did.

The platter of tamales was passed from person to person, a green salad appeared on the table, and diet soft drinks were poured into colorful plastic glasses from two different sixty-four ounce bottles. When this group got ready to eat—before the chewing started—the clatter was intense, and sometimes Rico experienced it like a fog of noise over the table. Just as it would begin to clear, one voice would rise up, and it was always Rosalita's and she always said the same thing. Rico knew it was coming. "So how was everybody's day?" she would ask, her voice animated as if she really wanted to know, and maybe she did. But tonight Rico didn't want to answer, and before the fog had even begun to subside, he blurted out, "Who believes in destiny?"

To Rico, it seemed as if all activity stopped for a heartbeat, the platter pausing in midair, glasses freeze-framed on their way to lips, even the disk jockey on the oldies radio station that Rosalita always had blaring took a little silent swallow before he started up again. And they all turned their heads to face him, even little Jessica.

"Rico," Rosalita said with a curt little laugh, "eat your tamale." But Maribel, who was optimistic by nature, her eyes wide, asked, "Papi, did you win the Roadrunner Cash?" and he had to shake his head and say, "Sorry, *mi hija*, not today," to which she replied, "Shit," and everybody laughed.

"I believe in destiny," Lucy announced, somewhat urgently.

"You've got your destiny right there in that high chair," Rosalita said, and Rico didn't want to admit he heard bitterness in the words, but he did. He saw Lucy turn toward her mother, saw the way the blood moved into her neck, turning it crimson in just a few seconds. But before she could say a word in retaliation, Elena leaned over and kissed Jessica on the top of her head and said, "She's everybody's destiny," and Rosalita looked down into her plate and focused all her attention on cutting her tamale.

"Why do you ask, Papi?" This was from Ana, who was looking at him curiously, as if he were a specimen in one of those medical laboratories at UNM that all the nursing students had to march through from time to time in their biology classes.

"I was thinking about it today while I was working," he said truthfully. "Why do things happen the way they do?"

"You going philosophical on us, Papi?" Ana asked.

"It's a fair question," Rico replied. Part of him regretted even bringing the matter up, but a stronger part wanted to push it farther, so he added, "I want to know. Who here believes in destiny—besides Lucy?"

"It's official," Ana said in a loud stage whisper. "Papi's in his midlife crisis." Everyone laughed, and Rico did, too.

"What's going to happen to me?" he asked.

"I'll look it up in my psych book and get back to you," Ana responded.

"God is in charge," Maribel suddenly contributed, a strange intensity in her voice. "There's no such thing as destiny, just God's will."

"And I think everyone has the same destiny," Elena said. "The grave."

Silence descended over the table like a light snowfall.

"Elena, *mi madre*, you sure know how to wreck a party," said Rico, though he said it with a big smile in his voice.

But that night, long after everyone had gone to bed, Rico stretched out on the couch, and for the first time he thought about dying. His father had died young. His mother seemed to be well on the way, and she was only in her sixties. What words would he want etched into his gravestone, he wondered. Here lies Rico Garcia. He worked hard all his life? He never cheated on his wife? He had a madman inside him and he never let him out? He wanted more than "Beloved husband and father" and the dates of his birth and death.

Rico closed his eyes. It was late, and the house was quiet. He could hear the sound of his own heart beating. Listening to it soothed him, and he began to drift toward sleep, a process he looked forward to at the end of each long day. He enjoyed the unexplainable images that presented themselves in his mind, the way they made no sense and no apologies. Tonight he felt almost as if he were marching toward some new place far beyond the shapes and colors he saw inside his head, marching to the beat of that little trap drum in his chest. And when he had gone so far he could barely hear the beating anymore, he saw the words of his epitaph, or heard them, or maybe just felt them. He wasn't sure how they came to him, but he knew what they said. They said, "Rico Garcia. He surprised us all."

That made him chuckle just as he plummeted into a deep sleep, right there on the couch. For the first time since he and Rosalita got together, he never made it into the bedroom, not all night long.

1974

I NEED water, I need food, I need to stay alive, he thinks as he lifts his head slowly. It has taken so long, so many aching hours or maybe days, to figure this out. For all that time he has been wishing to die without allowing those words to form in his mind. But he knows it won't happen. Nothing comes that easy for him. Ever.

In the air, interlaced with the smells of sweat and filth, the faint scent of rice with cumin hovers. He rises to his feet and begins to flow like one rivulet of dirty water toward the knot of men at the far end of the compound. There are ten toilets there, ten for a thousand men. He will find them and relieve himself. He will join the line for rice and water. He will find a way to survive.

He allows his eyes to rise to the top of the wall, a barrier so high there is nothing visible beyond but sky. No one ever escapes from here. They had impressed that, if nothing else, upon him on the first day, the day he received his number. The day he was assigned to a cell with five other men. When the darkness came and they were forced to go inside, when they all laid down at once, parts of their bodies touched each other. It was that close, that small, that unbearable.

How has this happened to him?

He cannot permit himself that question.

He cannot face the answer.

He stands behind a man whose black hair looks wet with grease. The man's feet are bare. He wears a shirt thick with grime which is buttoned to the neck and at the wrists. The man's right hand is mangled, scarred over. When he reaches for the tin plate, he balances it on his arm.

The rice looks as if it had been cooked in dirty water, but he eats it anyway, standing up among a thousand men, searching for one who looked like him.

White.

But he sees no one.

M ARGARET FELT no sense of wariness as she moved to the kitchen door and opened it to Rico. The screen door, with its flimsy wooden frame and screen popped out in two places, now stood between them, offering very little protection. She didn't feel she needed any, so what did it matter. Even Magpie, asleep on the floor of the living room, failed to stir.

"I've come to say I'm sorry for what I said last night," Rico began. He had actually practiced a more flowery speech, but it vanished from his mind the moment he saw her. "I had the wrong idea, and I ended up making an asshole out of myself." Here he stopped talking. He could see Margaret quite clearly through the screen, and he hoped to detect a look that indicated he'd made the right decision by returning, that they could start over again, fresh. But before he even had a moment to check, he heard more words coming out of his own mouth. ". . . which is not unusual," he added, and then he smiled. It should be pointed out that Rico was a good-looking man. He stood just a fraction under six feet but seemed taller, perhaps because he'd inherited a slender, muscular build from his father. He had interesting angles in his face, along with high cheekbones, deep dimples, and a beautiful set of teeth, all of which gave him a certain flair, while the tattoos and the well-defined muscles telegraphed the bad boy that he wasn't now and had never been. Back in the days when he and Rosalita had been passionate, she had said on more than one occasion that the only reason she didn't leave him during the rocky patches was that she couldn't bear not being able to look up and see that face several times a day. All this was meaningless to Rico, who thought he looked like every other Chicano guy his age in the South Valley. Maybe today, though, he let his smile linger a second or so longer than he would have if he hadn't heard so many times that it could cast a spell on a woman.

"Don't worry about it," Margaret replied. "It's okay." She could have added that she'd heard comments like that scores of times from men on the subway or drunks in the bar and had never, not once, received an apology later. She could have confided that this was virgin territory, his little display of regret, and, in truth, she felt a bit stunned by it, but what for? To admit such a thing was an invitation, and Margaret tended to be stingy with her invitations. Always had been—ever since, standing at the window of Donny's apartment in Hell's Kitchen, she'd watched her mother and father wave goodbye from the street, never to show up again. But, invitation or not, she did feel touched by Rico, and the specific place it registered was in the tips of her fingers which moved toward the latch on the screen door and flipped it free. She opened the door and stepped outside.

Rico backed up, a wave of exhilaration, subtle but powerful, sweeping him farther away than he needed to be to let the door swing along its path. "I'd like to teach you to weld," he said, "now that I've got it straight that that's what you want."

Margaret held her breath. Here was a dream come true, a rare event in her experience. Yet it was hard for her to accept it. She felt afraid, and she learned instantly that it was just as difficult to say the word yes as to desperately want to hear it.

"I can pay you," she said as a way of making it easier on herself. "What do you charge?"

And now Rico had a decision to make. The idea of money exchanging hands had never once occurred to him, not in all the imagining he had done on the way over here this morning. He was used to giving everything he had to women, used to that particular feminine expectation that seemed to him to come with a chant of *more, more, more*. But here was a woman offering a fair exchange. It seemed wrong to take it—not macho enough perhaps—but he knew that that reaction was tightly wrapped up in his previous fantasies and this idea that she was his destiny, and he made a choice then and there to surprise himself and say yes to what she offered.

"How does ten bucks an hour sound?" He made more than that in the garage when he was working, but there wasn't always work, so it evened out.

"Great," she responded. "More than fair."

She extended her hand to him to shake, the way two men do when a deal is struck, and he reached for it with the same gravity he would put into any deal-closing handshake. "My name is Rico Garcia," he said, and then he added, "*a su servicio*" because that was the way Elena had taught him to introduce himself when he was a little boy. And he felt happy, like a little boy, in this moment.

"I'm Margaret. Margaret Shaw," she said, and she smiled and Rico felt like all the stars in the sky were on his side.

"We'll start on Monday," he said. "Come by my shop in the morning."

"What time do you get there?"

"Eight, eight-thirty."

"I'll be there at eight-thirty," she said. "On the dot."

"*Bueno*. See you in a couple days," he replied, and then he turned and walked away. He climbed into his truck, feeling sure of his direction, the way he had when he laid the first cement step on the walkway to his house just after he bought his piece of property. Even then, his neighbors had stood at the fence, peering in, and said, "Rico, you *vato loco*, who puts in a walkway before a house?" Rico had not bothered to reply. What was the use of explaining that this was something he could do right now, get it done, if others couldn't see that already? What was the use of explaining that his vision blurred when it swept past the immediate moment and the few that followed? Rico had lived his whole life as a man without a long-range plan. He had enough to do just managing the day.

On the other hand, he remembered, vividly, each and every instant that had passed already, as if they were carved into stone tablets which could never wear away. He often wondered how he could possibly have enough room in his head for all the memories, large and small. He remembered the birth of each daughter, of course, the hours of agony Rosalita went through, swearing up and down each time that she was finished with giving birth;, but he remembered, just as clearly, the little dresses each daughter wore for the first day of kindergarten. He remembered the entire sermon Monsignor Frank gave at his father's funeral mass, and he could still recite the times tables he learned in the third grade. He remembered the sound of the Rio when the dams were open and the water eddied through the roots of the cottonwoods that had fallen over at the edge of the bank, just as well as he recalled the look on Elena's face when he'd told her Rosalita was pregnant and they were planning to move in together without the benefit of holy matrimony. So many moments lined up behind him, each one lit with a spotlight any time he chose to turn it on, and yet the future was nothing but shadows. Except that now, there was one little beam shining brightly, and if it had a label it would've been, "8:30 Monday morning."

Rico parked in his usual spot behind Garcia Automotive, unlocked the security gates, and went right to work. Saturdays were always the easiest, the day his customers showed up for routine oil changes and tire rotations. They sat in his office with their takeout cups from the Barelas Coffee House, thumbing through old magazines or just staring out the front windows at the foot traffic waiting for him to finish. He worked with speed and efficiency, and he always kept his mind on the job. But today was different. His mind drifted. He had never taught anyone to weld, and now, as he replaced the drain plug on an oil pan or poured the dirty oil into the recycle barrel, he found himself wondering how to start. His own father had taught him to weld so long ago that Rico could not remember the sequence of lessons, and he took his skill so much for granted that he never broke down the steps, one by one. He wanted to present the material in an orderly manner, lay it out in such a way that Margaret would grasp the basics quickly. But not too quickly, he smiled to himself.

"You got a shit-eating grin on your face, bro'," said Benito Aragon, a man Rico had known since they were both eight years old. He carried a bag from the corner grocery store in the crook of his arm. "There's only one thing puts a shit-eating grin like that on a man's face, bro'," Benito continued, stepping farther into the garage. He placed the bag on the concrete floor and pushed his sunglasses up onto the top of his head. His shaven head had progressed to the stubble stage, and he wore a pair of long, baggy red satin shorts that made him look like a wannabe basketball player for the UNM Lobos.

"Don't talk to me about eating shit, you sick fuck," Rico responded.

Benito placed his hand dramatically over his heart. "You killed me, bro'," he said, and then he stepped forward and he and Rico shook hands, a complicated series of movements left over from their teenage years that ended in a stylized hug. They saw each other every couple of months, usually when Benito was walking home from the *mercadito* with a six-pack and stopped in the garage. "So who is she?" Benito persisted. "I know you, Rico."

"You don't know shit, Benito."

"When I see my man smiling at the recycle barrel, I know what I know."

Rico laughed. In thirty-five years, he had never confided one personal bit of information to Benito and he was not about to start, but he did feel compelled to say something, so he settled on, "I was thinking about teaching."

"Teaching or teachers?" Benito replied. "Oh, I got it, I got it. You suddenly remembered that student teacher we had for New Mexico history in the ninth grade, right? Miss McKenzie? Better known as Senorita Double-D. No wonder you were smiling." Benito cleared a spot on Rico's workbench and hoisted himself up to sit there. "She was the only reason I finished the ninth grade."

"You finished but you didn't pass," Rico reminded him.

"How could I? I only went to one class. But go ahead, ask me something about New Mexico history."

"Who's the governor?"

"You mean now? Fuck if I know."

Rico figured there was a fifty-fifty chance that was true. Benito had his hands full: first he'd married a bitch-on-wheels who convinced him to sign over his truck to her, and then packed it up with everything they owned and took off. His second wife came with four kids, the youngest of whom had promptly been hit by a car—a drunk driver—and was now paralyzed from the waist down and in a wheelchair. The driver did six months in county. That was ten years ago, and Rico knew that Benito still harbored fantasies of killing him and dumping his sorry carcass in the middle of the desert for the vultures to finish off.

Benito stayed for two oil changes and even helped rotate the tires on an old '75 Caddy in mint condition. Then he ambled on down the block, stopping to watch a pickup basketball game his son was playing in, wheelchair and all.

MEANWHILE, MARGARET busied herself by hanging a hammock between two elm trees in her yard. She had bought the hammock from a Mexican street vendor at an outdoor *mercado* on Old Coors Boulevard for twenty dollars, and she had no idea whatsoever if that was a good price or a ripoff fit for a *gringa* from New York. It was woven in bright tropical colors and came with a little pillow sewn into one end, as if it were important to the weaver to point the resting person in one direction only. Margaret felt a stab of guilt as she twisted the substantial hooks into the flesh of the big trees in her yard. It seemed selfish and wrong to wound them in such a way, but she pressed on. She had never had a yard, a tree, or a hammock to hang in her whole life, and it seemed magical. It was not the magic of travel billboards or subway ads, though, which seemed to focus on couples in bathing suits, margaritas, and white-tipped waves in the background. This was the magic of being off the ground and also horizontal, of staring upward through a maze of leaves and seeing patches of pure cerulean blue, of having the supreme luxury of time and space. She would become a woman resting in a hammock under a Chinese elm tree not far from the Rio Grande. She would hear the monkeys from the zoo as she daydreamed.

Besides, having a hammock was a family legacy of which there were precious few in Margaret's life. In the months after her parents left for India and before they disappeared, she had received a long letter with a photograph tucked into the envelope. In it, her parents relaxed in a wide hammock, Vincent settled into it on his back and Regina on her side next to him, her face pressed into his chest and their legs intertwined. Vincent's arms were wrapped around her, and in one hand he held a tall bottle of Kingfisher beer. He was smiling at the camera, while Regina's face was barely visible. Vincent had written little messages on the picture, like in a comic book. Out of his own mouth came the words, "I love you, my sweet little girl!" and out of Regina's came, "We miss you every day, every minute, every second! Don't grow up too much before we get home!" On the back of the picture, in Vincent's hard-to-read scrawl, it read, "Mommy and Daddy in Goa, thinking of Margaret with Grampy in New York." Donny had hung it on the little vanity mirror in her bedroom, where it stayed for a good ten years before she finally tucked it into a box of mementoes which included all the gifts from India; and then later—after Donny's death—his gold-plated pocket watch, his certificate of U.S. citizenship, and a small stack of family photos, mostly people Margaret didn't recognize who lived, she assumed, in County Cork, Ireland.

When she finally got the hammock strung up, taut and secure, she climbed in, placing her head on the little pillow and letting her arm trail over the side to ruffle Magpie's fur from time to time. She felt like a pretty magician's assistant in a levitation act. She felt like a new baby in a cradle of love. High above the trees were white clouds which slowly passed over, first removing and then releasing the blue sky into the little patches between the leaves. A great peacefulness worked its way into her, maybe from the ground up, maybe from the sky down, maybe it hovered in the air at that elevation, she didn't know. But absorbing it, she felt invited to close her eyes and gently rock in a drifty, dreamy way, and when she did, who should appear in her mind but Rico. "I got the wrong idea and made an asshole of myself . . . which is not unusual," he had said. And the words were true and he meant them and she knew it, and something in the visual of him outside the screen had hit her hard.

Maybe in some way he reminded her of Donny in that moment. Her grandfather had a humble streak that ran neck-and-neck with his rough-and-tough side. He would yell at her for something—which she probably deserved—and then later stand before her, filling up all the space by the side of her narrow bed, and say how sorry he was; how he didn't know what he'd done wrong with her mother, how he had contributed to the personality of a woman who would run off and leave her daughter with a man who clearly didn't have the skill to do a good job of raising her; how he desperately wanted to do everything differently now—first and foremost was not yelling—and then he would ask for her forgiveness. Every time it happened, Margaret felt her heart stagger until, somewhere along the line, she'd find her voice and say, "Don't worry about it, Grampy. It's okay," and he would lean in and kiss her on the cheek and Margaret's heart would ache more for him than for herself, even in those times when she felt he had been unreasonable and maybe even cruel. The truth was, she loved her grandfather three times the normal amount. She loved him as Grampy but also as a father and a mother.

Of course, she didn't love Rico. She had erased him the instant he'd left the yard and climbed into his truck yesterday. Erasing was a skill Margaret had, her way of keeping power. Even as a little girl in the Catholic school Donny sent her to she'd watched in fascination as the lessons of the day were erased from the blackboard, one after the other, by an energetic nun with a man's name: Sister Mary Edwin, Sister Alphonsus, Sister Marie Peter, and so on. She had even volunteered to clap the erasers at the end of the day. She would stare into the puffs of chalk dust looking for the remnants of math or geography or religion, watch it all rise up and fall away while she held her breath and slammed the erasers together again and again. She'd gone through a phase of doing homework, all the long division problems neatly laid out, and then erasing them so the page in her notebook was as clean as she could make it. And later, in her painting, she often began with an image, a shape, a design, a mark, something that simply asserted itself on the canvas, and then spent the whole painting making it go away. She had even tried to write about it—her obsession with erasing—for one of Nick's alter-assignments, as he called them, where he would force his students to use their lesser skills to express what went into their painting. She'd gotten an A-plus on that paper even though she was registered as an auditor, not a matriculated student, in the class. She knew about erasing—the reasons for it and the best ways to do it.

But there he was in her mind, Rico Garcia, like a slow motion trapeze artist keeping pace with her as she gently rocked from side to side. Perhaps she responded to the sadness she saw so clearly in his eyes, though it was not the kind of sadness that cried out for rescue. It was the kind that built up over time until it simply was. She had it herself and she knew it, but green eyes were different than brown eyes. They suggested the hope that associates itself with springtime, the hint of growth and possible abundance. Brown eyes had seen too much. They appeared on the older souls, Margaret thought, the ones who were compelled for good reason to batten down the hatches from the first moment they arrived in life.

Margaret opened her eyes and glanced down at Magpie, in whose mud-brown eyes she had been lost many times. "You want to try to get in the hammock, Mag?" she asked, knowing that it was probably not an easy thing for a dog to accomplish. But Magpie declined. She rolled over on her back, her four legs pointing skyward and her long tongue hanging out the corner of her mouth until it almost touched the ground next to her head. Margaret shifted onto her stomach and reached down to pat the silver fur on her dog's belly. "We might have a new friend," she said. "We'll have to see."

1974

WHEN THE night is very dark and the silence is as penetrating as it ever gets, he crosses his hands over his heart and thinks of the woman he loves. This brings a pain so searing that only his intense need for privacy prevents him from moaning, thrashing, beating his head into the concrete wall.

She had been sitting next to him on a bus, her overnight bag—with tiny round mirrors embroidered into it—wedged into the tight space between them. It had been a long ride, and she was sleeping, her head pressed into his shoulder and her hair, which smelled of lavender, stuck along the length of his upper arm in the sweat. He had been nervous. Wired. His eyes, hidden by dark glasses, moved from one side of the winding road to the other.

One more hour, and it would be done, he thought.

One more hour.

But before the hour passed, the bus had stopped. Men in uniforms got on. They walked straight down the aisle and yanked him to his feet. He had seen them coming, and he slid the bag onto the floor, tried to kick it under the seat.

She had woken up then, sat up the way he had seen her sit up a thousand times, fully alert, and he had heard her catch her breath.

They were pushed down the aisle of the bus. Pushed off it.

All the people riding the bus had looked down or looked away as they were shoved past.

Behind them, one of the officers bent down low to retrieve the bag from the floor. He carried it in front of him, as if it smelled bad.

She had reached for his arm. Her fingernails dug in, drawing blood.

She screamed his name as they were placed in two separate police vans.

He had tried to fight his way to her, but he had been knocked down to the dirt, threatened with a gun.

He has not seen her again.

He presses his hands into his heart and tries not to move.

On Sunday, Margaret woke up moody. After she had taken her morning shower, for example, she threw her towel to the floor and studied her naked body in the mirror on the back of the bathroom door. This was a sure sign of a coming storm. Whenever she experienced the urge to stand outside herself and technically review her body, which in these moments she tended to equate with her cage, her jail cell, or her hostage closet, she was already in trouble. It meant the restlessness, the discontent, was upon her, and she was trapped in it. Over the years, she had experimented with all the usual ways out— alcohol, exercise, drugs, sex, furious painting sessions, various shrinks, even a short-lived dip into transcendental meditation, but nothing worked. Often she would get itchy and begin to scratch herself in search of a little relief, a quasi-solution which had left unsightly scars on her arms, shoulders, and upper back. When she'd worked at the Stereophonic Lounge, she would become impatient and snap at bar patrons, but fortunately it was a place where the regulars protected her at these moments—loudly warning each other and even the newcomers to tread lightly when ordering drinks because the bartender was seriously on the rag. Sometimes she intentionally broke something, though over the years she had learned to make it something unimportant or at least replaceable.

The one thing that did help—if she could find her way there—was to connect this foul internal weather in some soulful way to her parents, who, she reasoned, must have felt something similar when they took off for India. Surely, nothing else but this, nothing less than this, could have made them get on the train-to-the-plane in New York and disappear forever. The only time she could forgive them, or even understand, was when this wild restlessness rushed over her. In those moments, if she could keep her vision clear and find something brand new to do, the tornado moved on with minimal wreckage.

She pulled up her black jeans, put on a sports bra, and slipped her arms into a baggy V-neck T-shirt. As she stepped into the kitchen, she happened to glance up through the window, where, in the distance, the tops of the five dormant volcanoes on the West Mesa quietly waited to resuscitate themselves and show the land developers, particularly those intent on putting a highway through the sacred petroglyphs, exactly who was boss. "Magpie, let's go somewhere," she called, and within two minutes they were both in the car backing out of the driveway. She wound her way north to Central and then headed west, racing up the Seven Mile Hill, past crumbling motels with big shiny trucks with license plates from Chihuahua, Mexico, angle-parked in front of every door. It was barely seven in the morning, and no one was stirring. Even the gas stations and mini-marts were empty. She noticed a street sign for Paseo des Volcanes and swung a hard right into what appeared to be a lunarscape. One road, the one that she was on, progressed, straight as an arrow, into the big nothing. It was completely still. Even the tumbleweeds along the barbed wire fences on either side of the road had stopped tumbling.

After a few miles, a dirt road angled off to the right toward the volcanoes, and Margaret took it. It occurred to her, as she slowed down to negotiate the ruts, that this was her very first experience of a dirt road. It seemed impossible, but there it was. She was raised in the New York City backwoods, where every square inch was paved, if not occupied by a fifty-story building. It had probably been two centuries since there was any loose dirt in the city, aside from the parks, whose footpaths were paved, too. The exact opposite of where she now found herself, she thought. Funny, but she didn't miss the city one bit. She had always assumed it was woven into her identity, inseparable from who she was. But here in the desert, it seemed like a mirage that she had suddenly stepped out of. She parked not far from the base of the biggest volcano of them all, facing east toward the Sandia Mountains that rose up like a natural barrier between her and her past, and collected her backpack from the floor of the car. It contained a bound sketchbook, a bottle of black India ink, a Rapidograph pen, and two bottles of spring water. As she climbed out of the car, Magpie scrambled into the front seat and jumped out the driver's door a second after Margaret. There was a large sign listing all the rules but they ignored it, particularly the leash law which seemed absurd, given all the empty space.

They had never climbed a dormant volcano before—naturally—and Margaret found it difficult to keep her footing. Broken bits of lava, centuries old, shifted, her feet slipped, and before too long she was ascending the steeper parts with one hand and sometimes two on the ground before her for balance. Meanwhile, Magpie, a city dog after all, stuck her nose under every rock, which evoked images of sand-colored scorpions and angry tarantulas on tall hairy legs, ready to strike, and Margaret had to turn her face away so as not to be neurotically overprotective. Somehow, huffing and puffing, they made their way to the top, which actually wasn't very far, though once they got there it seemed that the West Mesa, which stretched in all directions before it met the walls of the city to the north and east, was part of another, lesser world. She found a rock with a good backrest, facing east, and settled down to do some serious looking. One thing Margaret knew about herself was that her eyes went everywhere. Where other people saw a simple edge, she saw a series of shadows laid out, one more intense than the other, and a drop-off that typically pitted two radically different colors against each other. Where other people saw a tree, bare in winter, and dismissed it as such, she saw a riot of color—purples, greys, blacks, dark blues—shimmering against a sky that looked as if it had been carved in bas-relief out of library paste; where others saw the Hudson River and perhaps categorized it as a grey stripe separating Manhattan from New Jersey, she saw a shifting orgy of iridescence which could only be captured one nanosecond at a time and never fully. Her natural impulse was to hold her breath in an effort to stop everything so she could look longer and see more. "Take a breath, me darlin'," Donny had insisted over and over again when she was a small child. "You'll pass out of the picture if you don't." But Margaret held out. She tried to make time stop. But it never did. By the time she was a teenager, she gave up trying.

She started with a slow 180-degree scan, north to south and back again, just to allow the landscape to imprint itself in broad strokes of color first: the light beige sands of the mesa; the darker tan of the city of Albuquerque, low to the ground and so infused with the palette of the desert that it almost disappeared; the greenbelt along the river; the rising mountains, slate-colored in this moment; the sky, a psychedelic shade of sea-blue. Above, a few hawks rode air currents across her visual field, and a few black crows squawked from the top of weathered fence posts; while a cow, here and there, munched anemic desert grasses.

Where was she? She closed her eyes and watched the complementary colors of all she'd seen appear on the screens inside her eyelids. It was a phenomenon that could keep her occupied for hours: open her eyes, see the green stripe of the river; close them, it turned red. Open her eyes and stare into the blue sky; close them, it turned orange. She didn't know why, or care. She took it as a reminder that all things change constantly, depending on a million things, such as perspective, light, time, water, wind, angle, and the ability to notice in the first place. Again, she stared intensely into the sky and then closed her eyes to pleasantly drift in a sea of orange, which carried her along for a while, backward in time, and then delivered her to a memory.

Soon after her parents had dropped her off with her grandfather, she and Donny had had their first incident. Donny had long ago painted one wall of his tiny kitchen a deep shade of burgundy in an effort to tone down the morning brightness, which got on his nerves after a long night in the Bit O' Blarney bar. He also had a broom with an orange handle which he usually left propped up against it. Margaret had found both shock and comfort in the collision of those two colors—the deep red and the fluorescent orange. She would sit at the kitchen table eating her morning cornflakes and watch them vibrate.

One day when she came home from kindergarten with Donny, who was a little short of breath from climbing the four flights to their apartment, he had unlocked the door and pushed it open, stepping back so she could enter first. Immediately, her eyes moved to the burgundy wall, but the broom was gone, and all she saw was the wide expanse of deep red, with no hope in it. She collapsed to the floor and began to sob.

"Margaret, honey, what is it?" Donny had asked, dropping to his knees beside her, so stunned he didn't even think for a moment to collect her into his arms. "Tell Grampy what's wrong, Margaret? Do you hurt? Tell Grampy where you hurt."

But Margaret couldn't utter a sound, couldn't even raise her eyes from the linoleum floor, with its specks of blue and green and white. Waves of grief, one after the other, slammed her down and kept her there. Donny gathered her up. He sat back on the floor, holding her so tightly she finally felt safe enough to whisper, amid great splashing tears, "What happened to the broom, Grampy?" And he had held her even tighter and roared with laughter, surprising her since she felt so much in the grip of tragedy.

"Grampy swept the floor, that's all, my darlin'," he said. "We still have the broom," and he got up, lifting her with him, and closed the door to the building hallway, and there behind it was the broom. "We can put it wherever you want it," he whispered into her hair, which was damp now, as if all the exertion of crying had caused her to break into a serious sweat. "That broom is here to stay."

"Put it where it goes," she had sobbed, her voice shaking and her arms wrapped around her grandfather's neck, as if he were a rock in a great sea of misery and she had to hold on for dear life.

He grabbed the broom. "Tell me where you want me to put it, honey," he said, and she had vaguely pointed and he placed it against the wall. He had a look on his face that told Margaret, even at that young age, that he didn't know whether to laugh or cry, and she had climbed down and adjusted it; and then he had scooped her up again and carried her to the living room, which he was in the process of converting to her bedroom, and sat with her in his lap for a long, long time.

That moment between them had become a bit of a land-mark, so tender that it took years for them to even make a joke about it. Margaret remembered the first joke, too. Donny had held up the broom—which by that time had lost many of its bristles—and the ones that were left stuck out at every possible angle, so using it for its original purpose was a waste of time. "Margaret, me girl, I'm afraid to bring it up, but I think we're in desperate need of a new broom," he had said, and she had glanced up from her bed, where she was lying on her stomach reading a school book, and growled, "That broom's not going anywhere"; there was silence for a few beats and then they both began to laugh, loud and long, and Donny said, in his musical Irish brogue, ". . . unless you're riding on it, me girl." Still, he never threw it out. In fact, Margaret still had it in her storage unit in Queens. They even had a private reference for it called "a case of the orange broom." Whenever one of them would feel unusually, unreasonably, or inexplicably sad, he or she would admit to having a case of the orange broom, and the other would be extra kind until it passed over.

Margaret opened her eyes again. After Donny had died, in the absence of anyone to be especially kind to her, the sadness that came with a case of the orange broom had transformed itself to rage and often self-destruction. But sitting here, on the top of a volcano, knowing that it had once, in a fit of pique, spewed molten lava all across the countryside but hadn't done it lately, she felt happy. She opened her backpack and took out a bottle of water, which she poured into her cupped hands for Magpie to drink from.

And then she started to draw.

Now THAT he knew for sure that there was a next step with Margaret, that it would be taken at precisely eight-thirty the following morning, Rico thought about her less. All in all, he was a man who preferred reality to fantasy, who only reverted to fantasy if there was no chance of reality anywhere in sight. When he did indulge in fantasy, he tended to be uncomfortable and was soon looking for a way out. For Rico, the tension between what he had—which he knew was a lot—and what he might be drawn into in his imagination, was formidable and worth avoiding. He didn't want to entertain the notion that there was an unlived life to slip into, and he knew instinctively that if he visited it too often the color might drain out of his real one, a possibility that he simply couldn't risk.

So on Sunday he did what he always did on Sunday: he got up early and took Elena to eight o'clock mass at the Holy Family Church on Atrisco Boulevard. He sat in the pew with her and performed all the requisite motions—standing, sitting, kneeling over and over again—but he was not a believer, at least not in the way she was. His mother found great comfort in the Catholic Church. She often had a rosary wound through her fingers, and she lit candles every week, even though she could barely see them and Rico had to guide her hand in the right direction. She knew all the responses, of course, and beat her heart with great vigor during what was still called in his youth the "mea culpa." He studied her out of the corner of his eye during this part, wondering why she felt so guilty about what he knew, and she knew, she had no control over. And during the Sign of Peace, she always hugged him tightly and said, "Te *quiero, mi hijo, te quiero,*" to which he replied, "*Te quiero también, Elena, mi madre.*" It was true. He did love her rather fiercely.

It was on the drive home from church that she would usually speak quietly for a few minutes about Fernando, his older brother who had been dead for twenty-six years—more than half of Rico's life. Rico remembered him well, and his feelings were mixed, to say the least. Perhaps it was the times, which were hard for a *cholo* born too greedy and too macho for his own good. Perhaps it was simply an accident of personality or some unavoidable genetic glitch that made Fernando turn out the way he did, which was bad—more than bad—through and through. From an early age, Rico had learned to avoid him whenever possible, to stay hidden or fuse himself to his mother or father. Even so, he took more than his share of beatings, heard more vitriol than anyone needs to, and lived his early life with only one clear goal: to be the opposite of Fernando. His daily plan included not being near his brother, not being associated with him in any way, not getting dragged into anything he hadn't chosen for himself, not causing any heartbreak for his parents. He was seventeen when Fernando died at twenty-two, stabbed to death in the state lockup in Santa Fe, where he was doing his second bid, this one for aggravated assault and armed robbery.

When his parents sat him down and gave him the news, Rico's first reaction was overwhelming relief, though he never admitted that to anyone out loud. How could he explain that the relief he felt was for Fernando as much as for himself or anyone else. He knew his brother could never last the way he was—it could only get worse, no matter how much praying his mother did on her knees up at the old church in the badlands of Chimayo. Fernando used to mock Elena when she made her annual pilgrimage to that little chapel, which was famous all around the world for the miracles that somebody somewhere insisted had happened there.

"Score me some smack while you're at it," Fernando would taunt. "You're heading to the heroin capital of New Mexico.

More overdoses there than anywhere else in the whole state, right out the front door of that church whose holy red dirt you waste your time believing in."

"I'm going to pray for you, Fernando," Elena would respond, calmly. "I'm going to pray you find your way."

"I know my way already. My way is money. My way is fucking as many women as I can and getting high. My way is the party way," he would say, and to Rico it sounded as if he wanted to drive her into the corner of the room with his words and pound her with his strange fury. He had never actually hit her, never even threatened to, though the same could not be said about Fernando and his father, who went at it until they were both bloody. Teeth were loosened and noses were broken during their fights. But Manuel could not control his son, and after a while, he accepted that and politely asked him to move out and never come home again, and Fernando obliged. No one in the family had seen him for over two years when he died. They brought the body back to Albuquerque and had a funeral service with exactly three people in attendance. They buried him in a hastily purchased family plot in a cemetery near the Big-I, where I-40, going east and west, and I-25, going north and south, intersect. Elena had kept fresh flowers on his grave until she lost her vision and could no longer drive a car to get there.

So whenever she and Rico would be cruising down Bridge Boulevard on the way home from church on Sunday, and she would say, seemingly out of nowhere, "He was a nice little boy, Fernando, smart and cute. He changed overnight when he was around eleven or twelve. I don't know what happened to him," Rico would pretend he'd never heard it all before. He had no memories of his brother as a nice boy, though he had distinct memories of thanking God, whether there was one or not, each and every time Rosalita gave birth to a girl. Girls could be trouble and they could cause their share of pain, but very few could match the heartache imposed by a genuine bad boy—a bad son or brother.

Elena would mull over the points along the path to Fernando's demise: the dangerous crowd he found or that found him, the drugs, the fighting, dropping out of Rio Grande High—which was something Rico had in common with his brother—the first prison sentence for dealing crystal meth. When she finished her litany, tears glistening in her eyes over the fact that her son had died at the hands of a man who was much worse than even he was, Rico always said the same thing, though he honestly didn't think his mother found comfort in it or even remembered it, week to week. He said, "Elena, *mi madre*, I think it's better to get killed than it is to kill someone, and we know he was heading in that direction. We know he would've got there, and this way he was saved from that."

He meant it, too. Every time he saw the nightly news, which often featured a camera in the local courthouse recording inmate after inmate stepping up to the podium in his orange jumpsuit to be charged, Rico couldn't help but see his brother's face superimposed on each one; and when he heard their list of crimes, he felt sick inside, sick enough to switch the channel and say, again, that if that shit passed for news, they were really scraping the bottom of the barrel.

It was inevitable that his spirits were sinking, or had already sunk completely, as they pulled back into the driveway after church—as if church itself was a stick Elena used to pry open the lid they all tried to keep jammed down over Fernando's memory; and once his ghost got out, it took a while for it to evaporate again. Rico would walk his mother to her *casita*, promise to come back later to pick her up for a big homemade supper, and then busy himself around his property, no matter how hard he had to look to find something constructive to do. His compound was the best kept place in the whole South Valley, he thought, perhaps a bit cynically. Who else repainted the metal on the casement windows every year? Who else had upgraded from an entry gate that just got dragged along to one that slid on compact little wheels? Who else could say they hand-built not one but two buildings from the ground up, collecting the adobe by the shovelful?

Rico opened the door to his own house, which was still quiet, though Jessica and Lucy were already up and dressed. "*Buenas dias, Papi,*" Lucy called from the kitchen. "How was church?"

"The same as it always is," he replied. "A job."

Lucy laughed. "If *Abuelita* knew how you feel, she wouldn't make you go."

"Let's make sure she never knows then," he said, opening the door to his bedroom and tiptoeing in to strip off his church outfit and put on his work clothes. Rosalita was sprawled out on the bed, as if she automatically doubled her space the minute he got up. She was a heavy sleeper, and he took a few seconds to watch her. She had on a short-sleeved nightgown with tiny flowers all over it, and her hair, which she kept long, looked like a black cloud on the pillow. She was just thirty-nine years old and had already put in twenty-three years with him, most of them good. They had raised three daughters, facing all the problems of parenthood together as a united front, and the girls were proof that they did a passable job. But now he felt he hardly knew her. She had become a woman who would fling her legs and arms wide when she was alone in a bed, no longer a wife who wrapped herself around her man and couldn't sleep unless he did. She rarely talked to him anymore about anything important, went along as if it were perfectly normal never to mention such things as no sex for four years, or a mother-in-law who has needs Rosalita far too often had to handle alone. It was eerie for Rico, and came with a sense of unacknowledged danger, as if her personal tectonic plates were shifting way below the surface and a tidal wave was not only inevitable but on its way.

He had not told her about the welding lessons with Margaret. Perhaps that was slightly deceitful. He didn't know. But she had become so cut off from him, so mysteriously private and locked into herself, that it seemed unnecessary—even pathetic—to go out of his way to share something new in his life with her. He felt, and it seemed true to him even when he thought about it at length, that she didn't care what he did as long he paid the bills and showed up at the dinner table every night like a husband and father should.

Carefully, he hung up his dress shirt and blue jeans, creased along the legs from Rosalita's iron, and put on an old brown T-shirt and a pair of cut-off sweat pants. As he turned back around, he saw that Rosalita's eyes were half-open in a dreamy way, and she was watching him or at least looking in his direction. It stopped him, that look, made him consider climbing back into bed with her. But then, without even a word, she shifted her position, rolled onto her back, and just stared straight up at the ceiling.

Rico left the room, weighted down by the broken Fernando-record he heard from Elena every week, and Rosalita's whatever-it-was-that-was-eating-away-at-her, and a day ahead of him with nothing beyond yard work. But, he reminded himself as he pushed through the back door, there was always tomorrow.

At eight-thirty.

1974

AND HE has a little girl.

A little girl, far away, and he might never see her again.

It is unbearable to think of her, back at home in the big city, perhaps looking out the window from a fourth floor apartment. Waiting.

His throat constricts, closes off, and he cannot say her name, not even whisper it into the thin mat he sleeps on, face down. When he thinks of her, sweat breaks out along his hairline. He cannot breathe.

A wife, and a little girl.

Gone.

Nothing left but time.

WHEN RICO arrived at Garcia Automotive at five to eight in the morning and hoisted up the garage doors—making it official that he was open for business and glad of it—in his mind he had already laid out his lesson plan, if it could be called that, for his first student. He had an idea of what Margaret hoped to accomplish, at least in the beginning, based on the rusty parts she had so carefully situated on the concrete pad in her yard. The shapes she seemed so obsessed with made no sense to him, but he hadn't paid any attention whatsoever to the whims of modern art, or any other art for that matter; and, besides, he didn't need to know the why, just the how, and in that department, he was more than competent.

He watered the spider plant that had been hanging in the office window for five years, emptied the garbage can—which as usual overflowed with the takeout coffee cups of his Saturday customers—and then went outside to collect the trash that had blown against the fence or into his small parking area, or perhaps been thrown there by passersby, over the weekend. He checked his appointment book, which looked healthy with jobs for the week, slipped into his work coveralls, which he left on a hook on the bathroom door, and settled down in his chair to watch for Margaret. He wanted to see her as she approached, take in, in a relaxed manner, the way she moved toward his door, experience the burst of energy that he imagined she would bring to him.

He rocked back in his rolling office chair so his feet dangled a few inches above the floor. It was a crazy thing, he mused, how much a middle-aged man, a father and a grandfather for

God's sake, could look forward to seeing a skinny middle-aged woman, one who had already made it clear she had no interest in him, stroll around a corner. And it wasn't because she was trying to attract his attention, either. Margaret wasn't working much on her appearance, he had to admit. *Chicanas* tended to put more time into it, with their polished nails, gold earrings, high heels, and tight pants designed to show off their rounded hips and fleshy thighs, which they were proud of and rightly so; while Margaret looked, both days he'd seen her, as if she hadn't changed her jeans in a week and had no plan to. She wore baggy T-shirts that hid whatever equipment she had, and her long hair looked like it might not object if she dragged a comb through it more often.

Within ten minutes, she appeared on Barelas Road, coming at a fast clip, a walking speed that the new people from the East seemed to think was normal. To Rico, she looked as if she was in a big hurry, though she was actually five minutes early and there wasn't really an official starting time anyway. She wore dark sunglasses like the Blues Brothers along with her usual outfit, and she carried a shoulder bag big enough for a weekend trip to Las Vegas, Nevada.

"Yo, Rico," she said as she came in, "here I am, reporting for duty."

"They really say that over there in New York? Yo?" he responded. "I thought that was only for the movies."

She laughed, a lovely sound that he had never heard before.

"Nope, all real," she said. "That and more." He had made no move to get up from his chair, so she added, in a conversational tone, "Ever been to New York?"

"*Mira*, I don't leave the South Valley unless I have to. I get lost in downtown Albuquerque."

Margaret smiled. Downtown Albuquerque consisted of a couple of square blocks of courthouses, a fourteen-screen cineplex, a few oddball businesses—such as a men's hat store and a Holocaust museum—and some restaurants that seemed to wrap it up by ten P.M., even on the weekend. It had pool halls and an Institute of Flamenco. Many of the buildings were painted with murals that looked left over from the sixties—big smiling suns, elongated androgynous humans falling through the cosmos, hot cartoon babes carrying signs that read "No glove, no love," and such like. Margaret adored it. Walking along Central Avenue was like entering a time warp or a dream that someone she didn't know had had a long time ago.

She fished into her bag and brought out a notebook, a pen, a bottle of water, and a scrunchie for her hair. Rico, with all the women in his life, was well versed in hair accoutrements, and he even knew the mythology associated with each one, such as why they protected the hair follicle from split ends or breakage, though he had no specific idea how such knowledge came to him. Probably through osmosis during the dinner table discussions he tuned out.

"You can hang your bag on one of the hooks in the garage," he said, finally standing up and moving in the direction of the work bays. She followed him, her step light and ready, as if she were on the verge of breaking into a run just to get there faster. He intended to emphasize safety first, warn her about the danger of serious flash burns from exposure to the hostile ultraviolet light in arc welding, about hot metal and the way it sears through flesh and ignites any combustible material, about vapors locked inside of some container you might have cause to cut or weld that explode like rockets and drive a man or an acetylene tank or anything else in the vicinity straight through the wall or roof. All welders had horror stories, and Rico knew for a fact that most were true, but when he turned to face her and saw her standing there, her notebook and pen in hand like a schoolgirl, he couldn't bring himself to start off by scaring her.

And he had a second lesson planned in his mind, a lecture of sorts in which he would outline and briefly explain the types of welding—fusion, gas, TIG and MIG electric, brazing, and soldering—and also throw around all the technical terms she could ever hope for; but something told him that Margaret needed her initiation by fire, not words, and right then and there he scrapped all the ideas he'd come up with about being a good teacher and just pointed to the low rider he was currently working on.

"The guy who owns this wants to put some big-ass tires on it," he said, "real fat, and they'll stick way out from the sides if I don't shorten the axles. So that's what I'm doing this morning—cutting out a chunk of the axle and then welding it back together. You can watch."

"Can I ask questions?" She sounded so businesslike that Rico almost laughed.

"Yeah, but I might not answer right away if I have to focus on what I'm doing."

She nodded and said, "Okay, no problem."

It was a strange experience for Rico to have any woman, and this woman in particular, in his shop. Rosalita rarely came here, and his daughters only stopped by every blue moon when they happened to pass along Fourth Street and felt a sudden urge to say hello to their Papi. A woman changed the atmosphere in the garage, invaded it somehow without meaning to. She made it feel like a radio was playing even though there wasn't one. It would take getting used to, this sense of double the usual presence.

"Come here. I'll show you how to set up," he said.

Margaret moved to his side and paid strict attention. She was a person who liked to learn something new. The first time she'd entered an oil painting class, for example—from the moment the teacher arrived in the studio—she'd felt perilously close to bursting into tears and she had to work hard to overpower them, knowing that very few teachers, or fellow students for that matter, would automatically recognize them for what they were—little watery statements of happiness and gratitude. Such gratitude brought with it the image of a door opening, a door she hadn't previously known existed, and Margaret always hoped that she might find freedom behind it. Consequently, she rushed into learning as if she were simultaneously running out of a burning building.

In that, Donny had told her, she was like her mother, who had impatiently learned to read before kindergarten, who took to scampering, her arms extended out to the side, along the tops of railings like a tightrope walker, who actually convinced him to scrounge up the money to send her to a wilderness training program in Utah when she was only fifteen. Regina, Margaret thought, was more a daredevil than a model student like she was, but Donny told her that it was the same passion taking a different form, and she believed him.

So when Rico started in, Margaret opened herself totally to the lesson, which came at her fast even though he delivered it in that crazy New Mexico accent she had always—from the first time she heard it in their old stand-up act—assumed was a Cheech and Chong joke. Donny, a big fan of comedy, had one of their records from the early seventies, and every time they listened to it together, they howled with laughter. Donny lamented the demise of real stand-up, which had been replaced, he said, with what he called drive-by humor.

Standing in Rico's garage, Margaret felt as if she'd stepped into a tornado of important information, and she was immediately swept up in it: this is how you mark a full acetylene cylinder; this is how you mark an empty one; this is why you never tilt it or lay it down; this is how you secure it using chains; this is why you crack the valve to blow out dust in a regulator; this is the chart that lists the melting points of various metals; this is the chart that shows which goggles you need, depending on the job; this is why you don't overheat lead when you solder; this is the range of electrode sizes used in arc welding. On and on it went, Rico just chatting away as he set up his equipment, and Margaret hanging on to the details by her fingertips.

Rico hoisted the low rider up on his hydraulic lift and pointed out areas he had already welded. He did quite a business with the low rider subset, diehard motorheads who fixated on every detail. He did bodywork, too. In fact, he said, he liked aluminum body TIG welding more than anything else because aluminum felt so pliant under his fingers. For small art projects, Margaret would probably braze and solder most often, which was something she could do on that cement pad in her yard, he added, but big welding jobs were out. Too many sparks. Too many things to catch on fire—including her.

By the time they knocked off at noon, Margaret was quite overwhelmed. "I never knew it was so complicated," she commented as she replaced a pair of protective goggles on a wall hook. "Or so dangerous, either. What am I getting myself into here?" For a long time in her art life, she had wanted to expand past the two dimensions of painting into three, to encourage her creativity to make more demands on her and take up more space, all the space it wanted. But she hadn't really known what she was inviting. Now that the three-dimensional urge had taken hold of her, she couldn't shake it, and didn't want to. But today she felt a little daunted.

Rico, on the other hand, had felt like he was blushing half the morning because no sooner would he make some kind of general explanation about welding than he'd hear an alternate meaning, some undercurrent, in his own words. His every reference to fire, to heat, to melting together seamlessly, it was all too close for comfort to the language of sex. When he was showing her the basics of electric arc welding, and he had to explain that space was necessary between the hot electrode and the metal that was waiting for it, that this space was essential for the electricity to arc in, he felt the inches between them fill with a current hot enough to melt metal—and he almost forgot to mention the part about temperature control being the single most important thing in welding. The odd thing was that, he had totally removed from his mind, as if with a cutting torch, the possibility of sex with her. But doing that had paradoxically made everything but her seem sexy, and now he felt like a horny teenager who couldn't even look at one of those yucca plants in his own backyard, the kind that grow a thick seed stalk to the tune of two feet a day, without feeling like he needed to run off somewhere and beat his meat. Feeling this way was a blessing, of sorts. After Rosalita had turned away from him, he'd had to wrestle with his own desires for a long time; and then, as if they'd decided to cooperate with him or had given up in defeat, they simply stopped. Rico was only forty when this happened. He could get it up, but he didn't particularly want to. For what? He never talked about it because it was embarrassing. Now, out of the blue, he was embarrassed for the opposite reason. What middle-aged man has time to worry about a constant hard-on?

"That's it for today," Rico said when they finally broke for lunch. "It's noon. I have other things to do this afternoon."

She dropped into his office chair, leaving him to sit down on one of the folding chairs. "Can I buy you lunch, Rico?" she asked, very casually, as if in New York women took the leading role all the time.

"I have something I brought," he said, and then, because he was essentially an honest man, he added, "My wife packs a lunch for me every day."

"Oh, you're married?" There was no subtext of disappointment in her tone that he could detect.

"Not legally. But for a long time. Three daughters, all grown now."

"And you're still together. Wow, that's impressive," she said, and she seemed to look at him with the kind of respect some women show when they're telegraphing to the man and simultaneously to themselves, *Hands off!* "What's the secret?" she asked.

"Put up with whatever gets thrown at you and keep your fucking mouth shut," Rico said, and Margaret threw back her head and laughed again.

"I knew it!" she said. "I just never heard anybody admit it before." She had little lights in her eyes, like torches.

"You never got hooked up?"

"I've been hooked up, but . . ." She looked around the room as if the end of her sentence would appear by magic on one of the walls and she could read it to him. ". . . never satisfactorily," she concluded. "I think I have a piece missing in that department. Hey, maybe you could weld one on for me."

He knew it was a joke, that there was not one iota of genuine suggestiveness in it, but her words hit him right in the solar plexus. Rico had been hit there in the past, mostly by his older brother, and he knew what it meant to take a physical blow so intense that the whole world stopped dead in its tracks while you made a decision about whether to fall down or stay standing. Luckily, he was already sitting, so all he had to do was respond in some way that kept this little conversational ship afloat.

He settled on, "It's probably the muffler," and then she laughed again, and Rico felt like he was batting a thousand.

"You assume I have a big mouth," she responded, "and here I've never even shot it off in front of you."

This time he didn't have a comeback, so he just smiled at her like he had his secrets, and she smiled back. There they were, a couple of welders, he thought, and suddenly he found himself looking forward to talking over the tricks of the trade with her in the future when they were equals instead of a teacher and student. "Let's make a plan for your next lesson," he said. "I was thinking three times a week for a couple weeks until you get the gist of it."

"Sounds good. What works for you? I have no schedule at the moment, so I'm wide open."

Rico was about to say Monday, Wednesday, and Friday, which seemed like a reasonable plan, but before he formed the words, he realized he didn't want to go two days without seeing her, so instead, he said, "How about Monday, Tuesday, and Wednesday mornings?"

"Okay, good. So I'll see you tomorrow." She collected her bag off the floor where she had dropped it, reached in, and produced her wallet. She extracted thirty-five dollars and handed it to him.

This was a difficult moment for Rico, reaching up and accepting the money, but he made himself do it.

"Thanks so much. It was a great first lesson," she said.

He folded the bills and put them in his pocket.

"I'm going to the library today and take out a book on metals," she added, as she stood up and hefted her bag to her shoulder. "I can see I need to do some serious studying." She took a few steps toward the door.

"Margaret," Rico said, just wanting to say her name out loud, realizing that it was the first time he had ever done so.

She stopped her forward motion and turned to face him.

"What the hell do you have in that bag?" he asked. "It looks like it weighs fifty pounds."

"Just the essentials," she said, and then, without thinking, she lifted it off her shoulder, turned it upside down, and dumped it out on the ground between them. The contents formed a mountain of rubble: a notebook, a water bottle, a sketchbook, pens and ink, two rolls of cherry-flavored Lifesavers, a comb and brush, a wallet, a checkbook, a ring of keys, a novel, some sunscreen, Chapstick, sunglasses, a watch with only one wrist band, a folded road map of Albuquerque that appeared to be plastic-coated, even a dog collar attached to a leash. Pennies, nickels, dimes, and quarters rolled away from the mound into the corners of the office, along with a cylinder of something called Rescue Remedy, which landed close to Rico's feet.

He reached down into the mess and picked up what could only be described as a medium-size dust bunny. Holding it between his thumb and pointer finger, he said, "I may be wrong, but I think this is something that could be thrown out."

Margaret chuckled as she began to collect all the paraphernalia from the floor and shoved it back into her bag. She couldn't and wouldn't tell him that, starting in high school, when she and her best friend, Christina, would dump their purses out on their beds a few times a week and study the contents for the purposes of trying to figure out who they were, she was a goner if anyone ever expressed an interest in what she had in her bag. No matter how many times she looked at the contents, she could never get over the phenomenon of carting around such a big bagful of stuff. And something about Rico encouraged her to reveal herself, a little at a time. He seemed slow and steady, as if he knew the reason for this *mañana* attitude that was so pervasive out here in the west.

Still, once she had rounded the corner toward her house and gained some distance to reflect on that recent moment, she was more than a little surprised at her own spontaneity. True, it had happened at the end of a long morning of listening, watching, and absorbing, when she was so filled up she probably needed to spill something off, and just the action of turning anything upside down was a relief.

She turned into her yard, where Magpie lay sprawled on the other side of the closed driveway gate. "Hey, big dog," she called, and Magpie began to thump her tail into the dirt without getting up or even raising her head. Margaret squatted next to her to scratch her ears and ruffle the fur of her chest and belly. She had read that once dogs passed puppyhood, their owners rarely touched any part of their bodies except the head, and she had promised herself that she would be the exception. She regularly gave Magpie leg and foot massages as if she were the uncontested queen of the canines.

Then she walked over to the cement pad and stared for a few moments into her collection of rusty parts. Putting them together in some new form seemed daunting now that she knew that metals all melted at vastly different temperatures, which meant you had to know in what order they could be welded, as well as what could not be welded together at all. She didn't have any idea of what metals she had represented there on the concrete pad, which were ferrous and which weren't, or which parts, if any, could still contain vapors ready to ignite and blow her and her welding fantasy to the ends of the earth.

But staring into her collection of rusty parts was not unlike examining the contents of her handbag. It was fascinating to Margaret, an identity scattered there, waiting to be assembled.

1974

"*P*RISONS ARE different here, man. They keep you locked up for years without even charging you with anything. Nine out of ten of the inmates in this shithole have never been charged. No Legal Aid lawyers to help stupid American hippies who deal drugs, either." The man pushes his long blonde hair back off his forehead. "You gotta find a way to cope, man."

They are the first words he has heard in English after what he thinks, if his counting is right, is seventeen days and nights. The words hit him hard, in the stomach, like a sucker punch. "How long have you been here?" he asks. His voice sounds odd, like someone else's.

"I don't know. I stopped counting. Years."

He doesn't want to believe it, but even a peripheral glance at this man before him, so dirty, his skin baked and cracked like the deserts to the north, tells him it is true.

"How do you keep on doing it?" he finally asks. "Get up every day and do it?"

"What else is there?" the man says, and he laughs. His teeth are stained, brown. A few are missing. He extends his hand—a simple gesture, so familiar—and says, "I'm Will."

"Vincent."

Strange, but there in the hot sun, he can't think of anything more to add.

"Come on, man," Will says. "Let's find a place in the shade to sit down." He starts off, through the crowd of men squatting in the dirt. "There's a guy from France here, too," Will says over his shoulder. "Jean Pierre. I'll introduce you."

Vincent follows, barely able to keep his balance as he picks his way through wave after wave of prisoners. All adrift.

As MARGARET walked to the library, she smiled to herself. It was not even a mile away from her little adobe house, but even so, one after the other, she crossed streets named Iron, Lead, Coal, Silver, Gold, and Copper, as if the whole city were laid out to remind her of the metals of the world, just in case she forgot what her next step was as an artist. Never before in her life had she felt such a sense of humor in a city, as if it were compelled to play a joke on her. She wanted to learn to weld, and who should she stumble across but Rico Garcia, whose blackboard was the underside of an old car that had to be chopped to accommodate fat tires. She wanted to go to the library, and every corner presented her with a street sign pointing the way to the very subject she was on her way to research. How did something like that happen?

Maybe I belong here, she mused, and that idea caused her to stop dead on the corner of the old Route 66 and look around. Albuquerque was a dusty, working class city, sprawled out in a big natural basin that gave it some protection from wind and weather but also caused the yellow smog to lie just above the building tops in the heat of the summer. On the streets, men wore cowboy hats, cowboy boots, and big silver buckles on their belts, and they weren't on their way to a cos-tume party either, as she had assumed for the first few days after she arrived. Prairie dogs popped up and took over school yards and vacant lots, the professional baseball team was enig-matically named the Isotopes, and each and every meal served in a restaurant seemed to be automatically accompanied by either red or green chile. How could a New Yorker, born in

Chinatown and raised on Forty-Eighth Street between Eighth and Ninth avenues, adjust to all this vacant space? Even the sidewalks downtown were all but deserted, right in the middle of the work day.

Margaret entered the Main Library on the corner of Copper and Fifth Street, which felt like libraries everywhere: cool, quiet, and somehow undisturbed and ancient. She intended to consult a librarian immediately, to be efficiently pointed toward the stacks where the secrets of metals were revealed after having been categorized according to the Library of Congress or the Dewey Decimal System. But on the way to the main desk, she passed a table full of new library acquisitions, where she noticed a coffee-table book on low riders. She opened it and thumbed through. The pages contained glossy, four-color photographs as carefully staged as any in a fine art magazine, and she found herself absorbed enough in the images to begin, here and there, to read the printed commentary that accompanied them. Within a few pages, she read, "This classic 1966 Chevy Impala utilized three different welding techniques. The frame was arc welded, the exhaust system oxyacetylene welded, and the aluminum body TIG welded by Rico Garcia, a master welder known throughout the Southwest as 'el rey' when it comes to low riders."

This astonished Margaret, who now carried the book to a nearby leather-upholstered reading chair and sat down. Rico was famous. Of course, he had gained his notoriety in a field that she didn't even know was a field. She had never thought about it, but if she had, Margaret would've voted "no" if anyone had asked her if the subject of low riders would rate its own library book. And she never thought that welders got credit anywhere for anything, even though it could truthfully be said that they held the whole world together. Not to mention the fact that, while Rico had said he often worked on low riders, he never hinted that it was the kind of craftsmanship that got him included in a book that cost—and here Margaret had to check the front flap of the book—just five cents under forty dollars. Would she have ever asked him to teach her to weld if his reputation had preceded him? She doubted it. Margaret was too sensitive to the patina of success, of making a mark that others noted and applauded, of the way—once that happened—the person was promoted to some league that was simply out of her range.

Now, turning pages in the book and seeing Rico's name again and again, and toward the back, an actual photograph of him at work in Garcia's Automotive, she felt uncomfortable. She decided to simply sit in the chair and wait for the tight grip she was experiencing, particularly in her shoulders and jaw but also on her mind, to loosen, which might take a while. She couldn't will it away, and she couldn't relax it away, because this sense of being yanked from a happy place to a problematic one was the antithesis of relaxation. It made her nerves feel invaded by a toxic foreign substance, like acid. It made her feel as if she had to escape, when she hadn't even known she was trapped or locked up. And arguing logically to herself about the foolishness of her reaction wouldn't help much either, because she knew that talking herself out of this feeling meant convincing herself that Rico's presence in the book was less important than she wanted it to be, for his sake. She wanted to be happy for him and she was, but in some way it seemed to Margaret that when the spotlight shone on someone, it simultaneously cast her into darker shadows; there was only one way out of the shadows, and that was to disappear into them once and for all. To disappear, to be forgotten, to emerge somewhere else with all that tension and worry packed away somewhere secret—that was her cycle and her destiny.

She glanced up. She happened to be sitting in front of a huge two-story window, and the intense sunlight outside came as a shock. It created bright shadows on the floor, patches where the old wood seemed polished to a golden gleam, one of which stretched to a point just inches away from Margaret's feet. She closed the book, held it to her chest, and waited for the light on the floor to slowly engulf her. When it did, she got up and asked the librarian where the books on metals were, and then she lost herself in them for the whole afternoon.

When she was ready to leave, she had a stack of books—including the oversized one on low riders—that became heavy enough as she walked home to warrant a break, and she stepped into the Flying Star Café on the corner of Silver and Eighth Street. It was inviting, with its large windows and the upholstery in its booths featuring comets, stars, and little rocket ships that seemed to suggest that the patrons could sit there and go somewhere else at the same time.

She got in line at the counter and, suddenly realizing she was hungry, ordered dinner—a salad which included dried cranberries as well as a julienne of jicama—and then settled into a back booth to cogitate the nature of metal. Sometimes Margaret became captivated by a theory or an image or an idea, and today, as she pored over the pages devoted to metals, pages she found hard to understand even when she read them slowly and spent time studying the illustrations and pictures, a perception had formed in her mind and slowly seeped everywhere. She had no idea if it was accurate, something that would be covered in Physics 101 if she'd ever taken it, or totally erroneous, but she had arrived at the conclusion that all metals are constructed of the exact same basic material, just arranged in different ratios. She had no image for this basic material, but maybe it originated as some kind of ooze, whatever dreams are made out of, or perhaps some form of lava that erupted from a giant mind somewhere else and flowed through space onto this planet. She didn't know. But what had occurred to her was that the secret of welding was to create little tunnels and bridges, footpaths and skyways, from one metallic landscape to the next. The point, she decided as she buttered her dinner roll and took a little bite, was to attach piece to piece in such a way that a flow was introduced, a type of communication, rather than a wall that could not be scaled or a scar so deep it lost feeling and eventually became numb.

She would ask Rico, she thought, as her salad was deposited on her table by a waitress with at least four rings in her lips and tattoos that formed permanent long sleeves, complete with a little rickrack border at her wrist. Her discomfort regarding Rico and his notoriety had vanished, and the part of her that felt like withdrawing from him, had withered away almost without her noticing. Maybe it was the blazing New Mexico sun, which made shadows form and disappear with such rapidity that becoming lost in one, or attached to the darkness, was essentially a short-lived endeavor.

Margaret ate her dinner and then went home. When it cooled off, she and Magpie walked around the neighborhood, pausing to watch a pickup football game in the grassy yard by the zoo entrance, in which all the players were women— most of them hefty—which probably came in handy in such a rough game, Margaret thought.

AFTER MARGARET'S lesson, Rico focused on his work obligations, just as he did every day of his life. One time, years before, a new neighbor, a grown man from Mexico who was renting a room down the block, had identified himself as a "bus burro" in a local restaurant. Rico had laughed and so had the man, but the truth was that Rico was feeling more and more like a bus burro in his own life. He needed pleasure. He needed time off. He needed a Sunday without church and a Saturday without work, and a few days here and there when he didn't have to scrub his hands and fingernails with gritty orange cleaner before he could feel good about picking up a knife and fork at the dinner table.

His mind drifted back to the cylinder of Rescue Remedy that had rolled out of Margaret's bag toward his feet. What was Rescue Remedy, he wondered. Did it work, and if so, how? In his whole life, Rico had never felt rescued by anything other than his own willpower, the mighty force that stood between him and the many faces of trouble. It was willpower and nothing else that propelled him to place one foot in front of the other every day and just keep going. He never had the illusion he was working toward some specific end where life as he knew it would transform into something new and better, where he could lock up the garage and get on a plane for parts unknown with his pocket full of cash. No. For Rico, it was the beaten path, and that was that.

It had occurred to him, when Margaret mentioned that her schedule was wide open, that she didn't have a job, and he wondered how she pulled that off. She wasn't rich, obviously, with that disgraceful old car and that ancient adobe rental that, he had noticed, had duct tape stretched across a baseball-sized hole high up in the front window. Yet she had time to mosey to the library for the afternoon, to learn to weld, to move to New Mexico from New York, and who knew what else. From his observation, she only had herself to think about, which made a big difference. He himself had people coming out of the woodwork, and so did everyone he knew, most of whom, or perhaps all of whom, were *chicanos* from the South Valley.

Rico was squatting down in front of his tool cabinet, collecting a timing light from the second to bottom drawer, when he sat back on his heels for a moment to reflect on this. Was it true that he didn't have even one Anglo friend or even friendly acquaintance to his name? He'd known a few in school, but that was more than twenty-five years ago. He had a few Anglo customers and several new Anglo neighbors and they were cordial enough, but he didn't know them personally. He had noticed, though, that they didn't come in packs, big families that included several generations all under one roof. They were more solitary as a rule. More disconnected, it seemed, though another way of looking at it was more unencumbered. More free.

Margaret seemed free for sure, but what did he really know about her? He knew nothing. Whatever was happening between them, whatever kind of friendship was brewing—if there was one brewing at all—had begun in the moment when he rerouted his embarrassment and shame into an apology, showed up at her door and, without saying the exact words, asked for forgiveness. It was a strange place to start. It was as if they had to start over before they had even started the first time. But having started at a low point, maybe even the bottom, they couldn't go anywhere but up. There was more to it than all of that, too. It had to do with the belief that he really did deserve a second chance, and she deserved a second chance to get to know him, too. It had to do with standing up and saying no to the force that wanted to mow things down before they even had a chance to grow.

He straightened up and returned his attention to the engine he was in the process of tuning up. He still did his tune-ups primarily by sound, which was possible because most of his customers drove older cars, the kind they loved and wanted to keep alive no matter what. These cars whispered and sang in Rico's ear when he worked on them. They complained, confided secrets, and sometimes asked for help. He knew they were just machines, but Rico felt that each one had a personality, a presence like no other, and by the time he closed the hood and sent them on their way, he always knew them a little bit better than he had on their last visit, something he certainly didn't feel about their owners, who all seemed to have much the same concerns: "Oh no, how much will that cost me, Rico?" and "Is that the very best you can do, Rico?" and "Could I pay you half next week, Rico?" Over the years, he had learned how to say yes and how to say no, whom to trust and whom to doubt, and how to make it clear that he was not a man to fuck around with, should that particular message be called for. In that, he had advanced much farther than his own father, who got screwed left and right because he was too nice a guy; or else, perhaps, because he just didn't have it in him to protest, having used up all his energy trying to control and then reject Fernando.

Sometimes Rico thought he got his tough streak from his older brother, that it was developed and tempered like steel under fire. The extreme duress of Fernando's presence, like a whip delivering a never ending series of lashes, created in Rico a kind of endurance and strength, but also a cut-off point, one that could not be safely passed by anyone. If he got pushed, he retaliated, pushed back with all the pent-up fury of never having stood up to his brother, not to the day he died. How could he? Fernando was a force of nature, like a tornado intent on leveling whatever crossed its path, like a fire intent on consuming the houses of the rich who dared build on the edges of the forest. Rico was helpless before his older brother, but through the years—exactly ten from the time Fernando changed until they laid him in his grave by the Big I—he grew harder inside, as if his arteries and veins were lined with lead and his nerves with carbon steel. It gave him a place to stand up straight in this world. In fact, Rico, in his generous moments, considered it a gift, the one and only, from his brother, and even felt grateful. All he had to do was look out the doors of his garage to see men so beaten down by life that they did nothing but wander around, wearing filthy army jackets that no longer zipped closed and carrying dirty bedrolls strapped to their backs. The Albuquerque Rescue Mission was just a few blocks north. Rico was one of the local business owners to whom Father John made a personal visit every Thanksgiving, asking for a contribution toward the annual dinner at the mission, and Rico always handed over fifty dollars cash.

Speaking of cash, he now had thirty-five unexpected dollars in his pocket and the promise of more. He wanted this money, which Margaret would hand him hour by hour, to be just his. It probably wouldn't add up to any more than a few hundred bucks all told, but he wanted to keep it apart from household finances and the demands of his flock of girls. He didn't want to waste it on some new tool or some operating expense for the garage either. He wanted to stash it somewhere and wait until the precise minute that it became clear to him how to spend it, and then he wanted to slap it down and walk away with whatever it was he wanted. For the first time ever, he needed a hiding place, and he looked around the garage with a sharp eye, noticing his city business license, which was, according to the instructions, prominently displayed in the work area. He took it down off the wall, pried the piece of cardboard backing out of the cheap frame, and pressed the bills inside. It made him feel good to know it was there.

Driving home that evening, waiting to make a left onto La Vega Drive, Rico happened to notice Wilfredo coming up the *acequia*, the irrigation ditch, on his old nag Negrita, and he made a split-second decision to make a U-turn when the light changed, park in the dirt lot at the head of the trail by the river, meet up with Wilfredo, and go along for the ride. This was an unusual, but not a rare occurrence. Rico felt a small sense of responsibility for his young neighbor, who lived alone with his mother, Dora, and seemed to crave some man-to-man contact. They had done building projects together, played one-on-one basketball in Wilfredo's driveway, and attempted to keep Dora's Chevy Cavalier in running order through routine maintenance.

He had already parked the truck and was waiting when Wilfredo crossed the ditch and arrived at the entrance to the trail. "Yo, Wilfredo," Rico called, trying out a genuine New York vocabulary word, "you got room for two on that stallion?"

Wilfredo broke into a grin that stretched from ear to ear as Rico came toward him. Wilfredo rode bareback, probably because there was no money for a saddle. There wasn't really money for a horse either, but Dora had inherited this one as part of the deal when she bought the property. It wasn't so easy for Rico to swing up behind Wilfredo, but he would never tell him that.

"Take care of your *cojones*," Wilfredo advised as Rico got situated, and they both laughed.

"You take care of yours. You might need them some day." It was a thing they always said when they got on the horse.

Wilfredo made a clicking sound, and Negrita headed for the dirt path to the Rio. It was dusk, and the cottonwoods along the riverbank were filled with huge black crows. They squawked up a storm, making such a terrible racket that once in a while Rico felt an uneasiness about moving past them deeper into the *bosque*. There were so many of them—thousands and maybe tens of thousands—and if they should take it into their heads to dive-bomb intruders on their home turf, there'd be nothing left but bloody pulp. Rico had never heard of such a thing happening, but he knew that nature was unpredictable, and all the flying, walking, and creeping beings who lived by the Rio, whose environment was getting destroyed, were getting desperate. Anything could happen.

Still, Rico enjoyed these rides with Wilfredo. He could sense how important it made the young boy feel to be in charge, to hold the reins and control the speed of the animal. And just riding along the river was soothing. The bouncing of the horse seemed to jar loose the tensions of the day, and the little breeze created by the forward movement blew them away.

"*¿Qué pasa contigo?*" Rico asked after a while. "Anything new?"

"I have a *novia*," Wilfredo responded. "I think."

"No shit," said Rico. "Aren't you a little young?" And then, before Wilfredo could even answer, he added, "Stay out of that game, *hombre*. Once you get in it, you never get out again."

"I haven't really been *in* it," Wilfredo said, with great emphasis on the word *in*, and Rico laughed and replied, "Are you talking dirty, Wilfredo?"

"No, Rico. I'm just telling you," he said.

They slid off Negrita, and Wilfredo led her down the bank to a place where the water formed a good drinking puddle.

"How old were you when you had your first *novia*?" Wilfredo asked.

"At least twenty. Maybe thirty," Rico responded.

"Come on, Rico, tell me the truth."

"I don't remember, Wilfredo. Older than you, though." He watched Negrita slurp up the muddy brown water of the

Rio for a while, and then said, "What's her name? This girl you like?"

Wilfredo turned to him. The sun was heading for the horizon in the west, and one ray of it slanted across Wilfredo's face, lighting up the sweat along his hairline and turning his skin a shade of gold. He looked so innocent, so childlike, so unequipped for what he was rushing toward that it was all Rico could do to keep a straight face. "Jennifer," Wilfredo said, as if he expected all the angels in the celestial heavens to start strumming their lutes in her honor.

"Jennifer," Rico repeated, and out of respect for Wilfredo, he added, "that's a beautiful name."

He said Jennifer, but in his mind he was thinking, Margaret.

1980

SOMETHING HAPPENS to time in here, Vincent muses. It loses its meaning. Next week, last week, next year, five years ago, ten years from now. They all melt together.

Here you are, surrounded by a thousand guys, all in limbo.
You disappear.
You don't even remember who you were.
Years go by.
Years and years and years.
Go by.

Rico and Wilfredo rode Negrita a few miles along the river, past where the footpath was overgrown and, for a few hundred yards, became difficult to make headway. They pressed farther, knowing that it opened up again into a wonderland of sunflowers growing every which way. This was perhaps the most magical place in the world, Rico thought. Because of the lay of the land and the bend in the river, there was no sign of humans nor their habitat anywhere—just the river, the golden sunflowers, the blue sky, and the tops of the Manzano Mountains to the south, way off in the distance. Quiet and peaceful were words that should have described it, but they had lost their ability to capture this kind of beauty. Better to bring Margaret here than try to describe it to her.

Rico had a temptation, passing but acute, to mention to Wilfredo that he had made a new friend himself—not a *novia* by any means, but a female through and through. He stopped himself because it seemed—and was—pitiful to confide in an eleven-year-old boy. He had never been the type of man to tell his secrets. What he did was nobody's business, and how he felt, overall and moment-to-moment, was not for public consumption either. But suddenly he just wanted to have a reason to say her name out loud.

When he arrived home just before dark, the whole house was deserted. Elena, Rosalita, Lucy, and Jessica were out having their pictures taken at some charity event sponsored by Elena's church called, "Mothers Through the Generations"; Ana was taking a night class that didn't release her until after nine; Maribel had a job at PetSmart and, though she got off work at seven, she rarely made it home before eleven. To be in the house all alone was a rare event, and Rico found himself wandering around, actually opening doors and peeking inside as if he had no idea who lived behind each one. They had a nice home here. They had furniture they had selected rather than inherited or collected out of junkshops as they did in the early days. The house was orderly, at least to the extent that it could be given the presence of a two year old. There were finishing touches, like a vase of fresh flowers on the kitchen table, collected from the garden outside, and seven little pots with cactuses growing in them on the window ledge. Photographs of the girls in various stages of development were framed and rested on several of the horizontal surfaces.

He sat down on the couch. It was silent, with the radio off for once and no chatter, no TV blaring, no baby screeching for whatever reason. He folded his hands in his lap. What next, he thought. Twiddle his thumbs? Rustle up something to eat? Take a long, hot shower? Take a cold one? He unlaced his work boots and took them off, and then he stretched out on the couch, adjusting one throw pillow under his neck and another one under his knees. He could hear the ticking of the kitchen clock, the hum of the cool air coming through the swamp cooler vent in the ceiling, and the motor on the fridge turning on and off at intervals. It was almost like a musical concert, he thought—a buzz here, a tick tock there, a crescendo of noise rising and falling. Dogs were barking off in the distance too—which happened one hundred percent of the time in the South Valley—and cars whose mufflers needed replacement passed by on the street. He felt a sudden urge to listen even more closely, as if once he quieted down in a quiet place—which was unusual in itself—he couldn't stop. He even became aware of the sound of his breathing, the way it whistled a little as it formed airstreams out of his nostrils.

He listened even harder, feeling suddenly convinced that he was heading toward a place he'd never really had the chance to visit before. He closed his eyes, and it felt like a thick curtain had fallen from the top of the window frame, blocking out the details of the trumpet vines that practically cascaded in thick vines into his living room. He felt completely alert, just lying there like a lump on the sofa, as if his senses had just awakened after a long, long nap. It seemed to Rico that a space had cleared in his head; he was moving through it with no particular goal in mind, but with the same kind of curiosity that might make him pick up a stone in the yard and turn it over in his hand for no reason.

It was somewhere in this silence that he heard a message, though it didn't come in the form of words and there was no voice attached to it. It came in the form of a certainty, a direction, a knowing that he could not escape or ignore, not if he wanted to have any respect for himself as a man and a husband. It had to do with Rosalita, with trying one more time to penetrate the shell she lived in. Because now Rico was wondering if she had somehow found for herself a place like the one he was in at this very moment. If she was so absorbed in some internal process, some way of being that had so little connection to the outer world that she had all but disappeared from it. If that was why she seemed like a ghost or a shadow.

His determination to talk to her coalesced into action, so when she went into the bedroom that night to slip into her nightie and climb into bed, he followed her, closing the door behind him. She turned from him as she quickly undid her blouse, removed her bra, and pulled the nightgown on over her head. Then she lifted it to undo her slacks and slide them down over her hips.

"Are you coming to bed already, Rico? It's so early for you," she said. He could tell by the way she moved like a cat toward her side of the bed that she knew he was up to something, though she had elected to play it as if it were normal for him to come in and close the door. This had not been normal for four years now.

"Rosalita, I need to talk to you," he said.

"It's not a good time, Rico. I'm tired. I have to be up early for work."

"It is a good time," he countered. "It's the perfect time."

Rosalita snapped back the summer bedspread and got into the bed. She propped the pillows up against the headboard and leaned against them. "Okay," she said. "What is it that's so important?"

Her tone, which was full of annoyance, seemed like a high wall to scale, but Rico moved to the bed and sat down next to her. "I want to talk to you," he said.

"We've established that. So go ahead. I'm listening. Start."

It seemed almost impossible to begin, given the feeling of resistance in the room. "Rosalita," he said, "I have to tell you that . . ." Here he stopped. There were so many ways to go from here, so many emotional strands to follow, but each one was so entangled that they all felt dangerous to him. He reached for her hand, and she let him have it. He had touched her hand, even held it occasionally, countless numbers of times, even after she disconnected from him. But now he turned it over and rubbed her palm with his thumb. He looked at the lines there, her whole past, present, and future story to a gypsy fortune-teller, but a mystery to him, except that the skin still felt so soft, like a young girl's.

"What is it, Rico," she asked, and this time her voice was just as soft as her skin.

He looked up and saw a fluttering in her eyes that reminded him of the woman she was before she entered the deep freeze state. He felt tears, hot as molten metal, fill his eyes, though, thank God, they didn't spill over. They glistened there, though, a source of extra tension for Rico, who had probably not cried in front of Rosalita more than five times in all their years together.

"Rosalita," he began, and then he added, "*mi alma, mi vida, mi corazón*," just because he had used those words so constantly in the old days, "I have to tell you that I can't go on the way we are anymore. I can't."

She looked as if she was holding her breath. She said nothing, but her fingers in his hand suddenly felt cooler.

"I don't know what happened to us—to you, Rosalita. But it has to change because I'm going crazy." He wanted to tell her how mystified he was, how hurt if he had to be truthful about it, how his patience had finally come to an end, how their marriage had become a kind of mockery of the love that united them in the first place. How he was perilously close to thinking of himself as a man stripped of his balls, and, if he had the courage, he wanted to say how angry he was and how disappointed—things that he knew she would perceive as fighting words when all the rest were feeling words. But instead of all this, he said, "I think about sex all the time, Rosalita. Too much. I'm having fantasies, weird fantasies, the kind that make me wonder if I'm normal anymore. I'm getting a hard-on every time I turn around, and, Rosalita, I can't hold out any more. This is it, *mujer*. Either you get over whatever-it-is you're in and we start up again or . . ."

He had no idea how to finish the sentence. He was not a man who had a plan in mind when he brought up a subject. He had a bad enough time just putting the words together in a coherent sentence when he was under stress like this. Her summer nightgown had fallen a little low on one shoulder, and her hair, already brushed out, looked like an intense shadow designed to match her eyes.

"Is there something you want to do to me, Rico?" she asked, and her voice sounded genuine, as if she were posing a real question, maybe one with a little humor it in, too.

"Yes," he said. "Everything."

"Then go ahead," she said. Just like that.

"Take that nightgown off," he whispered, and she obediently lifted it over her head and dropped it onto the floor next to the bed. He hadn't seen her bare breasts, except by accident, in years, and his hands moved to them. Then he fell across the bed toward her, gathering her in his arms, burying his face in her neck, breathing her in, lifting her hair, and then whispering into her ear, "Where have you been, Rosalita? Where have you been?"

Margaret had been in the same position on the couch for three hours, poring over the library books on the nature of metal, before she noticed that the pillow she'd wedged in behind her back against the wooden arm of the futon couch had slipped. The arm was digging into her back right across the place where the lower ribs attach, and she finally, with a little groan, pushed herself forward for relief. She had purchased this couch at the St. Vincent de Paul used furniture store for thirty dollars. The workers there, all of whom looked like recovering alcoholics, had tied it to the roof of her Dodge Colt Vista, and back at home she had dragged it inside by herself. It was comfortable and it looked clean, the latest, and perhaps the best, in a long parade of futon couches that had come and gone from Margaret's apartments over the years.

When Donny died, Margaret had continued to live in their place on Forty-Eighth Street, the only home she'd known for fourteen years. It had all the essentials necessary to make her feel comfortable—a coffeemaker, a queen-size bed that had been his, a color TV and radio, plates and pots, drawers full of clothing and painting supplies—but it didn't have Donny, and just being at home there made her ache inside, an ache so deep she once caught herself reaching into the knife drawer with the idea of cutting it out. Her high school friend Christina, who was in her first year of college at the University of Pennsylvania, spent most of her spring break at Margaret's, packing up Donny's clothes and shoes, and lugging the boxes down the four flights of stairs to the street, where they hailed a taxi and took them to the Salvation Army drop-off point. Afterward, they had sobbed in each other's arms as they scrubbed the apartment, top to bottom, which was Christina's idea. She referred to it as a ritual cleansing, which Margaret thought was funny, though she didn't say so.

At night, they would break into Donny's private scotch stash, twelve-year-old Glenlivit, even though neither of them liked the taste. In any case, it wasn't the taste they were after— it was the place it took them, very efficiently. "The quickest way out of New York," they called it, though, truthfully, Margaret had no desire to leave and Christina missed the city so much she was thinking of transferring to NYU at the end of the year. But they needed and wanted to get to the place where they could cry even harder at the kitchen table, tell each other Donny stories, because both had loved them—told in that brogue of his that made them all seem funnier—and both had loved him.

"Remember the one about his grandfather?" Margaret would say. Donny's grandfather had been shot by a neighbor in a drunken party brawl. When he recovered he had to appear as a witness in court, where the judge had asked, "Is it true that you were shot in the fracas?"

"I think it was a little above the fracas," Christina would reply, imitating Donny's brogue, and they would both laugh and cry and pour another drink.

"Remember the leprechauns?" Christina would counter. One time when they were high school sophomores, they had come back to Margaret's apartment to find Donny and his Irish friend Pat Connelly parked at the kitchen table having an intense conversation about leprechauns. The girls had found that hilarious, and Margaret had said, "I can't believe I come home and find two grown men in a serious discussion about the wee little people in the green suits."

"They don't wear green, girls, they wear red!" Margaret would recite, and off they'd go again, into peals of laughter, a far better ritual cleansing than any amount of scrubbing the kitchen or washing the windows.

When Christina returned to school, Margaret fell into a black hole, into the dark night where it was more than she could manage to get out the door once a day to make a grocery run to the corner. She stopped eating. She stopped going to work—and she had a good job for someone inexperienced, as a go-fer in a company that published three different arts and crafts magazines. She also stopped attending her painting classes, which, after a few weeks, brought Nick, her teacher, to her door. She would never forget the look on his face when she answered it.

"Oh my God," he had said. And she had tumbled into his arms as if he were her best friend, and said, "My grandfather died, Nick," and then proceeded to faint, something she had never done in her life. It had simply taken everything out of her to say those few words. He had done all the right things: carried her to the couch, wet a washcloth with cool water and pressed it to her forehead, cleaned up the kitchen and made some food from scratch. He had drawn her a bath and made her get in it, collected the dirty clothes from the floor and taken them to the Chinese laundry on the corner. He even contacted the counselor at the School of Visual Arts, begging her to make a house call, even though Margaret—as a part-time student—didn't actually qualify for her services.

Margaret, even in her fog, had suspected at the time—and later Nick confirmed it—that rescuing her in that moment had almost done him in. He had never before seen anyone who had gone over the edge. He had made a concentrated effort in his own life to stay as far away from the edges as he possibly could; but he forced himself to help Margaret, to pull her gently back. Once she was on her feet again, he took off running, and they barely spoke for over a year, by which time he had married another woman.

It took eight months for the sharp, deep ache of no-Donny to begin to dull, and then Margaret decided that she could not live in the apartment anymore. So she sublet it illegally for close to three times what she paid in rent. The monthly profit subsidized a smaller place in an unimproved building in the flower district, and then one in the East Village, and then a one-bedroom in Queens, and then a studio in Brooklyn, and so on. She held onto Donny's apartment for nine years before the management company found her out and threatened legal proceedings if she didn't surrender the keys immediately, which she did. She had stood in front of the building and looked up at the window where, twenty-three years before, she had watched her mother and father wave goodbye and disappear forever. She never returned to the block where she and her grandfather used to walk, hand in hand, back when she had thought that he was a giant, maybe the biggest and strongest man in the whole world.

Margaret shifted the book off her lap and stood up. It was late, past midnight, and the windowpanes looked solid black in the slits where she hadn't quite closed the curtains. She walked to the kitchen door, Magpie dutifully trailing after her, and went out into the yard. The rusty parts on the cement pad drew her to them, as if they were sending a message that they were impatient to be assembled. They wanted her to breathe life into them, she thought. She had assumed, when the urge to go three-dimensional first overtook her—long before she had the space and time to do it—that she was artistically fed up with a flat surface and needed to break free of it. But now she knew that it was more. It was also about paying close attention to connection, to the mysteries of how to position parts so they were built to withstand all kinds of pressure, so they were built to last.

She picked up an old gear. It looked like a circle with a hole through the middle, some spines connecting that hole to the circumference, with a railroad track around the edge. She wanted to transform it into an ear on a being that was somewhat recognizable, but not quite human. She wanted to find a way to connect it so it seemed suspended in air, barely touching the other parts. And she wanted to bury this being in such a conglomeration of parts that it would take time to find it, even if you knew where to look. She had to admit that she didn't even know what kind of metal it was, and therefore could not speculate on its melting point or anything else. Margaret had always entered her paintings from a place of not-knowing. She had no plan for them, wouldn't think of making one, and was constantly surprised and always thrilled when they squirmed out of her control and did what they wanted. She wished, many times, that she could apply that model to her life in more ways than art. In her painting life, she never knew where she was going and she loved it that way. In her other life, her so-called normal life, she tried to manage it, saving money in her coffee cans, trying to dress up whatever apartment she was in to create a passable home, showing up on time for work, and having the integrity—rare in a bartender—not to steal even one dime. There was a wildness in her, but she kept it confined to her art, and sometimes she wondered what would happen if she just took the lid off the rest of her life and let the wildness in there, too. Perhaps that was coming toward her in some way, for suddenly, in her artistic life, she was imagining finished products before she even had the technical mastery to put them together. If her art became more orderly, more predictable in some way, would her other life get wilder, she wondered. Was she ready for that?

She climbed into the hammock and rocked back and forth like a metronome counting out the minutes until it all would unfold.

1985

V INCENT STANDS next to Will at the prison gate to say goodbye to Jean Pierre. They have known each other for ten long, long years. In each one of those years, Jean Pierre's family has traveled back and forth from Marseilles to India, hired lawyers, offered bribes. Jean Pierre has never given up hope, something Vincent surrendered long ago, but not as long ago as Will did.

Jean Pierre wears clean clothes, brought in a small bundle by his father, who now sits inside the room marked "Processing," staring out at his son, who will leave with him on this day. Jean Pierre has received a shave and a shampoo. He wears white sneakers.

His hands are shaking.

"I'm not gonna hug you and get you dirty, man," says Will. "You clean up good."

Jean Pierre laughs.

"Fuck some mademoiselles for me," says Will. And then he turns and walks away.

Vincent steps forward. He is overwhelmed with sadness but he manages to say, "I'm happy for you, Jean Pierre," even as his eyes fill with tears.

"I remember the address," Jean Pierre says. "429 West 48th Street, New York, New York. I'll send a letter. Don't worry." And then, on an impulse, he reaches up and lifts off the silver chain with the St. Christopher medal he wears around his neck. He places it on Vincent, like a blessing. "I hope you find your way home, mon ami," he says. "I hope you find your wife and little girl."

They hug, as if one of them is going to the gallows.

Then Jean Pierre disappears through the door, and Vincent is left standing in the hot sun, staring into the window of the

"Processing" room, where men in khaki uniforms block his last glimpse of Jean Pierre.

He hears two days later, though he never knows for certain if it's true, about the accident, the collision of a battered taxi carrying two foreign passengers and a bus on the winding road to Siruguppa. His hand moves to his throat, to the St. Christopher medal, and he wishes Jean Pierre, who believed in it so completely, had kept it.

He wants to give it back, to give it away.

But he is afraid to take it off.

Rico arrived at the garage the next morning in a black mood. And the fact that he knew he should be feeling good, maybe even happy, only made him angrier. His life had been out of control in one way, and now it was just as out of control in another. Before last night, he had felt blocked out of something important. He had felt rejected and confused and, at times, very lonely. Now he felt enraged.

The ice between Rico and Rosalita had been officially broken. She had responded to him in a way that seemed genuine, and while he held her in his arms, as she moaned quietly into his chest—trying to muffle her own sounds because all the girls were home and sitting in the living room not very far from their bedroom door—he felt a deep and powerful love flow between them. This love asked for no explanations. It stood outside the perimeter of the last four years as if time had no relevance whatsoever. It knew that forms came and went, including the many forms of relationship and love, sex and marriage. They had been in one phase. It had ended, and now another had begun. Why ask questions?

And Rico hadn't really asked any last night, just the "Where have you been, Rosalita?" that he repeated twice before he fell into her and got lost. She had not answered anyway, except to say, "Waiting for you to come get me," which, at the time, had a sexy edge because he was already on top of her at that point, and she had already opened her thighs to him, wrapped her legs around his hips and made it more than clear that the waiting, four years' worth, was over. Rico had felt himself bear down and lift off at the same time, and after that he had felt as if he'd been sucked into outer space.

But later, after Rosalita had fallen asleep, her face pressed into his chest and her hand low on his stomach, so low that her ring and pinky fingers rested at the edge of his patch of pubic hair, Rico had begun to feel something else, and it wasn't good. He had imagined this moment for four years, the moment when Rosalita's winter would turn to spring, and everything between them would at last come back together. He had thought he would feel very good when it happened, but now that it had, Rico felt violated, used by Rosalita, as if she thought it was a fine thing to end her ice age and melt in his arms, offering no apology for all those cold years and acting like nothing had changed in the meantime.

But something had changed, Rico thought. Him. He had changed, moved away from her, perhaps as far as she had moved away from him, though he had been so preoccupied with his own feeling of rejection and felt so much the victim that he had not noticed how far he himself had traveled. Last night had been a point of honor for him; he'd made his last and final attempt to reach her, to pull her back. He'd done it as a gesture of respect for his wife, one last attempt to salvage what they'd had together for nineteen years before he let her go once and for all. But he had never once asked himself if he still wanted her. Rosalita, herself. Now, based on this ice blue anger that made him cold, made him reach for the summer bedspread and pull it up across his chest, hiding that hand on his stomach, he had to face the truth: maybe he didn't want her anymore. Maybe it was just too late.

He barely slept.

Beside him, Rosalita was peaceful, her chest rising and falling, and her arm folded under her head to form a little pillow. Rico wanted to shake her awake and demand an accounting of the last four years. He felt as if she'd been traveling in some foreign country and had arrived unannounced back at his door last night. She came in and acted as if she'd never been gone.

Rico felt he had a right to a lengthy explanation, an apology, a play by play that would take the sting out of all the nights he'd been turned away by her, all the nights she'd clung to the edge of her side of their bed, where there was no likelihood of a chance brushing up against each other. He tossed, he turned, he got up three times for a glass of water, but he never settled down to sleep—though he did pretend to be off in dreamland when Rosalita got up at five-thirty for work. She had never put her nightgown back on, and now she pranced around the bedroom nude as Rico watched out of the slit in his eye. And she looked good too, a curvy woman with shapely legs and an ass that could still inspire a little loving slap or two. She collected her work clothes and shoes and left the room, closing the door behind her with a soft click. That was when Rico opened his eyes fully and took to staring at the cracks in the ceiling plaster.

When he heard her car start up, heard her open and close the driveway gate, and take off up Riverside Drive, he finally got out of bed. He took a quick shower and put on his clothes, very aware of the pressure in his chest. If he were a tire, he would've been inflated far past the optimum amount, he thought, though there was no release valve that he knew of for the human heart. It was just ten after six when he heard Jessica calling to her mother, and he knew they would appear in the kitchen within a few minutes to begin the new day, just the same as all the rest. Today, though, he did not feel up to facing Lucy's morning grumpiness or Jessica's babyish exuberance. Quietly, he let himself out the door and got into his truck. He had two hours to kill before he opened the shop.

Before he even knew what he was doing, he turned into the driveway of Albuquerque High School, and swung around the back to the kitchen where Rosalita had just begun her work day. The double doors to the service entrance were wide open and he could see several of the food service workers inside, all in their white uniforms complete with paper hats that looked like cheap French berets covering their hair. Rosalita was one of them. She stood at a long stainless steel prep sink washing a thousand juicy red tomatoes. Beside her stood her friend Sonia, who had worked for the school as long as Rosalita had. It was Sonia who noticed Rico as he came through the door and said a few words to Rosalita that made her look up in surprise, dry her hands and come toward him.

"Rico, did something happen?" she asked, and he saw fear reflected in her eyes and even the set of her jaw, and for good reason, probably. He had only shown up at her job three times, and for each one bad news had driven him there: his father's death, a broken leg for Maribel, and an allergic reaction for Ana that had her in the emergency room for one whole afternoon and night.

"Everybody's okay," he said, "But I need to talk to you for a minute. Outside."

Now she looked perplexed and, Rico thought, a bit annoyed. But she turned and called, "Be right back" to Sonia, who nodded and then added a little wave to Rico, which he returned. They stepped into the parking lot.

"What is it, Rico?"

Now Rico felt embarrassed, as if it were a stupid thing, a bad idea to come here, and he'd just figured that out. But since he was here, and since he knew why he came, he plowed forward.

"I have two questions," he said. "Why did you let me fuck you last night? That's one question. The other is, Why haven't you let me touch you for four years?"

Rosalita drew in a breath and then let it out.

"Rico, is this the right time for this?"

"I've been living on your time schedule for years, Rosalita. Now you can live on mine for a few minutes."

She reached up to her hat and took it off, as if wearing a paper kitchen beret was just too much at a moment like this. "But I'm at work," she said.

"Then go in there and tell them you're taking the day off. Tell them something came up."

She appeared to think that over for a few seconds, but then said, "Should I tell you the truth?"

"Sí, Rosalita. La verdad, por favor."

"I got tired of my life, tired of our life, and tired of you. I wanted to get away, and I knew I couldn't. It wasn't anything bad you did, Rico. You're a good husband, a good father. And you're my friend." Here she reached partway toward his hand. "But none of that was enough. And I . . ."

She hesitated, and Rico had a feeling bad news was coming.

". . . and I met somebody at the same time, another man, and I had to make a decision about whether to leave you or go behind your back, or just let things go on as they were. It was a very hard time for me, Rico."

Now Rico held his breath. He felt as if his skin was being ripped off in strips exposing whatever is underneath to the heat of the desert sun. He felt hot. He waited.

"In the end I decided to leave everything as it was. But it wasn't the same after that. I couldn't pretend that it was." She shifted her kitchen hat, which she had balled up like a Kleenex, from one hand to the other. "I wasn't ready for that."

"So you lost both ways," Rico said, and even though there was an edge of anger in his voice, the words themselves had kindness in them.

"And so did you," Rosalita responded. She did not add, "I'm sorry."

Not that Rico was waiting for those exact words in that particular moment. He may have driven to the school for the express purpose of forcing them out of her, but now he had heard too much, not only what Rosalita said, but all the agony behind it, all the waves of sorrow, all the questioning she had done in private, maybe to spare him, maybe not. Standing there, with his perfect hindsight, he suddenly remembered the way her eyes had been so clouded over during that time, the way she used to stare at the television as if she were seeing through the picture tube to some other world, the way she took to holding one of the throw pillows on the couch in front of her heart with her arms crossed over it. He remembered watching her as she did the dishes, washing the plates over and over, making the same circle on them with the sponge as if she had totally forgotten where she was. He had studied her from the kitchen door, wondering if she would ever snap out of it, whatever it was.

"You could have told me, Rosalita," he said.

"No, Rico. I couldn't." She moved slightly so she stood in his shadow. "I can barely tell you now."

"And all this leaves us where?" he finally said.

"Nowhere special," she answered. If he had been more like Fernando, he might have smacked her a good one in that moment. He might have hit her hard enough to knock her down, and then climbed into his truck and tore off without a backward glance. He might not have shown up at home for a week, if he had been more like Fernando. It wasn't that Rico didn't know or understand the feelings that make a man act that way. He did. But he didn't respect them.

"This is a lot to hear," he finally said.

"Now you know," she responded, and she reached forward and touched him on the hand. "I hope it's better for you, knowing." Looking down into her eyes, Rico felt somewhat steadied by her gaze. He could see the concern she had for him. He could also see her fear and dread, and something in that simple truth paralyzed him for a moment.

And then they were interrupted by Sonia, calling from the kitchen door. "Rosalita, are you coming in? I'm sorry, but we're behind in here and . . ." She stopped talking when they both turned in her direction. She stepped back inside the kitchen, disappearing into the shadows.

Rosalita returned her eyes to Rico.

"Go ahead," he said, with a nod in the direction of the kitchen door.

"Okay," she replied, and then she turned away. Before she entered the kitchen door, she spun around and stared at him as if he were a vision or a mirage in the middle of the parking lot. Then she went inside.

Rico climbed into his truck. He turned the key in the ignition and felt comforted by the smooth sound of the engine coming to life. When he arrived at the edge of the parking lot, he had no idea which way to turn on Indian School Road, though he'd driven up and down that street a million times in his life. Finally, he made a right, and after a series of unplanned rights and lefts, he ended up in the parking lot of the Frontier restaurant—right across from the university—a local eatery that sat a hundred people at a time and usually had the food ready for pickup within a minute of when you ordered it. Often it was ready before you even got settled into a booth in the back. Today Rico ordered a sticky bun and a coffee, which he carried to the farthest dining room, and sat down under a painting of Elvis Presley that was at least eight feet high and six feet wide.

The Frontier was crowded, as usual. Study groups with books spread far and wide occupied several of the big tables, and there were mothers with babies and young lovers and old men with stained shirts all around him. Busboys pushed overloaded carts through the narrow aisles, clearing off the tables with the precision of robots, and the speaker above his head produced a static-riddled version of "My Green Tambourine." The racket pleased him. It pushed any possibility of thought out of his mind, but it couldn't control the black mood which pressed in from the edges, just like the black background of the painting above his head was closing in on Elvis. On the opposite wall a life-size portrait of John Wayne, all cowboyed up with both pistols drawn, appeared ready to blow Rico's head off. Rico, who felt as if he'd already been in one shootout today, barely picked at his sticky bun. When he left forty-five minutes later, more than half of it sat uneaten in a sea of coagulated butter.

He drove west to Fourth Street and turned south. He had actually forgotten about Margaret, and it wasn't until he arrived at the garage almost ten minutes late and saw her standing out in front that he remembered it was time for her second lesson. "Shit," he said as he pulled into his parking spot. Then he said "Shit" again. He put the truck in park and got out.

"Yo, Margaret," he said as he came toward her.

"Yo, Rico," she replied with a smile, but then the smile disappeared and she took a half step toward him, and added, "What's wrong, Rico? What's happened?"

This stopped him, an almost imperceptible pause in his forward motion. How could a woman he barely knew read him like an open book? He had spent his whole life perfecting his poker face. He had learned to control every muscle, including the vestigial ones that sometimes urged him to show his fangs and growl. But she seemed to look past it all into his heart, which, while not breaking, was at least seriously stunned. And then the completely unacceptable happened. He felt his throat tighten and his eyes fill up, and there he was, having to reach up to brush tears off his cheek while pretending to adjust his sunglasses.

"*Nada*, Margaret," he said. "Sorry I'm late."

He stepped around her to work the key into the lock. Behind the security bars was a small window, and he could see himself reflected in it. Perhaps it was the wavy quality of the old glass, which hadn't been changed since his father had bought the shop, but he looked shell-shocked in the reflection, like a man who's already been knocked out, but hasn't fallen down yet. It made him mad to see that reflection, and the dark mood grew even darker, right before his own eyes. He could also see Margaret, a slim presence at the periphery. She had that heavy bag hanging from her shoulder, and in that split second, it crossed Rico's mind that maybe she carried the weight of the world in it, that she was some kind of angel sent to help him. He dismissed that thought quickly, though. What kind of a man looked for an angel to rescue him?

He pushed the door open, stepped in, and flipped on the lights.

Margaret followed him inside. He was intensely aware of her behind him, as if the energy around her, that yellow glow she seemed to have, was pressing up against his mood. "Want me to set up?" she asked.

"*Sí, claro*," he said.

She went into the work bay and hung her bag on the hook. Then she hit the lever for the hydraulic lift, stopped it at precisely the right moment like a pro, and began to pull the TIG welding apparatus, with its foot pedal amp control and its argon hoses, away from the wall to a convenient place under the car. Rico, across the garage at the bathroom door, lifted his coveralls off the hook and stepped into them, zipping them up just as she turned to him, ready to go.

"You learn fast," he said.

"I've got a good teacher," she replied, and then she added, "*el rey.*"

Women have a way of smiling a half-smile, one that seems to be connected somehow to the outside edge of their eyes, which they use when they know they have something on you, Rico thought. This smile makes their eyes gleam more as their lips curve upward in the slightest way, and it creates an intense charge in the atmosphere between the woman and the man she's smiling at. It could almost, but not quite, be called flirtation.

"I read about you in a book at the library," she continued. "I had no idea you were famous. If I'd known, I would never have hustled you to teach me to weld. I would've been way too intimidated."

Suddenly Rico felt dizzy, and he leaned against the workbench for balance. Everything was speeded up, swirling around him like he was some cartoon character, maybe Wile E. Coyote, who had just been lassoed by a cowboy in a passing pickup truck and was spinning mightily along the side of the road. His wife had just announced that, for her, their last four years had been a complete write-off. She had said that they were "nowhere special" in their lives together now. But here was another woman, a woman he had mistaken for both the Virgin of Guadalupe and a rescuing angel, who was giving him that half-smile and a compliment, too. And just a few moments ago, she had taken one look at him and known something was terribly wrong and asked him what it was; and Rico appreciated that because for four years everything had been wrong with him, and his own wife had failed to bring it up.

"Yeah, I'm '*el rey*' to the low riders and '*el nada*' everywhere else," he said, because he had to say something, and that was the first thing he could think of. There was a certain buoyancy to the words too, as if leaning against the workbench permitted him to launch them with more lightheartedness than he could realistically muster in the moment otherwise.

Margaret threw back her head and laughed. It took five years off her face when she did. "Hey, I'm going to embroider that on a nametag for your jumpsuit there," she said. "Really."

"This is not a jumpsuit, Margaret. Jumpsuits are for *maricones*. These are work coveralls," he replied in a stern voice, which made her laugh again. And the ring of that laugh echoing around the work bay wedged its way into his mood, lightening it up, mainly, Rico figured, because he was where he was, making jokes with Margaret, and not in the past—or the future either, for that matter.

"Ready to rock and roll?" he asked; she nodded, and he stepped up next to her, commencing the job on the axle that they had begun just yesterday. Today it would be done, and then they could move on to the body work, which was probably more in line with what she needed to learn for her art projects. Having her next to him, staring upward into the underbelly of the Chevy as he worked the cutting torch, sparks flying everywhere, he felt as if they were making some crazy offering to a fire god from long ago, maybe in some ceremony at the rim of the volcanoes on the West Mesa, in hopes of holding off the eruption.

They finished just before noon, and, like yesterday, she collapsed into his rolling desk chair while he landed in one of the folding chairs. He was delighted and amused by this little display of oblivion and selfishness on her part, how she automatically assumed she was the one in need of the most immediate relief and comfort. In fact, she did look rather overwhelmed, as if she had a bad headache or had been staring into the sun for three hours of intense driving.

"I am *so* out of my league," she said. "I hope I'm not driving you crazy."

Suddenly Rico remembered his first few lessons with his own father, how the whole language of welding was like Chinese to him and he had no idea what to reach for when his father asked him to hand him something. He had just dropped out of high school and was only fifteen when he went to work full-time in the garage, though fifteen then seemed older than it did now.

"It takes time," he said. "Let it come in its own time."

"Hey, I'm a New Yorker. I'm in a rush," she said.

"No such thing as a rush," he answered. "There's always *mañana*"; and even as he said it it occurred to Rico that he actually lived his life that way—perhaps to his own detriment, as his four years of patience with Rosalita no doubt proved. It made him feel sheepish, and he fixed his eyes on the cement floor for a moment.

"So," Margaret began with a little shift in her voice, as if she were preparing him for a change of subject, "how does it feel to be captured for all eternity in the pages of a book?"

"It feels like nothing," Rico said. "I never even saw the book."

"You never saw the *book?*" Margaret repeated. "Why not?"

"The guy who wrote it, you know, he invited me to a bookstore where he was signing it, but I didn't go. It wasn't like I was going to buy it. He told me it was, like, forty bucks. And after that, where would I see it?"

Margaret shook her head. "The *rey* without an ego," she said.

"Margaret, speak English, will you?" he said. "Or Spanish."

She shifted forward in the chair and reached down to the floor where her big bag was waiting in a pile. "All is not lost," she said. "I just happen to have a copy on me." She reached into the bag and extracted a book that looked, on first glance, too big to fit in there. "Ta-daaaa."

She placed the book on the desk and opened it to a page marked with a yellow sticky note. Rico stood up to cross to the desk, bringing his folding chair with him. She had rolled her chair close to the desk too, and soon they were sitting elbow to elbow, the book spread open between them.

"Here you are," she said, pointing to a full-color picture of Rico squatting down next to the fender of an old Impala. He wore goggles that obscured his face, but he was still recognizable with his tattooed arms and long ponytail. He leaned in to get a better look, and so did she, and that was when he heard the car pull up, stopping in front of the garage office, in front of the window where he and Margaret were framed like a painting. Rico glanced up and saw, with a thud in his heart that felt like an electrical short circuit, that it was Rosalita.

1988

VINCENT TEACHES *the illiterate prisoners how to speak, read, and write English. He does this to pass the time. He does it to make some form of contribution.* He does it because the prison officials give him a small cell of his own, a closet really, where he is frequently visited by one of the prison cats, an orange tabby he calls Gladys. Gladys, like all the cats, helps with the rodent problem. She also helps Vincent feel more human.

He is working with his students in a corner of the prison compound, drawing the letters of the alphabet in the dirt with a sharp stick, when he sees Thomas Yazzie for the first time. Thomas lingers at the edges of the lesson. Watches. Offers nothing.

He is dark-skinned, black-haired, like everyone else, but there is something different about him. Different enough that Vincent takes notice. When the lesson is over and the men disperse, Thomas moves forward.

He is Navajo, it turns out. An ex-soldier who has seen too much and done too much and desperately needs healing. He has left the army, finished his tour of duty, received his DD-214, and headed out to see the beauty of the world as a way of counteracting what he'd seen and done.

He came to India.

He needed money, and he made the same mistake Vincent had made, fourteen long years before.

"The prisons here are different," Vincent tells Thomas, who, he learns, arrived just nine days ago. "They keep you here for years before they even charge you with anything." He offers his hand. "I'm Vincent," he says. "Let's go find a place in the shade to sit." He begins to cross the dirt yard, stepping around squatting men who play a game involving little piles of stones and a great deal of yelling.

Thomas follows as quickly as he can.

Rosalita never took her eyes off Rico's, not from the time she opened the door and got out of her car, to the moment she stepped out of the sun and into the office of Garcia's Automotive. Rico watched her coming with the same sense of trepidation and dread he might feel about the approach of a tornado from across the plains. He had no doubt how the former Rosalita—the Rosalita from before this morning, last night, or the past four years—would handle her entrance into a scene like this. It would involve screaming and yelling, and she might even come at him, her arms flailing. But her hot Latina blood appeared to have cooled to the point of neutrality over her long winter, and now Rico had no idea what she might do.

When she stepped across the threshold, he said, "*Hola*, Rosalita," as if nothing at all were wrong with her finding him huddled down at his desk in the middle of the day, shoulder to shoulder, with an Anglo woman, one with long black hair, green eyes, and lips the color of peach blossoms.

"*Hola*, Rico," she said, and her voice had a quality in it that made Margaret sit up straight and glance at him, as if she was waiting for him to present her with an explanation of what was happening.

"Rosalita, this is Margaret," he said. Then he turned to Margaret, whose face was not more than a foot away from his, and said, "Margaret, this is Rosalita, *mi esposa*."

"Hi, Rosalita," Margaret said with an easy smile. "We were just looking at this book I found in the library. Rico's in it. Come see." She said this naturally, as if she were an innocent person, which she was, though how could Rosalita believe this. She said this in a voice that somehow reduced the visuals of this moment to unimportance, as if she had the power to take the questions hanging in the air and drive them all like a drill into the book on the desk. She even slid out of her chair and made a gesture toward it, as if it were a seat she had just been warming, waiting for Rosalita to come along.

"Rico, what's going on here?" Rosalita said.

Rico stood up. "She just told you. We're looking at this book."

"It's about low riders," Margaret supplied. And then she repeated, "I found it in the library," as if she had a limited vocabulary and, under tension, had to resort to repetition.

Margaret, with her years behind the bar, knew very well that, when the force field suddenly charges up between a man and a woman—and even more so, a husband and a wife—it's time to beat feet. And, just by the nature of being a bartender and an attractive woman, especially in her younger years when the rage she felt seemed to telegraph itself as sexy wildness, she had often been the spark that ignited trouble, which she had no interest in doing anymore. She was finished with trouble, had left it behind her in New York, and now all she wanted to do was clear out fast. "Time for me to take off. Thanks a lot, Rico. I'll leave the book so you and Rosalita can take your time looking at it," she said, purposefully making no reference to the nature of their relationship, which truly was only teacher and student though it felt, even to her, like more. She simply hefted her bag onto her shoulder, said, "Nice meeting you" to Rosalita, and left. Both Rico and Rosalita were stone silent as she crossed the parking lot and continued up Barelas Road.

"So who is she?" Rosalita finally asked. Normally such a question comes with a scarlet edge of anger in it along with a list, being composed on the spot, of suspicions, but Rosalita's had none of that. It barely had curiosity. In fact, as Rico scanned her tone for hidden meaning, the only word that came to his mind was defeated.

"She's a *gringa* who wants to learn to weld," he said. "She lives in the neighborhood."

Rosalita sat down in the chair Margaret had just vacated. "Have you known her a long time?"

"Not even a week," said Rico, all the time feeling as if he were walking blindfolded along the edge of a cliff.

"Are you going to teach her?"

"We already started." It felt good to say it, Rico noticed. "Yesterday."

Rosalita looked up at him, as if she were doing some mental calculations, and then she said, "Oh. That explains last night."

"Now you know," he said, echoing her exact words from just a few hours ago, and then some vindictive streak in him, the same one that everyone possesses, prompted him to continue with the rest of the words she had used on him this morning. "I hope you feel better, knowing, Rosalita."

Some moments between lovers are like storms, where winds whip up debris that might have been settled for years, and some reach the freezing point, where, in the face of repeated cold blasts, the lovers can only run in opposite directions for cover. But some have no air in them at all. They are the quiet, suffocating ones that seem inescapable, insurmountable, and hopeless. They are the ones that feel like a trap, or quicksand, or drowning. This is exactly where Rico and Rosalita found themselves. They should have been at each other's throats, but instead they spoke in quiet, civil tones. They should have held knives to each other's heart, but they didn't, because both knew that the knives were already embedded and all they could do together, at least in this precise moment, was bleed.

Meanwhile, Margaret walked home in an apprehensive mood, as if whatever Rico and Rosalita were not saying was ricocheting off the concrete block walls all around her, and she had to keep her guard up to fend it off. Back in the bar business, she had a name for what had been hovering in the atmosphere of the garage, preparing to incarnate: stingrays—or, if they were particularly vicious, killer stingrays. If she was on the receiving end, ninety-nine percent of the time the sender of the stingrays was female, though, given the right circumstances—which usually arose when a girlfriend or wife Margaret had never known existed showed up unexpectedly—males were more than capable of generating them too, and theirs were always of the killer variety. Oddly, Margaret did not know if she herself was capable of it. As she strolled the four blocks toward home, she attempted to remember any time or any place when she had shot off a round of rays toward anyone, and she simply couldn't. She was jealous by nature, she thought, but in a more theoretical way. In real life, when the stingrays started, she erased whatever had caused them from her consciousness and just went on.

The initial scene with Rico, when he had shown up in her yard expecting her to fuck him stupid, was one she had erased, but now she felt a need to conjure it up again for the purposes of reexamination. Once you got to know Rico, she mused, he did not come across as a horndog, or even close to one. But that first impression could certainly be filed under that heading, and his wife—who was so pretty, who looked like some feisty Mexican woman in an old western movie, one who could ride a horse like a circus performer, wear her hair braided, piled up on top of her head, and tote a rifle for the purposes of running bad hombres off her land—had stepped into the scene as if she'd been there before, perhaps so many times that she had run out of energy for it. Her stingrays were present but weak. And Rico had not sent out any at all.

Margaret turned onto her own street, where an ice cream truck blasting the song "Greensleeves" at top volume was parked mid-block surrounded by children who apparently had never heard of the concept of getting in a line. They clamored around the little service window on the side of the truck, over which the owner had screwed a heavy wrought-iron grate, impatiently attempting to pass their money through the bars and receive their pre-packaged ice cream treat. Margaret had to weave her way through them. She glanced at the side of the truck where the ice cream choices were stenciled. They all came on popsicle sticks or in pointy sugar cones. She had loved pistachio ice cream as a child, primarily due to its vivid and unexpected color, though she never ate it after age five, probably because of the one clear memory she associated with it. On a hot summer day, she and her father had descended the six flights of stairs from the loft where they lived, and walked a few blocks to a sidewalk café in Little Italy. Vincent had ordered a big dishful of pistachio ice cream for her, complete with a cookie that could be used, at least for a while, in place of a spoon. That was the day that her father had told her that she would be living with Grampy for a few months while he and her mother went on a trip to India.

"Can't I go?" she had asked, over and over, and Vincent had said no, it wasn't a good idea. India was dirty and disease-ridden, dangerous and poor. It was no place for a little girl. "Are there any little girls there?" she had asked, and he had said yes, but they belonged there, and Margaret, just five years old, had tried to find a way to say, "I belong with you and Mommy," but she couldn't quite locate the right words. So she ate her bowl of ice cream instead, and she felt, with each little bite, like she was swallowing sorrow. The children around the ice cream truck showed no such sign of sorrow. They opened their treats and tossed the wrappers to the ground, where they remained, poised like a flock of pigeons waiting for a breeze.

Margaret walked a few more feet and turned into her driveway. As she passed through the gate, she called for Magpie, who ambled toward her from under an elm tree. "Hey, big girl," she said as she squatted down to give her a hug. "How's dogworld?" Magpie rolled over so Margaret could more easily reach her underside, and Margaret vigorously petted her for a good minute and then said, "Let's go inside and rest up for a long walk when the sun goes down."

On the way in, she found herself singing the words to "Greensleeves," which she couldn't even remember learning. "*Alas, my love, you do me wrong, to cast me off discourteously,*" she sang to the accompaniment of the music from the truck which still hadn't moved, though the crowd of children had diminished to just a few stragglers. ". . . *For I have loved you well and long, delighting in your company.*"

That is a very sad song, she thought, as she flopped down on the couch and stretched out. She felt depressed just singing it, perhaps because of the little scene she'd just witnessed between Rico and Rosalita, perhaps because discourtesy weasled its way into all love relationships sooner or later, perhaps because there was always somebody who had loved somebody else, delighted in his or her company, and then got shafted.

Aside from Nick, with whom love had repeatedly blossomed, burst forth like a tropical flower which, despite its beauty, had never been picked, Margaret had experienced true love—the kind seen in movies, twisted with passion and drama, thirst and hunger—only once. And truthfully, when she looked back, which she tried not to do very often, she felt lucky she'd gotten as far as she had with it, given her lack of preparedness for the black chasm of fear that had cracked open inside her, right along with her heart. This man's name was Harold, and he was a musician, a saxophone player whom she'd met in the Stereophonic Lounge when he came to hear a ragtag blues band that had, shortly afterward, received a lucrative recording contract and vanished forever from the local venues.

He was twenty-seven, two years older than she was, when he sidled up to the bar and ordered a Slow Comfortable Screw, a drink that gained its popularity mainly, she assumed, because people liked to ask for it. It made them feel lawless, which was helpful on a night out in a bar. She worked the bottles like the pro she was, using her stainless steel shaker to mix the ingredients right in front of him. The sloe gin, the Southern Comfort, vodka, and orange juice—it looked like a recipe for trouble as she poured it over the ice and shook it with a suggestion, perhaps, in the shaking, of a hand job just for him. Then she drained it into the glass she had already placed on the coaster, filling it to the brim without even one spare drop left over.

"Hope it's slow enough for you," she cooed, as she raised her eyes to his and held them there. For some reason, no doubt associated with the lighting, her eyes looked greener in the dark bar than anywhere else.

"Oh, no," he sighed, as he gazed into them and simultaneously slid a ten dollar bill across the bar, "I had hoped for something more original from you."

"Then you should have started with something more original," she replied, with a little glance toward the drink. "I base my badinage on the line that's fed me."

"Badinage?" he said.

"Look it up. Get back to me," she replied with a sexy little smile in her eyes. Margaret herself had only learned that word a few days before when she read it in a trashy novel that someone had left on the seat in the coffee shop where she frequently had breakfast. When she had read it, she'd thought it referred to some S&M practice. That didn't fit the context of the story, so she had consulted the dictionary.

"Oh, I know what it means. But I haven't heard it used in a sentence since the last Merchant-Ivory film."

Now she smiled. "Please pass the badinage," she said, and he replied in an assumed British accent, "Sorry, darling, we seem to have run out," and then they both laughed. That was how they started, a combination of sexual innuendo and merriment, all mixed in with an unusual vocabulary word. Three years later, it ended rather differently.

But those three years! Margaret had felt herself falling through space toward him, right then at the very beginning, and had surreptitiously reached for the edge of the rinsing sink under the bar to steady herself. As for Harold, he had fallen in love with her from the back, before she'd even turned around from the other end of the long bar and noticed him waiting there. Her black hair, which brushed the waistband of her jeans like a curtain that had been pulled closed for privacy, had not prepared him for such pale skin or those eyes which seemed to have the history of Ireland in them. And when she'd moved toward him, her hips had swayed from side to side like a model on a runway ramp in Milan, and Harold got it, what happens when women lead so subtly with their hips. So ordering the Slow Comfortable Screw was truly a wish in search of fulfillment, though it should be said that it was also his favorite drink at the time.

When he had turned on his barstool away from the bar and toward the music, Margaret had studied him carefully in profile. He was olive-skinned and thin with wild curls that spiraled off his head in shades of burnt sienna. He wore a black V-neck sweater, well-fitted, and a complicated watch that looked as if it had better things to do than tell time. He drank slowly, putting away just two drinks over the course of the three hours he spent at the bar. When the band packed up and left and he remained, she knew why.

He waited while she cashed out, and then they went around the corner to a basement after-hours club that she knew about, where they huddled into a back booth and confided secrets as if they were both going to be hung at dawn and just wanted someone, anyone, to know who they had been. This was unusual for Margaret, who, perhaps after watching sloppy drunks spill their stories for years and thinking it was actually quite pathetic, aspired to and practiced self-containment. But there was a warmth in Harold, a quietness and stability, that drew her out, drew her to him, even though they had no reason to think they might fit together. Harold had the pedigree—the degree from Princeton and the parents in the big apartment on Fifth Avenue. He had the trust fund, annual ski vacations in Gstaad, and intense parental expectations, which he was not currently fulfilling as an itinerant saxophone player.

With her vanished parents and dead grandfather, her classes at the School of Visual Arts leading nowhere except deeper and deeper into the paintings, and her tiny tub-in-kitchen apartment in Alphabet City—financed largely by the rental scam she'd set up around Donny's apartment—Margaret seemed to Harold like a character out of a story, perhaps "The

Little Match Girl." He had known other women artists, of course. How could he not at that time and place, when every other young person billed himself or herself as the next Gustav Klimt, minus the syphilis, or the next Charley Parker, minus that pesky heroin addiction? But to Harold, no one had ever seemed as genuine as Margaret or as beautiful or as talented, or, if the truth be known, as tragic, and he had to fight off the impulse to do such things as lay his expensive coat in a puddle for her to step on. By the time they emerged from the after-hours bar into the rush-hour foot traffic on Canal Street, he was a goner, sucked into love like inept flight deck sailors on aircraft carriers get sucked into jet engines; and by the time it was over, he was, like those sailors, shredded. Shredded by love. And so was Margaret.

The odd part was that, even at the end, neither blamed the other. Each felt totally responsible, as if every problem arose like a black tornado from one psyche only, and trapped them with no hope of escape and no way to save themselves.

But for a while, a few years, they were patched together like a crazy quilt, as if Harold's privilege and Margaret's lack were meant to even out for the benefit of both. Without feeling that it diminished her to say yes, she found it possible to accept his many gifts, such as a new winter coat, or sable paintbrushes that retailed for twenty-five dollars each, or a weekend in Montreal at the jazz-fest; while Harold experienced a frenzy of commitment to the artistic life just through exposure to Margaret and her passion for painting. This took precedence over everything, including him. He delighted in being ignored while she spent hours in the tiny airless studio she had kept on the Bowery since she was nineteen, not much more than a large storage closet really, in the back of a restaurant supply warehouse owned by a lifelong friend of Donny's from the old country. It cost her $250 a month, a sum which was often hard to come up with, but she managed it.

In the corner of her living room on Avenue B, Margaret had a six-inch slab of high-density foam, which served as both a bed and a couch of sorts. When she and Harold were in the apartment together, they rarely left it, as if it were a raft floating in the open sea a thousand miles from the nearest port. It was there that they pushed into each other, farther and farther, past anything healthy after a while, which is when it got dicey.

Harold compared the place they arrived at in their love affair to the molten core of the earth. Buried deep, hidden, burning at ten thousand degrees, it was simply not survivable. It should have been the place where they abandoned themselves, fusing into some other unit, a two-headed chimera that could take on anything, but to do that took courage, a sense of destiny, or a willingness to give up their previous lives. Neither knew how to do it. Margaret's core was fragile and fearful, certain she would never be safe, petrified, really, of being abandoned yet again by love. When she should have trusted Harold, she withdrew instead, tightened inward to steel herself for the next loss, a defensive move she did not even recognize for what it was. And as she withdrew, Harold stood helplessly by, dying more each day as his muse and his strength retreated. He knew that, without her, he was headed for graduate school— an MBA most likely—and a Wall Street future in his father's investment firm, where he would always be the son of the boss and never have to make his own way, like Margaret had to. He should have hung on to her, wrapped his arms around her waist and locked his fingers together in front of her heart for life. He should have wailed, screamed like a banshee, or howled like a lonely wolf, but he could not because he was paralyzed with the shame of the privileged.

In the end, each of their dreads came true. Harold disappeared down the stairs of her building on Avenue B. Margaret, her back pressed against the wall, let him go. A moment later, the phone rang. She answered it.

"Margaret, please," he said, "it's like you're all wadded up inside, tangled up in things you don't need to be afraid of with me. I love you. Can't you understand that? I don't want us to end."

"And yet you just walked out and slammed the door," she replied icily. She could hear the traffic on the street in stereo—through her window and in the phone. She could feel her breath burning in her throat.

Harold was silent for a few seconds. Then he whispered, "Margaret, please let me help unravel the wad you use to get through life. Please."

It felt like a knife shoved into her chest. "It's too late, Harold. Go home to your trust fund," she said.

She unplugged the phone, curled into the foam mattress, and barely moved for two days and nights. She lost the last of her hope and moved through her life as a woman who could not be reached. And Harold, though Margaret never knew it, developed a drinking problem, one that put him in rehab twice before he even finished his master's degree and stepped into the executive suite waiting for him just two blocks away from the New York Stock Exchange.

Through all of that, neither had ever resorted to stingrays.

Margaret finished one full rendition of "Greensleeves" before the truck pulled away from the curb, and the music faded in the distance. Memories of Harold lurked in the shadows of the words of the song, but Margaret was adept at keeping them there, in the dark. Besides, she had something more important on her mind: welding. Like a wizard, she raised her arms. "I dissolve all stingrays that want to come between me and my welding lessons," she said out loud, spreading her fingers wide, as if sparks were shooting from them.

After a little while, she fell into a deep sleep on the futon couch with Magpie on the floor beside her, and she didn't awaken until a beam of intense western sun enveloped her, nudging her awake with its relentless heat.

1989

*T*HEY FELL *into a friendship, Vincent and Thomas.*

"*I'll teach you how to jail,*" *Vincent had said, smiling a bit as he used the new verb.* "*And you can tell me about the world out there, if it's still out there.*"

"*It's out there, worse than ever,*" *Thomas replied.*

"*Not worse than in here,*" *Vincent responded.*

Thomas looked around. His eyes passed over the filth, the men in rags, crowded everywhere, the din and the dust and the relentless nothing, and he said, "*That depends on where you are. I've seen worse.*"

"*This is the worst I've seen,*" *replied Vincent,* "*but I'm used to it.*"

"*There's worse,*" *said Thomas.*

Vincent had looked into Thomas' brown eyes and known that what he had said was true.

Eight months later, he looks into those eyes again, deeply, as he wipes fever-sweat off Thomas' forehead with a rag that he keeps as clean as possible, given the circumstances. Thomas had sliced his foot open on a sliver of tin, the top of a can that had been buried in the dirt of the yard. It became infected. There was no medicine, no one to help. It went septic.

Thomas asks Vincent to find some paper and a pencil or a pen, and it isn't easy, but Vincent manages to trade two cigarettes, treasures in the prison, for a blank page ripped out of the back of a book owned by a man—a Brahman it is rumored—and he brings it to Thomas.

Thomas, who is barely able to sit up anymore and has stopped sipping water, takes the pen and draws a map.

No words had been exchanged between Rico and Rosalita by the time Margaret turned the corner and disappeared from sight. The book on low riders lay open on the desk, and there on its pages was Rico, the man known all over the Southwest as *el rey*. It was enough to make him laugh or cry; he wasn't sure which. He moved toward Rosalita, stepped behind the chair where she was sitting, and placed his hands on her shoulders. He began to press his fingers in, as if that could release the tension that had collected in the room. She groaned, a sound not unlike a growl, and then, as if she was embarrassed by it, reached up and put her hands on top of his, a light touch.

"So what's next, Rico?" she said in her new quiet voice.

Rico had no answer. He had to think hard for about half a minute. "Maybe lunch," he finally said, and Rosalita laughed.

"Always thinking about your stomach."

"Not eating lunch never solved anything," he said.

"Neither did eating lunch," she responded.

"At least it puts it off, Rosalita." He had the food she had prepared for him in the mini-fridge, but suddenly he didn't want to retrieve it, open the bag, unwrap something, and start chewing as he always did. "Let's go to the Barelas Coffee House," he said.

Rosalita turned in her chair to face him, a little glint of curiosity in her eyes, and said, "Okay."

So Rico locked up the shop, took his wife's hand in his own, and proceeded down the block toward Fourth Street. He hadn't had lunch outside the garage in years, and it felt somewhat liberating to saunter along with Rosalita, holding hands like a couple of teenagers. From behind his sunglasses, he took her in. They had been together more than half their lives. Anyone who thought about it for three seconds would assume that she was completely familiar to him, and she was. But she also wasn't. Thinking he knew her, inside and out, would be like mistaking a detailed map for a real place. Naturally, he knew her exterior very well, though even that was changing. Lines were etching themselves outward from the corners of her eyes, and here in the sunlight he could see a few silver threads in her lush, black hair. But the last four years had proven that what went on inside her was a mystery. If he could somehow slip through her skin and ride along her bloodlines into her brain and heart, he thought, there would be a universe inside that would make the solar system as he had been taught it in school seem like a small-scale model of the possibilities of space. Did she feel that way about him, he wondered, or was he just Rico, the same old Rico, who thought going through the motions was the same as really doing something?

"Did you take the rest of the day off?" he asked by way of opening the conversation.

"I finished the lunch prep, and then I said I was sick and they let me go." She paused a second and added, "I was worried about you, Rico. I had to see you, not to explain anything, because I don't know what to say. Just see you."

They had arrived at the door of the restaurant; he opened it and stepped aside so she could move past him. As usual, there was a line. The Barelas Coffee House was a place where deals were struck, even on the level of city government, though Rico was quite sure the politicians parked as close as possible and made a beeline for the front door rather than leisurely strolling down Fourth Street from City Hall, which wasn't very far. Inside, the closeness of other people and the clatter from the plates made small talk impossible, which suited Rico very well. He had no words stored up for use in the current situation, and he welcomed a time-out.

Soon enough, they were seated at a deuce along the front wall with a view to the street. The table top was yellow Formica with a little crumb-catcher band of aluminum tacked down around the edge. It was set with white paper napkins, where knives and forks rested. "All the comforts of home," Rico said with a grand gesture across the top of the table, and Rosalita smiled. The waitress appeared instantly, took a coffee order, and somehow transmitted that, if they knew what was good for them, they would be ready to announce their lunch choices by the time she returned. Both focused on the menu for a moment, and then, almost in unison, set them aside and glanced up.

They caught each other's eyes, silently acknowledging the moment of discomfort at the arrival of the inevitable, which in this case seemed to be conversation. Rico knew they were at a fork in the road: one way led straight into the heart of the issues swirling like smoke around them, and the other led away from them. Neither looked promising to Rico, as he lifted the paper napkin from the table and smoothed it over one thigh.

But Rosalita was ready. "No matter what happens," she began, "I'm glad about last night." She said this with urgency, as if she absolutely had to get it on the table before anything else, including their cups of coffee.

Rico knew in his heart that this was the moment he should say, "Me, too." Those words would cement some new stage of their life together into place, give them a foundation from which to start rebuilding. But he couldn't say them. The fact of the matter, which he only realized now in retrospect, was that he had not only been expecting, but counting on her to refuse his last attempt to reach her. Her no would be the "get out of jail free" card in a game of Monopoly. True, there had been great relief, enormous, heart-palpitating relief for him in their lovemaking; but it was also true that he had an unconscious back-up plan, one that involved the slow seduction of Margaret Shaw, and it had not been washed away in the wave of renewed closeness with Rosalita.

"I was surprised," Rico finally admitted. "I pretty much thought that part was over between us."

"Not quite," she said with a shy, sexy grin.

The waitress arrived with the coffee, and they both ordered Mexican food, though there were other choices on the menu. Rico watched his wife empty one packet of sugar into her cup and fill it with so much cream that it could barely be called coffee anymore.

"Rosalita," he said, "things are fucked up with me."

"Okay. Things are fucked up."

"I don't know what I want to do."

"Take whatever time you need to figure it out, Rico. You have it coming."

"What if I take four years?" He was beginning to feel like the words "four years" were some kind of chant that was always playing in the back of his mind. Four years, four years, four years. Even in this moment, above the racket in the café, he could hear it bouncing off the inside of his head.

Rosalita said nothing.

"What if I take four years?" he repeated, just slightly louder, as if he thought she hadn't heard him the first time, which he knew she had.

Rosalita took a long sip of coffee and then patted her lips with her paper napkin. "I have to pick my way carefully here," she said. "I don't want to say the wrong thing."

"I want you to say something," Rico said, "so just say something."

"Okay." She took in a little breath and then focused her eyes on his. "I was not the only person in the four years, Rico." And then, as if she had to clarify, she added, "You were there, too."

Rico reached for the underside of his chair and held on. He had seen war movies in which airplane pilots hit a button and their entire seats ejected like rockets out of the top of the plane seconds before it blew up or crashed into a mountainside or the sea; he was suddenly certain that what he was feeling was what they were feeling in that split second before blast off. And then, as if his whole life were about to flash backward before his eyes, starting with last night, he remembered her answer to his question, "Where have you been, Rosalita?" She had said, "Waiting for you to come and get me."

When he was a young man, just a few months after Fernando died, Rico had crashed his truck into an embankment along I-25. He didn't remember much about the accident, but one image had remained clear forever after. It was the way, in a fraction of a second, the windshield cracked into a thousand pieces and then shattered. After that, everything in his visual field went black, but he couldn't forget the way the silver cracks had manifested out of nowhere; that one pristine second before it all fell apart and all the pieces of the windshield scattered like memories that were unlikely to ever reassemble themselves. The truck was totaled, but he'd seen it later in the garage where it was towed, and the whole front seat and floor were covered with bits of glass that shimmered in the sun like diamonds. Staring into them, he had had a strange idea: if he could put them all back together again, would he have been able to avoid the accident in the first place. This thought had come to him like a wild bird.

Now, years later, gripping his seat in the Barelas Coffee House, Rico had a similar feeling. Every sentence out of Rosalita's mouth, or his own, was like a bit of glass on the passenger seat with the sun shining through it. She seemed to be saying that he had co-created the four missing years. It was just like a woman to fail to notice how much of himself he had sacrificed in that time, how challenging, and at times overwhelming it had been to hold their life together and wait. And wait and wait and wait. It had been hard, useless work and so consuming, and now she seemed to blame him for not crashing through to her, though he had tried for the better part of a year, until he just couldn't try again.

He let go of the chair with one hand and held it up to her, a "stop" gesture that she well understood. He would think about this later. He would. But not right now. Right now, he would remain calm. Fortunately, perhaps, the food arrived, slapped onto the table with precision by a waitress with an attitude of efficiency. He had an impulse to pick up the plate, loaded with beans and rice and tortillas, and send it flying, but he successfully fought it off. He didn't pick up the knife either, until he was sure he wouldn't throw it across the restaurant, just to see it embed itself in the wall. Because Rico was a man who didn't want to make a scene in public, or witness one, he ate his lunch in silence, and so did Rosalita. Then they walked back to the garage, where one of Rico's customers was standing outside the locked door. Rosalita got into her car and took off. Rico went to work, determined to keep his mind on the engine he was tuning and nothing else.

WHEN MARGARET awoke from her nap, her body sweaty in the heat of the late afternoon sun and her throat parched, she was overcome with a need to feel a breeze on her face, even if she had to get in the car and drive seventy-five miles an hour to create one. She took a long drink of water, refilled a gallon water bottle at the sink, and opened an ancient picture book called *The Wonders of New Mexico* that she had found years before in a box left behind by her parents. It had become a treasure, and she had pored over it for months before she left New York. She turned to the page for Jemez Springs, which was just over an hour from Albuquerque, higher up in the mountains, at about sixty-five hundred feet. The town, with its funky bathhouse from the 1870s, its local bar that looked as if it hadn't changed in a hundred years, and its spectacular rock mountains layered in multi-colors like some fancy dessert from Austria, seemed like an excellent destination. Plus, there was a river there, a good place to take a dog for a long walk.

Magpie, looking very alert, watched her as she studied the book on the kitchen counter. Margaret was positive that her dog could tell the future, which is why when she turned toward her and saw on her face what she called Magpie's "Am I going?" look, Margaret said, "Yes, you are." Magpie jumped to her feet and headed for the door, as if she'd been waiting for this moment all her life.

They got into the car, backed out of the driveway, and drove toward I-25, taking a not-quite-direct route that curved around toward Garcia's Automotive. She felt drawn there, as if by simply driving by she could advance her knowledge of welding and perhaps, she admitted, send some calming vibrations in Rico's direction. Something had happened to him in the past day. When he had gotten out of his truck that morning, she had seen it clearly: the Herculean effort it took to corral all his emotions and stuff them into his smile. And he hadn't fooled her with that adjustment of his sunglasses, either. She knew he had tears to wipe away.

In that moment, with Rico coming toward her, his whole body raw with pain that she could actually feel herself, Margaret had heard something unidentifiable snap into place in her own mind. It had to do with him, obviously, but also with something from long ago, a sense of something opening or closing. It had to do with an ache she recognized, as if aches resonate forever in some parallel universe, and poor lost souls wander into and out of them in a timeless kind of way, and then sometimes recognize each other from that other world in this one. She had seen Rico, coming toward her, his tears needing to be brushed aside so he could appear to be what he was not, and she knew his truth, maybe better than he did. It had to do with witnessing an ending of some sort. It had to do with that little girl in the window of Donny's apartment on Forty-Eighth Street, how she pressed her cheek into the glass so she could see all the way to the corner where Vincent and Regina had disappeared. It had to do with loneliness.

She had stepped back and given him room, pretended that what she had seen did not exist. But all morning, as she watched him work, as she stood slightly behind him and observed him as he expertly welded various metals together, she had the recurrent thought that some things simply cannot be put back together, no matter how hot the torch or how skilled the welder. Or perhaps they fit together, but the job looks sloppy in the end. Perhaps there are visible scars like welts. She planned to ask him, but his wife's arrival had prevented that.

She turned right onto Barelas Road, just planning to glance at the garage as she passed, but when she did Rico was right there in the parking lot, having just stepped out of the old Buick La Sabre he had moved from inside to outside. He stood still and looked straight into her eyes, and she knew she had to pull to the side of the road and say something sociable. He came to the passenger window and leaned into it slightly.

"What'up, Margaret?"

"*Nada*," she answered. "I'm on my way up to Jemez Springs to take Magpie for a long walk by the river. It looks like a beautiful place. I saw it in a book."

"You and your books," he smiled. "Don't cause any trouble up there."

"Did my books and I cause trouble around here, Rico? Things were a little tense when I left."

He shook his head. "It wasn't the book."

"Was it me?"

He shook his head again. "It's a long story."

"Maybe you should tell it to somebody."

"Does that help?"

"Actually, I wouldn't know," she smiled.

"I didn't think so," he replied.

They were both silent for a few beats.

"Though I do find it helps to talk to Magpie," Margaret said at last.

Rico turned his eyes to the big dog sitting erect and watchful in the backseat. "Can I make an appointment?" he said.

Margaret laughed. "She's got her paws full with me, but I'll see if I can squeeze you in sometime."

"How about now?" Rico said. And even as he said it, he knew that whether she said yes or no, he would be dropped off in some new terrain that he didn't feel ready for, but he still waited for an answer.

"You want to take a ride to Jemez?" she asked, as if she was seeking clarification only.

"Sure," he said, "Why not?" And then he waited.

Why not, Margaret silently repeated. There was the obvious reason, of course: his wife. But Margaret was tired of protecting people she had no intention of hurting. She wanted to act as free as she felt, so she said, "Okay, come on."

He broke into a wide, white smile. "Let me lock up. Take me a minute." He headed back toward the garage.

Margaret turned the engine off and the radio on. The *War and Peace Report* with Amy Goodman was on, but she was not in the mood for bad news from around the world, so she switched to an AM station that specialized in classic rock. This was a normal thing, she told herself, to go on a spontaneous walk with a new friend in the late afternoon on a gorgeous desert day. But it felt sharp around the edges. Besides, for Margaret, normal was singular, not plural. She had not expected this when she decided to drive past Garcia's, but here it was. She wasn't sure what to think, so she just turned up the radio and sang along to "Beast of Burden" by the Rolling Stones.

Meanwhile, inside the garage, Rico pulled down the service doors and locked them, shut down all his tools, and stripped off his coveralls. It was just after four in the afternoon, early to close, but he wasn't expecting any customers back today. He glanced in his appointment book for tomorrow, and then, at the last minute, picked up the phone and called home. He was relieved when Maribel answered. "*Hola, mi hija,*" said Rico. "*¿Cómo andas?*"

"*Todo está bien, Papi,*" she responded.

"Can you give Mama a message for me?" Rico said, rushing on before Maribel offered to put Rosalita on the phone. "Tell her I'll be home late tonight, after ten probably."

"Okay," said Maribel. Typical of a teenager, she didn't ask for an explanation.

"See you then," he said.

"Okay, Papi. See you later." He hung up, locked the door, crossed the parking lot, and climbed into the passenger seat of Margaret's car.

"Here we go," said Margaret as she pulled out into the street. "Everybody get out of the way!"

Rico smiled. "Do I need a crash helmet?" he asked as he put on his seatbelt, and moved the seat back a few inches so he could stretch out his legs in comfort. It had been a long time since Rico rode in a car that a woman was driving. In his own family, he was the default driver and everyone knew it. He liked to be behind the wheel, in control. But today he rested his head against the back of the seat and just looked out the window. There was a lot of traffic, several lanes bumper to bumper in both directions. Where had all the people come from? Just a few years ago, the transfer from I-40 east and west to I-25 north and south had been a simple two-lane exit and it had worked fine. Now roads swirled in a complex of ins and outs that rose several stories above the landscape, and cars were coming and going in every direction at top speed. His city, which he never thought of as more than a small town, was changing fast while he stood still.

As if she'd read his mind, Margaret said, "Did you know Albuquerque's the thirty-third largest city in the United States? Which is odd when you factor in that New Mexico is one of the lowest states in terms of population, only two million people in the whole state." She paused for a second, and then added, "though we do have more Native Americans here than any other city in the world. About forty-five thousand. And the highest number of PhD's in the country for its population. But the lowest ranking in terms of quality of education."

Rico looked at her. Through the window behind her, he could see the five dormant volcanoes in the distance against the bright blue sky. "Are you a history teacher or something?" he asked.

"No, I'm a bartender. Or at least I was one in New York. I'm thinking of getting out of that business."

Rico watched the way Margaret handled the car. Her right hand rested on the gearshift, as if she wanted to be prepared at any second to throw the Colt Vista into some higher or lower gear, and her left hand comfortably gripped the steering wheel at about eight o'clock. She drove well, changing lanes with confidence when there wasn't quite enough time. She had the driver's seat pushed way back, so her legs were almost extended straight to reach the pedals, and she constantly checked both her interior and exterior rearview mirrors. Watching her drive, he had the idea that she threw herself full-tilt into everything she did, which probably accounted for her memorizing all those statistics about New Mexico. She probably studied up on it long before she arrived anywhere near the state.

"You ought to become a courier," he said, "the way you drive."

"Are you making fun of my driving?"

"No. I'm admiring it." He threw her a smile big enough to display those deep dimples and she returned it, along with a little lift of her eyebrows. "I know a guy who's a courier. He drives all over the state—sometimes farther. He makes good money, too."

Margaret was actually interested. She could just imagine herself and Magpie on the road, doing eighty-five into the sunset. Or sunrise.

"What does he deliver?"

"Mostly paperwork. But a couple times, he took some camera equipment out to a movie shoot, and he told me one time he delivered a human heart for a transplant."

"Really? Wow."

She found it captivating: the image of a courier tearing along the highway with, on the front passenger seat or perhaps on the floor where it would not tip over, a heart packed in ice and headed for a new chest cavity.

"That must have made him feel important," said Margaret.

"He said it creeped him out."

"Really? Why?"

"He just said body parts give him the creeps. When somebody says something like that, I don't ask questions."

"But a heart," Margaret mused. She had once read a memoir by a woman who received a transplanted heart. Suddenly, this woman developed intense cravings for beer and honky-tonks, and she felt compelled to track down the donor of the heart in order to learn if these were his habits. She discovered the owner of the heart was a young man who died in a motorcycle accident. He had indeed been a party animal. Reading that book had inspired Margaret to wonder about hearts. Were all memories stored there? She pulled into the passing lane and whipped by a long line of cars doing about five miles an hour over the speed limit. When she pulled back in, she asked, "What do you think the heart is, Rico?"

"It's a machine. A pump."

"I see you're not a romantic."

"I'm a mechanic, not a poet." The fact was, though, Rico could have said plenty about the heart, about the weather it has, more tempestuous than any outer storm. About how the heart can feel on the verge of bursting open, spewing love like cherry blossoms, covering a whole landscape with little white fragrant flowers with pink crosses at the center. About how it can pulsate with hatred, too, which is what he sometimes felt for Fernando, a hatred so menacing he was scared of himself. About how the flow of blood inside it can suddenly stagnate, and the heart can go numb and lifeless, and all that can be done when that happens is wait and wonder. Rico had felt his own heart ache with love, ache with sadness, ache with pride, and ache with worry. He knew the heart was more than a pump, though he had great respect for a good pump. In his current state, though, in which the four chambers of his own heart were warring with each other—one filled with happiness at being in the same car with Margaret, one back on Riverside Drive trying to find a way back to his wife, one angrily chanting "four wasted years," and one just trying to keep the beat—Rico felt no inclination to provide details. Instead he said, "Why? What do you think the heart is?"

Margaret answered, "I don't know. I don't think I have one."

"You have one," Rico responded, "believe me." He had an impulse to place his hand on top of hers on the gearshift, perhaps to guide her into some form of downshifting that might find them on the side of the highway where he could do something right for once and show her that she was all heart, whether she knew it or not, but in that exact instant she moved her hand to the steering wheel. Soon, she exited at Bernalillo and turned left onto Highway 550, which, according to the map, they would follow for twenty-five miles before making a right at San Isidro up into the Jemez Mountains.

The stretch of road from the exit ramp to the place to the west where the Indian reservations begin is perhaps one of the ugliest in New Mexico, with strip malls and gas stations jammed up side to side, chain drugstores and banks pressing into each other, traffic light after traffic light where Mack trucks idle noisily. And then the housing developments start, one after the other, like prisons on the side of the road.

"Damn, I hope it's not like this the whole way," Margaret said as the fumes from an old pickup wafted in the windows. "This is awful."

"Keep going," said Rico. He knew that within a few miles, the highway would take them past the last McDonald's and Taco Bell, past the last casino, past the last stinking eighteen-wheeler at a traffic light, and past the last of the housing developments. They would climb a hill and at the top, the clutter of the modern world would cease to exist. It would collapse into a mirage, and the whole wide world would open up before them. Margaret's eyes would feast on the landscape, spread out in all the known shades of red and orange, brown and green, beige and blue. He could have told her what was coming, but he kept it secret, depending on it to overwhelm her, fill her heart—which she thought she didn't possess—with joy.

1989

"*T*HIS IS *where my grandmother lives on the Navajo reservation,*" Thomas *whispers, handing the map to Vincent.* "*If you ever get out of here, find your way to her and tell her what happened to me.*"

Vincent *cradles Thomas' head on his lap.*

"*Tell her I left this world saying her name. Alice. Alice Yazzie.*"

Thomas' *eyes move away from Vincent's.*

He *stares out above the prison walls and settles on a point in the sky. Vincent feels certain, in that moment, that he sees Thomas' spirit rise up and disappear into that bright blue point and instantly become a part of the whole, the sky over New Mexico too, where Alice waits and waits and waits for her grandson to come home.*

Vincent *has forgotten that he is an artist, but in this moment, he remembers. He turns the map over and, on the back, he draws a portrait of Thomas, who looks serene in his moment of passing. He keeps the map in his cell, between the pages of a book of short stories by Somerset Maugham, left behind by a Brit with family connections who was quickly released.*

WHEN Margaret had heard Rico say the words, "You have one, believe me," in response to her offhanded semi-joke about not having a heart, there was a quality in his tone of voice that reminded her of Nick, the way he would stand in front of her painting and stare into it with such intensity that she would feel compelled to give it a closer look herself. This sometimes went on for minutes, while the other students in the class busied themselves at their easels and resisted the urge to gather round their teacher to get a glimpse of what held him captive.

The words that Nick would say afterward varied. Once it had been, "Jesus, I wish I'd painted that." Another time he had turned to her and asked, "Can you take me with you in there, Margaret?" He had once mumbled, "I'm fucking breathless." But no matter what the words were, the tone was always the same: complete, absolute certainty. Nick had told Margaret privately that he thought she was a great talent capable—if she could handle the schmoozing—of a world class art career. Those words were essentially meaningless to Margaret, who was typically more concerned with how she would pay her studio rent, or how it would affect her painting if she used nylon instead of canvas and painted with wax instead of paint. Margaret viewed the "world class career" conversations as Nick's version of pep talks, and the simple truth was she didn't have the pep for them. But his certainty, his belief in her, that felt different. That felt real, like Donny's presence in her life felt real, like being more or less orphaned at five years old felt real, like having to hustle up a living felt real. Margaret appreciated the real things in her life because, to her, they were like islands in a big sea of doubt. Even if they were covered with brambles, she could climb up on them and find a place to rest.

So when Rico had said those words to her, and she had heard the certainty resonate in his voice, she had welcomed it, though she didn't let on. She felt his certainty like a jolt through her body, and she had reached for the steering wheel with her free hand to help contain it, to close the circuit so she could hold onto it for just a few beats longer. His certainty continued to vibrate inside her as they drove along the ugly strip in Bernalillo. Then, when they hit the precise spot in the road where the urban sprawl ends and a sublime replacement begins, she had felt it wedge itself into her heart and expand it, just like the view—which went from less than nothing to everything in one single heartbeat. She'd had to pull to the side of the road. She had never seen anything like this wide open space that suddenly unfolded like a giant magic carpet at her feet. She stopped the car on the dirt shoulder of the road, climbed out, and simply stood there, stunned.

Rico let her be, even as several minutes ticked by. She drank it in, as if she had been wandering out in that desert sand for years and had finally found a watering hole. When she returned to the car and got in, she had looked at him, the whole vista beyond him visible through the passenger window, and said, "I'm gone, Rico. I'm blown away." Rico had nodded once and said nothing, though later, after they had driven in silence perhaps ten miles farther into this landscape, she had said, "Thanks for letting me stand there by myself," and he had replied, "When you see something like that for the first time, anybody'd want to be alone with it."

Margaret had read that when Native Americans view a landscape, they see themselves in it, as one part of it, rather than perceiving it as spreading out like a fan before them. She had never understood that, being in the world naturally rather than standing apart from it, wondering what was going to pounce. But today, as she stood in awe by the side of the road, she'd had her first inkling. She had noticed that birds she assumed were hawks were lazily circling the valley, with its strange dirt towers and its snaking arroyos, and for better or for worse, she had felt a part of it, the whole design, including both the hawk and the mice scrabbling through the dirt, dreading the moment when a bird-shaped shadow enveloped them.

As they'd driven farther, past rock formations that, in layers, revealed the history of the planet, into the little village of San Isidro, where a police car was parked on the side of the road by a dangerous curve with a blow-up cop at the wheel, through the shabby Jemez Indian pueblo where corn grew green in the river valley, and into the red rocks, as high as New York City buildings and as orange-red as poppies, Margaret had felt truly transported. Before they even got to Jemez Springs, she pulled off the road into a turnout to the left, where the shallow river wound close. Margaret opened the back door and Magpie bounded out and headed straight to the water for a good drink. The river tumbled by at a fast clip. On the bottom, rocks and pebbles, smoothed by time and water, glowed.

"She looks like a wolf out there," said Rico. And it was true. With the river swirling around her ankles and her great head dipped down to slurp up the fresh mountain water, the freshest she had ever had in her life, Magpie appeared as wild and free as the landscape itself. Perhaps it was that wildness, inspired by river rapids and craggy mountains striped horizontally and a dog that looked like a wolf, that explains what happened next. Margaret stepped out of her flip-flops and, fully dressed, stepped into the river and laid herself down on her back among the glistening pebbles on the bottom. Her hair fanned out behind her as she closed her eyes. Rico, on the shore, immediately stooped down to undo his boots, strip them off along with his white athletic socks and his T-shirt, and follow. Just as he hit the water, he had a thought: I would follow this woman anywhere. This surprised him because he was not known for following. He had established himself as not-a-follower, growing up in the wake of Fernando.

He moved toward her and sat in the river beside her, and when she opened her eyes, so green they looked like mossy river rocks, he said, "We ought to bring an inner tube up here and ride this river back to Albuquerque."

"Yes," Margaret had said.

Just hearing a yes from her startled Rico, sent a hot sensation along the wires of his spine that completely negated the water so cold that, no doubt, his dick had shriveled up to next to nothing, which made it easier not to try to kiss her. But he needed to move into her in some way, nestle inside her spirit so she could get used to him, and he wanted to do that. He wanted to say something meaningful, but what came out of his mouth was, "This water is fucking freezing, Margaret."

"Yes," she said again. "Yes."

She had let her arms drift along with the current and now they were above her head as she lay there. Rico couldn't help but look, though he tried to do it surreptitiously. A wet T-shirt was a beautiful thing on a woman, and besides, he had never had one hint of her body underneath all the baggy clothes she wore. Now he saw that her breasts were small and her ribs were visible, even through the shirt, though perhaps that had something to do with the way her arms were raised up. Her shoulders were narrow, and so were her hips. The opposite of Rosalita, he thought, who had not one straight line on her body.

The arrival of Rosalita into his mind, even for one short moment of compare and contrast, created a ribbon of guilt that wanted to wrap itself around him. What was he doing, sitting among the pebbles in the middle of the Jemez River on a Tuesday afternoon at the very moment when, usually, he would be closing up shop for the day? What was he doing peeking at the tits of a white woman who had lain herself out in the shallow water like a fish? It felt wrong and it also felt right, and there was Rico, right in the middle.

"Margaret . . ." he said, suddenly overcome with a desire to tell her everything—especially about last night. "Last night I fucked my wife for the first time in four years," he could say, "and in a way I wish I hadn't, even though it was good, even though I fell into her like rain." But, with her head half under-water, her ears covered and only her face above the river line, Margaret hadn't even heard him say her name; and when she suddenly sat up, her nipples erect and beads of water like dia-monds running down her face, caught in her eyelashes, drip-ping from her chin, everywhere, he forgot about everything except her.

"Did you ever notice how your skin can be cold, but some other part of you way inside can be warm?" she asked.

"To me cold is cold," said Rico.

"But do you feel a need to get away from it?"

"Yes," he said. "Right about now." He stood up. His blue jeans were so waterlogged they felt heavy, and when he climbed out of the river onto a big flat rock on the shore, little puddles and streams formed all around him. The sun was hot, and it dried the drops off his chest and arms before Margaret even scrambled up onto the rock next to him and stretched out on her stomach.

Rico had a dragon biting its own tail tattooed on his upper left arm. Margaret, her arms folded under her cheek like a bony pillow, studied it with interest. She herself had no tattoos even though it had been the rage in New York for at least fifteen years. She didn't have any, mainly because she couldn't imagine not growing to detest a permanent image on her body. If every-thing changed but it, it would seem unreal and mocking. And if it changed over time—drooped, for example, or spread out or faded in color—then she would be sad at the inexorable march of time and the way it wreaked havoc on the human body.

"Tell me about your dragon tattoo," she said, resisting an urge to touch his arm and trace the outline with her fingers.

"I got it when my brother Fernando was murdered," Rico said. "A long time ago."

The word 'murder' should not intrude into this environ-ment of peace and serenity, one where clear mountain water rushes over rounded river rocks and creates a soundtrack so soothing it could probably put an insomniac to sleep in a few minutes. But somehow the hawks circling overhead, the mountains standing strong, and the overall serenity seemed able to absorb it as a fact of nature and, therefore, so could Margaret.

"Did it help?" she asked.

"I guess so. I never thought about it like that. I just knew I had to do it. I was only seventeen." In fact, it had been permanently inked into his arm within a week of Fernando's burial. He had walked down Isleta Boulevard, past the garages that specialized in *frenos y mofles*, past the tiny *mercaditos* and the new community center, to a tattoo parlor set up in the garage of an old adobe house with a yard full of dogs. Mario, the man who did the tattooing, seemed ancient to Rico though he was probably only in his thirties. The walls of his garage were covered with original tattoo designs from which to choose, but Rico had one folded up in his pocket, a page from a book he had never returned to Rio Grande High School when he had quit two years before. The book was titled *One World Through the Ages*. It was used in his global history class. The picture he carried—a dragon biting its own tail—was of an etching from Europe during the period of the Crusades. Rico never read the words in the book, but he liked to thumb through it looking at the pictures.

After they had received the phone call informing the family of Fernando's death, after he'd finally felt able to peel himself away from his father and Elena, who was devastated, after he'd closed the door to the room he had shared with Fernando during all the years of growing up, after he had sat on his bed experiencing what could only be called waves of relief followed by waves of guilt, he had suddenly remembered the dragon image in the history book. He had searched then and there for the book, found it in a pile of stuff in the corner, opened it, and turned to the picture. Staring into the circle created by the dragon biting its own tail took Rico somewhere he desperately needed to go in that moment, though he couldn't, then, say where.

"Why'd you pick the dragon?" Margaret asked.

"Fernando . . . it was like he was always eating himself alive," Rico said. "I picked it to remind myself what happens when you do that." But that was not all there was to it. There was something more that had to do with the peace the image had brought him the night that Fernando was stabbed to death with a shiv fashioned from a strip of stainless steel pried off the edge of a shelf in the prison kitchen.

"There's something hopeful in it," Margaret mused. "It's probably the circle. The circle's the symbol of wholeness, something that's complete."

"Says who?" said Rico.

"Says the people who think symbolically, I guess," she replied. "But I believe it." Margaret had never placed a circle anywhere in her artwork, not once in all her years of painting, which began for her in the fifth grade when Sister Mary Edwin had instructed all the students to bring a big shirt to school the next day, one they could use as a smock since they were going to embark on an art project. She'd had the students push the chairs and desks against the sides of the classroom and settle themselves on the floor. The project turned out to be finger painting.

"Not like when you were in kindergarten," Sister said. "I want you to paint the colors you think are inside you. Now, turn away from everybody else, and don't look at anyone else's colors. This is self-exploration."

When Margaret had slopped the first handful of red on the brown paper bag—which she had spread open and cut into a vague human shape according to Sister's instructions—she felt a bliss unknown to her before; and she wasn't home from school five minutes before she was asking Donny to buy her art supplies. She hadn't stopped painting since. She had heard a few years later that Sister Mary Edwin had renounced her vows and left "the blessed holy nunhood," as Donny called it, though something about the way he said it made Margaret, even as a little child, suspect he was kidding her about something.

Rico lowered himself down on his back on the rock so his whole front side was exposed to the sun. "Is this what you do, Margaret, when you're rattling around by yourself? Figure out if you believe the circle is a symbol?" He asked her this with a little edge of teasing, the affectionate kind that covers up a burst of appreciation.

"That and drive sixty miles to walk my dog," she replied. That caused them both to glance at Magpie, who was walking along the edge of the river, sniffing in every direction. "Ready to get to it?"

"Okay," said Rico, though he felt he could lie on this rock forever and look at her.

They both stood up, their clothes damp but not dripping any more, and started after Magpie. Since there was no real trail along the edge of the river, they picked their way among the rocks and sagebrush with Margaret in front. She couldn't see his face without stopping and turning completely around, and she only did this once when she said, "Rico, I don't want to pry, but if you want to say anything more about your brother, I want to listen."

When he had said that Fernando was murdered, Margaret had seen a lead curtain drop down over Rico's eyes, the kind that discouraged conversational probing. Yet it seemed odd to her to chat amiably about his tattoo while this more serious topic was still hanging in the air between them. She could certainly let it go, but she wanted at least to acknowledge it.

"Maybe sometime," he had said. "Not today." And she had nodded and smiled a little bit, a smile that said this was fine with her, and turned back around; and before she'd advanced even five steps, Rico said, "He was a good kid when he was little. He changed when he was about twelve." He didn't notice that he was reciting Elena's after-church litany as if it were his own.

Margaret kept right on walking, understanding that for some topics some people would rather talk into a person's back. "What made him change?" she asked, picking her words as carefully as she was picking her steps along the slippery rocks. "Something at home?"

"I don't think so. I was five years younger, so what did I know about anything? He seemed like a normal brother, and then he turned into a monster."

"Probably testosterone," Margaret replied. "Some kids just lose it at puberty."

"Fernando more than lost it," Rico said.

Then he told her everything, as if once he started to talk he could not stop. He hadn't really laid out the story of Fernando to anyone except Rosalita, and when he told her he was only twenty. The difference was when he told Rosalita—all those years ago, twenty-three if he counted—Fernando was the main character of the story, and now, telling Margaret, he was. To his wife, Rico had recounted the fistfights between his father and his brother, complete with bloody details. Now he talked about what it was like to stand in the doorway and observe them, how he had wanted to jump onto Fernando's back to help his father, but he had been too scared to do it because he was no match for Fernando. He knew he couldn't take whatever it was that his brother would unleash on him if he got involved. And how it was to see and hear his mother sobbing, sometimes screaming, the deep sorrow and helplessness that drove her to the church morning, noon, and night for all the good it did, then or now. How Fernando's wildness had forced Rico to be tame, maybe too tame for his own good. Rico had spoken so many words, his throat felt dry and he needed a drink of water.

All the while, Margaret listened with careful attention. She had heard a thousand sob stories in her years behind the bar, and, like all bartenders, she had developed a way to distance herself from them. Often she imagined she was a character in a movie, a bartender with a compassionate face who listened but never thought of the story again once the scene was over. But today, that was not the case. Today, she listened with a sense of awe, as if it was important to tell a story such as this one and important to listen to it.

After half a mile, Rico fell silent.

There happened to be a big rock, good for sitting on, right in front of them, and Margaret climbed up on it with Rico right behind her. It felt as if it had been heated up just for them, and she took a moment to shield her eyes, glancing toward the setting sun.

"It's such a sad story," she said, looking at him for the first time since he started talking. "I feel so sad for everybody in it, including Fernando. I can't imagine the state somebody has to reach to act like that."

"I don't know why I told you," Rico said. But inside himself, he knew perfectly well why he told her. He told her because he simply couldn't stop himself. He had no control around this woman, this *gringa* from New York. While he was walking along behind her, spilling his guts, he thought that if she had once turned around and looked at him, he would have had to run the other way—but she never did. And now, looking into her face seemed to be the most natural thing in the world. Just easy.

He hadn't thought this far ahead, but if he had, he might've imagined that if this moment which should be so hard for him was easy, then he might take a chance on leaning across the distance between them to kiss her lips, pulling her toward him, skinny little thing that she was. But these thoughts never formed. Rico felt spent, exhausted, used up. However, he didn't feel foolish—which he always thought he might if he ever opened up about Fernando—and he didn't feel sorry he had done it.

"You're so quiet," Rico said after a few moments of no sound but the river moving along its chosen path.

"I'm feeling for you, Rico," she said. "Sometimes it seems to me that every person is locked up in a prison that no one else can see. Every person." She herself could often feel the claustrophobia, the loss of freedom, the danger, and the regimentation of prison life though there was no sign of bars in her world. Except the drinking kind, which were their own prison, of course, though that was one she managed to avoid.

"Yeah. We need a mass breakout," said Rico.

"Maybe a riot," Margaret suggested.

"Maybe we're already in one," Rico replied.

They both laughed nervously because each knew that whatever was happening between them was creating a chance to break free in some way, though their ways were different, maybe.

They sat on the rock a little longer, until dusk, and then made their way back to the car. It was seven-thirty when Margaret pulled onto the highway and headed south. The atmosphere between them, with Rico having opened up about Fernando, was hard to mistake, especially as it got darker and darker. Margaret had always felt that darkness magnified all feelings and needs. It seemed dangerous to acknowledge the intimacy that had, like a lotus blossom, opened up, but impossible to ignore it in the dark. So when she took the left turn back onto Route 550, for that last beautiful section before they re-entered Bernalillo, Margaret said, "Rico, just so you know, I have a lifelong rule against getting involved with married men. I never break it." She took her eyes off the road for a few seconds as she said it. "Much as I might want to," she added.

"Too late. We're already involved." He watched her grip on the wheel tighten noticeably. "But I can keep my hands off you, if that's what you're worried about."

Obviously, that was what she was worried about. Yet his words, which should have calmed her, didn't. Perhaps she wanted to protest the ease with which he said them, though that would hardly be wise.

"Much as I might not want to," he added. He had turned his head toward her, and when she glanced at him he saw the crescent moon, which was just rising over the top of the Sandias in the distance, reflected in her eyes.

1990

*T*HERE IS *something else between the pages of the book of short stories. It is Vincent's most precious possession: a photobooth strip of Regina, his wife, and Margaret, their daughter. Margaret is only three years old in the picture. She is like a miniature Regina with her black hair and her green eyes, though they don't show green, either of theirs, in the series of four pictures.*

The images have faded, but Vincent keeps them alive in his mind.

After all the years here, where everything he knew has disappeared and his life is one that he could never have imagined and still can't though he lives it every day, he still dreams of Margaret and Regina, still holds them in his arms each night, still begs God to keep them safe.

Still loves them until it hurts.

WHEN RICO pulled into his own driveway, he saw that the lights were still on in his mother's *casita*, and he walked back there before he even checked in at his own house. As he approached her door, he heard the television, some crime show, no doubt. Elena liked to listen to the voices, though she could not see the faces of the actors with any clarity. She also missed the clues and the significant glances that were exchanged between pretty female cops with cleavage, not to mention the closeups of bloody corpses and the constant shots of autopsies in progress.

"*Hola, Elena, mi madre,*" Rico called as he came in the kitchen door.

"*Hola, Rico,*" she answered, not getting up. She was sitting on her old flowered couch, a cup of tea in her lap and her feet up on the coffee table. "You're home late."

"*Sí,*" he said. "I'm going to heat up this water and make myself some tea and sit down with you for awhile." The old Pyrex pot was still warm to the touch as he lit a match and turned on the gas. A box of Sleepytime tea was on the counter, and he opened it and dropped a teabag into a cup that was inscribed with the words "World's Best Grandmother," a gift from Lucy, he knew. He found the sugar bowl on the table and got a quart of milk out of the fridge in preparation.

Waiting for water to boil was a chore that Rico found agreeable, especially when the water was in his mother's old glass pot. He liked the way the blue flame from the gas stove was visible, spread out like thin watercolor paint on the bottom of the pot. He liked the moment when the water started to dance and then commence its churning. He liked the idea that the water became vapor, a mysterious transformation. Even the steam, rising like smoke from his tea cup, pleased him.

"What are you watching?" he asked, as he entered the living room and sat down on the opposite end of the couch. A commercial for some anti-depressant drug was blaring away on the TV, so he knew they had at least thirty seconds to chat.

"A murder mystery," she answered. To Elena, there were only two types of television shows worth watching: love stories and murder mysteries.

"You should have been a cop," Rico said, "the way you love murder mysteries."

"They didn't have lady cops in my time," Elena said.

"You know what one of my customers told me?" Rico said. "He used to be a cop in LA a long time ago, right? He told me when they first let women on the police force out there, they had to wear skirts and high heels and carry their guns in their purses. It was on the rule books, he said."

Elena turned to look at him. "Did you believe him?" she asked.

"Why would he make up something like that?"

"You never know about people," she said. The show came back on and Rico was relegated to silence for the next ten minutes. He often wondered how his mother coped, living in the realm of blurs and shadows. He imagined her view of the world came in patches of color and movement, perhaps the kind the monsoon rains made running down a wavy window-pane. She always seemed to be trying to see more, he had noticed. Peering, as if there was something to see through. Even now, she stared at the TV screen as if she were intent on memorizing every detail, though Rico knew for a fact that she couldn't even tell the men from the women. He sipped his tea quietly, as he was expected to do when her shows were on.

When it ended, Elena reached for the remote and expertly cut the power.

"Rosalita was here earlier," she said. "She walked me back home after dinner."

Rico knew, just from the careful tone of her voice—from the way it did not make its way up and down the musical scale as it usually did—that Rosalita had probably told her everything. He could feel the space between them on the couch fill with words on their way. He waited.

"Talk to me, *mi hijo*," Elena said.

He hesitated, trying to find the right place to begin.

"This Anglo woman, do you love her?"

Rico leaned forward and slammed his cup down on the coffee table. Some of the amber-colored liquid sloshed over the side onto the Mexican tiles he had set himself when he made this table as a birthday gift for Elena more than a decade ago. "Jesus, what was she doing talking to you about this?" he said, his voice exploding. Elena reached toward him, and the sight of her hand, hovering in the air as if she was trying to find his shoulder, or perhaps his face, and touch him—probably to calm him down—only made him more angry. He stood up. "Jesus," he repeated.

"Rico," Elena began, "I—"

"Give me some fucking room, Elena," he yelled. "I need some fucking room."

She sat back against the couch, dropping her hands into her lap.

"What the fuck did she drag you into this for?" He began to pace noisily, back and forth from the kitchen to the living room, as if by stamping his feet, like a bull in a pasture that's too small for him, he could shake off the pressure of living in a world of women who rushed around behind his back and told each other his business before he had even sorted it out for himself. "What the fuck is the matter with her?" Even Rico was struck by the venom in his voice, not to mention the fact that he had said the word "fuck" at least four times when he usually tended to maintain decorum in front of his mother. Seeing her sitting there, tiny, with her eyes downcast and her hands folded in her lap as if she were a Catholic schoolgirl being forced to sit at attention by some nun, tore him up inside.

"Listen, Elena, I have nothing to say about this right now. That's it." He stood stock-still, attempting to decide where to go and what to do next.

"She was upset, Rico. She needed to pour her heart out to somebody," Elena said calmly.

"She shouldn't have picked you." Something in all of this, Rosalita's breakdown in Elena's *casita*, felt dirty to Rico. Sneaky. As if she were martialing the troops, lining up the female family forces of guilt and pressure against him. "If she told the girls, I swear to God, I'll . . ."

He truly had no idea how to finish the sentence.

"I'm sure she didn't tell the girls, *mi hijo*." Now her voice was even softer. "She didn't even mean to tell me. It just happened." Elena was certain that that was an accurate statement. At dinner, she had noticed that Rosalita was far more quiet than usual, very preoccupied with whatever was going on in her mind.

"Where's Rico?" Elena had asked. It seemed so odd to sit down to a family dinner without him.

"He's coming home late," Maribel said. "I forgot to ask him what he was doing when he called."

"He's probably got a big job," said Elena. Her son was so predictable that no other option came to her mind.

"Yeah, probably," said Maribel. It was just by accident that Elena, who was sitting next to Rosalita, happened to hear a sharp intake of breath and a little bleat so soft it would have passed for silence in anyone but a blind person's ears. Elena had cocked her head in Rosalita's direction and heard it, even felt her efforts to return her breath to an even keel.

When dinner was over, amidst the chaos of cleaning up, the screeching of Jessica, and the banter of the girls, Elena had asked Rosalita to walk her back to her *casita*. Rosalita had risen from the table and come to collect her, offering her mother-in-law her arm, leading her out the back door and along the worn path to Elena's door.

"You didn't eat much," Elena had said as a way of knifing open the membrane that Rosalita seemed to have sealed around herself.

"I'm not too hungry, Mama. Rico and I had a big lunch today."

"You met for lunch?"

"We went to the Barelas Coffee House."

She knew that her son and Rosalita were not in the habit of meeting in the middle of the day to go to a restaurant. Rosalita was working at that time, and Rico tended to stay in the garage, where he could listen to the radio while he ate the sack lunch Rosalita prepared for him. "That's nice," said Elena. "Very romantic."

"Not really," Rosalita had said, and the tone of her voice was like a swinging door that could move in either direction: close down or open up. Then, just like that, she had said, "I think Rico has a girlfriend, Mama."

By that time, they were approaching Elena's back door. "Come in, Rosalita. Come in," Elena had said. And to her surprise, her daughter-in-law did come in, her daughter-in-law who was so very private, whom Elena felt she both knew and did not know, who, Elena knew instinctively, had not wanted her mother-in-law to come and live here in her domain, who had maintained her distance from the start.

Elena had opened the door and Rosalita followed her in. They went straight to the living room and sat down together on the old flowered couch.

"What makes you think this?" she asked.

"It's easy to think it when you've seen the woman, seen the two of them together like lovebirds." Rosalita was remembering the way they looked, framed in the big window of Rico's shop, that book spread out before them like a future together they were poised to step into.

"You saw them? Where?"

"At the garage. He says he's teaching her to weld."

"Maybe he is," Elena said, "but what kind of woman wants to learn to weld?"

"An Anglo with hair to her ass and no hips," Rosalita responded, and then she started to cry. "It's my fault, Elena. I know that."

"Don't talk about fault. It's nobody's fault. It's just the way things go sometimes." As she'd gotten older, Elena had stopped looking at the world as a reasonable place where things added up. Now she thought of it as a place where things happened, good and bad, to random people. "But are you sure?"

"I don't know how far it's gone," Rosalita said.

And then she had told Elena everything. Some of it Elena knew—such as the way Rosalita had turned off to Rico, though she surely did not know the cold spell had gone on so long. It was three years ago that Rico had told her about it. But the rest of it! Elena felt as if she had been swept into the television set, into one of those love stories she found so riveting.

Rosalita had cried, which was rare for her, cried so much that the top of her blouse was wet, as if she'd just come inside from a rainstorm. When the story was over, she had sat on the couch in silence for a good twenty minutes while Elena made some calming tea and served it to her in an oversize cup. "I never stopped loving Rico," Rosalita finally said. "Never, no matter what it looks like."

She had sipped her tea, slowly finishing it without either asking for advice or adding more details. Elena sat close to her on the couch and gently placed her hand on Rosalita's shoulder. Together, they watched the darkness descend.

After a while, Rosalita went home and Elena turned on her television show. Not much longer after that, Rico came in the door from who know where. Elena didn't ask, though she noticed that he smelled fresh, like the mountains.

"Rico," she said, "*Te quiero, mi hijo.*"

"*Te quiero, también*," he replied, and then he took off into the dark night.

MARGARET PEELED off her T-shirt and jeans, still slightly damp, and climbed into a warm bath into which she had dropped dried lavender. Little purple flecks floated in the water, releasing a scent so lovely that Margaret felt dizzy with sweetness. She closed her eyes and images flooded in: the spectacular jagged rocks of the Jemez Mountains, Magpie standing in the river drinking fresh cold water, she and Rico sprawled out on the rocks like lizards. She had never been in a more beautiful place, never even dreamed of one like that. Already she felt a longing to return, though the next time she would go by herself, just she and Magpie, so she could spend a whole day wandering.

Not that she regretted Rico's presence on her first venture into the mountains of northern New Mexico. Far from it. His heat, so steady and reliable, had warmed her every moment of their time together, made her feel safe and somehow free; and the things she had done, like immerse herself in the river, would probably not have happened without him. Margaret knew that, but she was certain that he didn't. Rico saw her as a free spirit, and for some reason, when she was with him, she felt like one. That felt good, very good, to a woman who had been burdened with a sense of sadness her whole life, who had felt that even her skin tone was pasty gray with sadness and smoke. Perhaps Rico would weld a new image of her, one that had no relationship to the old one, and she could simply step into it. It was a possibility.

The idea that an affair was not a possibility made it somehow perfect. She had been clear with him, and he had understood her. He had said he could keep his hands off her, and she believed him. But now, in the bath, her hands, all lathered up with soap that smelled like sagebrush, moved like Rico's might, all over her body, and she felt the heat they left in their wake, warmer than the water in which she was buried up to her neck, warmer than the sun that had warmed them on the rocks in the last moments of sunlight.

But for Margaret the best part of her day with Rico came later, on the way home, after they had pledged, for better or for worse, to lower the lid onto any possibility of a romance between them. This was new to Margaret, this mature sidestepping of a potential problem, erasing it without erasing the person who had brought it to her door. She had felt such a sense of space in her exhilaration that it was simple, even graceful, to segue into the subject of welding, which Rico more than anyone knew was her obsession.

"I've been reading a lot about welding," she began, "and I'm totally overwhelmed. Everything I read is so complicated. It's like . . . Remember this?" She took both her hands off the wheel and began to pat the top of her head with one while making circles on her stomach with the other. Rico noticed that she steered the car quite skillfully with her knees during this little demonstration.

"You shouldn't read so much," he said. "Just do it."

"I know you're right," she said, "but I'm addicted."

Margaret had worked seriously at her art life for eight intense childhood and adolescent years before she ever took a class or read one book that analyzed the hows and whys of oil paint. When she had finally signed up for a class, which happened to be the first one she took with Nick, she had worry and trepidation, even fear, that her experience of the paint, of the colors and the way they swept into each other, would be tainted by the shoulds, by what she should do. One benefit of being abandoned by her parents was that Margaret had grown up without the shoulds. Parents should stay with their children, but hers didn't. Grandfathers should be home in the evening to take care of little girls, but hers often wasn't. When Donny worked, Margaret stayed across the hall with a merry widow named Mrs. Sullivan who should not have let her watch television shows with adult content until eleven at night, but she did. Nice Catholic girls should not roll up their uniform skirts to reveal several inches of schoolgirl thigh, but Margaret had. Even Donny had told her, when she was just thirteen, that a good policy was to run the other way when she heard the word 'should.' "If it's got should in it," he said, "you can be sure you won't want to do it." This was in response to the nun's opinion that Margaret should enroll in some practical secretarial training courses, since it was obvious that she, with her tendency to daydream and her lack of interest in homework, was not college material.

Rico had just told her she should quit reading, and for some reason she was tempted to listen to him. But the words captured in the books on welding were portals into a new world for her. Reading them was like having a good dream and then waking up to discover it was real.

"There's a lot of stuff in the books about color," she said. "If you heat the metal to cherry red, this will happen. If you heat it to blood red, this will happen. To me, it seems like painting, except the emotions that the colors trigger happen in the metal instead of in the person looking at it."

Rico burst out laughing. "Jesus, girl, take it easy," he said. "It's just welding, It's not rocket science."

"How do you know it's not rocket science?" she countered. "Just because you can do it, it doesn't mean it's not complex, Rico. Probably a hundred years ago it *was* rocket science. Anyway, I'm not talking about science. I'm talking about art." She glanced at him. He had shifted slightly in the seat, and his back now rested partially against the passenger door. She saw him full-on, in the headlights of a passing car, and the way the light flooded onto him and then retracted made him seem like a spirit who could incarnate or disappear at will. "Talk to me about the art of it, Rico. Tell me everything you know. You didn't get to be '*el rey*' for nothing."

She looked so sincere that Rico felt called upon to come up with something smart. But he had never talked about welding to anyone, not because he was against it, but because no one had ever brought it up. Where should he start? Margaret waited silently while he searched for an entry point.

"Well," he finally began, "most people who're just starting out fuck up because they don't keep the base metal hot enough. You have to get it to the melting point and then keep it there, keep it steady. So the best thing to do is burn up some pieces on purpose, overheat them till they're useless, just wreck them, until you start to get the feeling of what's just the right amount of heat, not too much and not too little, and that takes time to figure out and it changes depending on what you're welding. So you're always keeping right on the edge, balancing, trying not to lose the edge and—"

As he spoke, it was as if there was another Rico emerging, one who had actually formulated quite a few theories, based on personal observation, and was actually able to get the words out in some way that passed for sensible. The more he talked, the more he wanted to say, as if Margaret had forced him to squeeze through the skinny center of some hourglass, and once he did, everything had widened and he had become giddy with all the room there was inside him. Every once in a while, Margaret would stop him and ask a few questions, but mostly she listened intently. He talked nonstop until she pulled off I-25 at Avenida César Chávez, drove up over the bridge above the old railroad yard, and arrived in front of Garcia's Automotive. She turned off the engine. For a second, Rico considered continuing, perhaps opening the garage door to take her inside for some hands-on experience, but he knew that would come soon enough, the next morning in fact; and he felt obligated to go home to Rosalita and whatever was in store for him there. He had never shown up late without an explanation, and, given the events of the day, he was certain Rosalita was stewing with images, not unlike the ones he had just lived through.

"How's that?" he asked as a way of ending his long monologue. "Enough to get you going?"

"Amazing," Margaret said, and Rico thought, She thinks I'm amazing.

He reached for the car door, got out, and shut the door behind him. Then he leaned in the window. "We on for tomorrow?"

"Definitely," she said in her New York accent that he had heard before only in the movies,

"Okay, see you then." He knocked twice on the door, then stepped back from it.

"Okay, see you then," she called. "Great day, Rico."

She drove off with images of melting points and molten metal and torches spitting fire and sparks.

1990

A NEW *warden arrives. A woman. She's progressive and experimental. She introduces meditation classes into the prison. She makes bathing mandatory once a week. She puts the prisoners on work details and they clean the place until it's shipshape. She conducts clothing drives and suddenly the men wear donated madras shirts and worn dress pants.*

She releases Vincent.

After sixteen years.

"You have been here too long," she says in her accented English. "I can't even find paperwork on your case."

Vincent stands in front of her desk, stunned.

"Go and collect your things," she says in a kind voice, and even as he's hearing it, it occurs to him that this is the first female who has spoken to him in all these years. "We can arrange transportation for you to Bombay, where you can go to the American consulate," she says. But Vincent says, "No, thank you."

He has to find Regina, and he thinks she must be in a prison here in Goa.

"How will you live?" the warden asks.

"I don't know yet." Vincent smiles a little when he says that. Just a little, because he is ashamed of his teeth, several of which are missing now. She gives him 500 rupees.

He leaves the prison with exactly three items, besides the clothes on his back: the strip of photos of Regina and Margaret, the St. Christopher medal, and the map to Alice Yazzie.

When the gate closes behind him, and he is herded into a van for the drive into Siruguppa, he feels like he is sleepwalking. He wonders if he's dreaming.

Rico was already in his shop, open for business, at five to eight the next morning. He made himself a fresh pot of dark roast coffee and sat down with a strong *café con leche.* Sitting at his desk, staring out through the big window, he felt like a captain at sea steering his ship through crashing waves. His job was to make it into port intact. That was the most he could hope for.

When he had left Elena's *casita,* Rico had felt angrier than he had in years. He had always thought the concept of a person's blood boiling was a joke, but that's what he felt. In the night, with the sound of the cicadas on his nerves and his own house outlined in darkness—the last place he wanted to go—Rico didn't know what to do. There was certainly no point in slamming his fist into the wall of the house or yanking up the flowers in Rosalita's garden by the roots. There was no point in crashing into the bedroom to force her to account for what she'd done. That would only wake the girls, involve each and every person in the family in his business, and half of what made his blood hot in the first place was the idea that his own mother knew private details of his life that he had not chosen to provide to her.

He got in his truck and left. With no idea where to go or what to do, he made turns with confidence, as if he had a destination, and in the end, he arrived in the parking lot of the cemetery in which his brother Fernando was buried, not far from Margaret's house. He had never come here on his own, not once in all the years since his death. The gates were locked, but for Rico it was easy business to climb over the fence. For just a second, as he came over the top, where the wrought-iron spikes threatened to spear him if he made a wrong move, it crossed his mind that he was about to enter the land of the dead. Outside, life went on. Inside, nothing was happening but the slow process of decomposition, if that even happened anymore with today's embalming chemicals.

When his feet hit the dirt inside the fence, he felt noticeably alive in the quiet, his the only heart beating in the place. He remembered the way to Fernando's grave—how they had driven for perhaps a quarter of a mile along the main driveway and then veered to the left at the Y in the cemetery road for about a hundred feet, how Fernando's funeral procession consisted of just the hearse and one rented limo in which he, his father, and his mother sat like stones. Fernando's grave was marked with a headstone that had an angel perched on top of it, a cherub sitting there naked and innocent, the antithesis of Fernando, if there ever was one.

It didn't take long to find it, though he was well aware how many more graves there were now, as if the dead as well as the living were crowding into Albuquerque. Rico stood for a few moments to stare at the gravestone: "Fernando Jose Garcia," it read. "April 10, 1960–December 6, 1982. Rest in peace."

"*Mucho tiempo, mi hermano*," Rico finally said, "but here I am."

Why he was there was another question entirely. Perhaps while his blood boiled some ancient family DNA got dislodged from wherever Rico had buried it. Perhaps the anger he felt, the urge to smash or break something, take some action that he would undoubtedly live to regret, connected him to Fernando in the only way possible for two brothers as different as they were. Perhaps the blood ties between them were stronger than Rico knew or could have guessed. Perhaps, once he told the story of his brother to Margaret, which, he reminded himself, had happened just a few hours ago, it was inevitable that he should find his way here. For whatever reason, here he was, standing graveside paying his respects, though that might not have been exactly what he was doing. Perhaps he was paying his disrespects.

He sat down on the gravestone next to the cherub. The angel's fat little legs dangled over the side, his ankles crossed. What now, Rico thought. He looked around. The night was dark, with only a few underpowered streetlights along the road, and a moon that was already on its way somewhere else. His dead brother was packed into a box at his feet, where he had been for a quarter of a century. There was no one anywhere in sight, and yet Rico felt crowded. He glanced down at the cherub, sitting there with him on a gravestone that only comfortably seated one, and without stopping to think, he reached over, placed his hand alongside the angel's head, and gave it a shove, just to test how easy or difficult it might be to send it flying across the cemetery to rest on somebody's else's grave for a while. It had no give in it, and he ran his fingers farther down to notice that the angel's head rose right out of the shoulders and chest, as if whoever made the original mold from which perhaps millions of concrete angels had been poured, had anticipated this moment, when an angry brother might arrive in a cemetery and suddenly get the urge to knock its block off.

Rico gave the head a few shots with the palm of his hand, but the angel just sat there smiling. He got up and gave it a good kick with all the force in his leg, but again, nothing happened. He was about to try again, when he suddenly began to laugh. It was as if he was a character in one of those bible stories Elena loved to listen to on books on tape—the one about Paul on the road to Damascus maybe, which she had recounted to him many times over the years. All night Paul had fought, man to man, with a devil, and in the dawn it disappeared and he was freed of his devilish desires. Here was Rico, doing the reverse, trying to pick a fight with an angel and getting nowhere. It was crazy. He began to laugh louder, and suddenly he was overtaken with great waves of laughter, so much so that Rico had to sit down on the dry earth, his back resting against the gravestone, his legs splayed open on Fernando's grave.

What was happening to him? Here he was, in the middle of a quiet cemetery, laughing like a hyena from the zoo when his life was in an uproar. For the last ten years of his brother's life, Rico had made it a mission to avoid him whenever possible; and now he was here at his grave, his hands resting in the pale desert grass that had taken root in the dirt where Fernando's body was lowered one unusually warm day in December many years ago. Margaret had said she felt sorry for Fernando. "I can't imagine the state somebody has to reach to act like that," she had said. Now, collapsed against his grave, Rico remembered Fernando before he went bad, when he was still a good brother, one who taught him how to swing a bat, who made him root beer floats with vanilla ice cream, who let him crawl into bed with him when Rico's bad dreams came. Rico had loved his older brother then, idolized him, even. Fernando seemed like the strongest boy in the world, the boy who was always there for protection. Remembering this, Rico's laughter changed, and suddenly he was sobbing, great wails that took his breath away. I never cried for my brother, he thought. And now suddenly he was.

He had not arrived home until well after midnight. He came in, bleary-eyed and dirty, and took a long hot shower. The house, with all his girls, was silent. He sat at the kitchen table in the dark for a while, and then he went into the bedroom where Rosalita appeared to be sound asleep. She was facing the wall, her body turned away from his side of the bed. She wore a nightgown that, in the dim light, made it look like her shoulders were covered with miniature roses.

As gently as possible, Rico pulled back the summer spread and sheet and settled next to her. It was a relief to stretch out. Rosalita did not stir. Her breathing was so rhythmic that he thought she might just be pretending to sleep, but if that was so, so be it. Let her sleep or pretend to sleep, he thought, not unkindly. It was easier for both of them either way.

But in the morning, before she got out of bed for work, she pressed herself up against his back and circled her arm around his waist. "Rico," she whispered into his neck, "I did something terrible, and I need to tell you. I was so upset last night that I talked to Elena. I told her too much. I told her everything. I didn't mean to, but I did. I'm sorry, Rico."

He had not been dreaming when she woke him. He had been in the delicious nothing of deep sleep, and he felt disoriented for being pulled away from it. "I already know," he mumbled without turning toward her.

"I'm sorry," she repeated.

"Rosalita," he said, not knowing where the words were coming from, "I think we've gotten to the stage where anything goes." Her arm around him tightened slightly, and Rico felt her whole body against his, her leg pushing itself in between his legs, and her foot running down the length of his calf to his ankle. He felt her breasts flattening against his back. Then her arm around his waist began to drop down slowly until her hand found his cock, which was half hard anyway, and she began to stroke him. He thought of stopping her, but why? It felt good.

"Fuck me," she whispered.

Rico shifted onto his back and Rosalita moved on top of him. She still wore her nightgown, but once she lowered herself onto his cock, she stripped it off and threw it toward the corner of the bedroom. Rico reached for her breasts as she began to slowly shift her hips back and forth. She seemed to have all the time in the world, the way she barely moved, as if even the tiniest rocking put her into some state that she wished to cherish for a while before she moved on. Her eyes were closed, her hair untamed, like a mane, and backlit by the sun that was just beginning to slant its way in the window.

She had been so far away for so long, as if her spirit and her body were living different lives, but now they had reunited and she was solid again like she always had been. Rosalita was formed from the earth, made from mud and rivers and vegetation that grew slowly. She was like an animal, living in nature and feeling every right to be there, alive and present. She was the coyote asleep in the river reeds, the stray cat suckling kittens under somebody's storage shed, the snake finding its way to the well where the water is pure and cold. He loved her. He did. He always had.

He wrapped his arms around her and rolled over, sweeping her underneath him, where her hair spread out on the pillow like ink. Her eyes were open now and so were his, and when they kissed, neither closed them.

"Rico, *mi amor*," she whispered as he pounded his confused love into her, inch by inch. And before she could say more, he kissed her deeply, so deep he could almost feel her throat with his tongue.

Later, after she had climbed out of bed, perilously close to being late for work, Rico fell into a satisfied sleep. It wasn't until he awoke an hour later that he realized she had never asked him where he'd been until nearly one in the morning. Lying there in the tangle of sheets, he took a moment to admire her courage in the face of all this unknown. Then he got up and went to the garage, knowing that Margaret would arrive for her welding lesson in a half hour. He sat at his desk with his cup of coffee, not wanting to miss the moment when she appeared on Barelas Road, heading straight to him at her New York pedestrian clip.

MARGARET HAD awoken early, at first light, and was already walking Magpie along the *bosque* before it had brightened enough to be called daytime. All night long she had dreamed of welding, of the fire and heat that fuses two parts into one forever. Her dream space was filled with colors—blood red and cherry red, lemon yellow and mustard yellow, blue and violet and purple. Acetylene torches and welding rods and beads of molten metal appeared at various moments to rearrange the molecules of color and then move on, as if invisible painters or welders were hard at work behind the scenes. She woke up happy. She had been suffering from an absence of dreams for a long time. Too long. For most of her life, when she closed her eyes at night, she went to a preferable world where all events were unpredictable and people who were forever dead in this world seemed to live on. But her dreams had dried up two years before she left New York. She would climb into bed and tumble into the blackness of sleep, and that was it. After her parents and Donny, she counted loss of dreams as the biggest tragedy of her life.

Now she'd had one, all color and flames, and it tempted her to close her eyes again and go back inward, maybe stay there permanently. But when she paused to glance around her bedroom, she couldn't help but notice that it was also a feast. She had painted the thick adobe walls a shade of spring green, and the ceiling was a deep dark shade of periwinkle. Above her head, a ceiling fan with its white blades circling created a psychedelic effect as it orbited around in the great expanse of periwinkle. With her foot, she reached for Magpie, who had taken to sleeping on the bottom of the futon mattress, and ruffled the fur along her dog's great neck.

"Let's get up and go to the river," Margaret said, and Magpie sighed, deeply, as if she'd had enough of a walk last night and preferred to sleep in. But once Margaret propelled herself upright, Magpie scrambled to her feet and waited by the door for Margaret to let her out. Margaret got dressed quickly. She was the rare woman who could be up and ready to go in five minutes—ten, if she took a shower, which she did not do this morning, having luxuriated in a long bath late last night.

They were perhaps a quarter of a mile into their two-mile walk when Margaret saw the coyote for the second time. Though she had no way of knowing if it was the same coyote who had captivated her a few days ago, she chose to believe it was, as if he was somehow her personal coyote, assigned to her for purposes known only to nature. He was ahead of her on the trail, close, perhaps fifty feet. He had probably been trotting along as coyotes do when he heard or smelled something amiss behind him, and had stopped to investigate because his head was turned around, back toward them, while his body faced away. Margaret stopped moving, though Magpie, who was off in the bushes investigating something mysterious, continued to thrash around, oblivious.

Margaret felt hypnotized by the gaze of the coyote. He seemed unafraid, though Margaret knew he would disappear the instant she made a move. She wanted so badly to be permitted to approach. She felt that, if he were to allow her to step toward him, it would prove she was a good person, a person even a coyote could trust. So she stayed still, and it crossed her mind that her standing still was what made him trust her even a little. Standing still had great power in its way. After perhaps twenty seconds, Magpie broke out of the scrubby growth onto the path, and the coyote turned his yellow head around and slipped into the undergrowth. Margaret walked along and was soon at the spot where the coyote had been. She imagined he was hidden, watching her, noticing the moment when her scent blended seamlessly with his.

As she worked on her whimsical morning sculptures, collecting twigs and sticks and stones and circling them around the base of a great cottonwood tree, Margaret's thoughts returned again and again to the idea that standing still, remaining in that unique moment of pure potential before action was taken, was the best possible moment to live in. This confused her, for at least when it came to painting, she had often felt the power of the forward movement, but rarely the lure of its opposite.

Margaret was used to having her dog and her thoughts as her main companions in life, along with oil paint, and therefore it was not the least bit unusual for her to simply sit down to mull over an idea or a feeling. Sometimes her mind felt so electric with activity that she could do nothing more than stand back and let it happen. Today was a day like that, and so, after she placed the last river reed on her morning sculpture, she parked herself on a tree that had keeled over into the river. The trunk was huge, and the bark had long since fallen off. Margaret walked out, which required a bit of balancing, about twenty feet over the muddy brown water of the Rio, and sat down in the crook of two branches. All around her, hearts were carved into the wood with names of lovers: Roberto + Maria, Jose + Dora, Mateo + Felecia, and so on. It seemed timeless to Margaret, who chose not to listen to the voice, cynical in nature, that wanted to raise such questions as, "Yeah, sure, Roberto and Maria. How long did *that* last?" Instead, she took her Swiss army knife out of her pocket. She had begun to carry it on her morning walks once it had become clear that she would occasionally need to strip bark from a sapling or cut a notch into a river reed in order to complete her day's sculpture assignment. She placed her thumbnail in the little notch on the side of the blade and opened it. What could she add to this surprising little love fest by the river?

She began to carve, not Rico and Margaret as one might expect, but rather "Regina + Vincent" in honor of her parents, whom she hadn't seen in thirty-two years. It was more work than she expected, and she suddenly understood why lovers so frequently opt for initials. But Margaret was nothing if not diligent. She dug the tip of the knife into the dead wood, and after a long time, she had both names inside a heart-shaped fence. All the while she carved, she thought about her theme of the day: the strange power of standing completely still.

By anyone's standards, she knew very little about her mother, the wild spirit, but she was certain that Regina had never stood still, not for an instant. She was restless, Donny had said, always wanting to be somewhere else, doing something else. As a little girl in pigtails, she wanted to be grown up. "She had no use for childhood, Margaret," Donny once said when Margaret was perhaps fourteen and pumping him for a few personal tidbits from which she could construct a mother. Then he told her a story: when Regina was just five years old—just three years before her own mother died, a victim of breast cancer at the age of thirty-two—the three of them had been sitting at the dinner table discussing Regina's first day of kindergarten, which was fast approaching. Regina had announced, with clarity and volume, that she wasn't going.

"You have to go, my darling girl," her mother had said. Her mother, Erin, was a woman who got a kick out of life, and she thought her willful daughter was adorable.

"I'm not going," Regina replied.

"You don't really have a choice. All the children have to go to school, like it or not. I had to go, and so did your daddy."

"That doesn't matter. I'm not going," said Regina. "You're not the boss of me, and you can't make me."

"Unfortunately for you, we can make you," said Donny, not in a mean way, but in the firm father-way he thought she needed.

Regina had pushed back a bit from the table. She had looked very pensive for, perhaps, Donny said, thirty seconds. Then she had turned to him, and very calmly asked, "Who are you, anyway? And why are you telling me what to do?"

Against their better judgment, both Donny and Erin had begun to laugh. Truthfully, said Donny, they tried not to, had even cast a warning glance to each other, but in the end they simply could not hold back.

Regina, obviously angered by their laughter, which she took as aimed at her rather than appreciative of her, hollered again, "Who are you? Why are you telling me what to do?"

Donny had said, in a voice meant to imitate the wrathful voice of God coming through the clouds toward some poor sinner, "I am the man who's taking you to school come Monday morning. And she—" here he gestured across the table toward his young wife, "—and she is the woman who's taking you today to buy a school uniform, including the beanie that you think is stupid. I have spoken!"

Regina had stormed off to her room and slammed the door, leaving her parents at the table, giggling like two fools.

But he had also admitted to Margaret that he later regretted it, making his daughter go to school. Within three years, her mother was dead. Every one of those moments, all three years, were precious, and, looking back, he wished Regina had had them. And then he'd packed her up and moved from Ireland to New York City. Who knew how that had affected her?

"Am I like her?" Margaret had asked.

"You look like her, spitting image," Donny replied. "But at least you can sit still."

What he didn't know was that Margaret had indeed received that wildness gene, but it had gotten trapped inside her body, making her a walking cyclone, even if she didn't seem that way.

But now she had made a move, packed up and took off for New Mexico, a place she'd never thought about living, until the idea—inspired by the image of coyotes running along the Rio in the middle of town—took root in her mind, crowding her so much that she finally gave into it. So here she was, a bump on a log in Albuquerque as the sun rose inch by inch above the Manzano Mountains.

"Let's take off," she said to Magpie, who was conked out on her side in the red mud by the river. They walked home at a brisk pace, arriving there at ten after eight. Margaret poured herself some cereal, ate it while propped up in the hammock, and then locked up the gate and started toward Rico's.

1990

V INCENT GRIPS *his 500 rupees as if they're made of gold. He has no idea how much money it actually is, what he can buy with it. He doesn't know how he will get more when they run out.*

He only knows that he must find Regina.

He must find her and set her free.

He wonders if she will recognize him after all these years. He has changed from a strong young man, with wild black curls, into a beaten man, skinny with missing teeth. When he looks into a mirror, which is rarely, he sees his hair has lost its color.

Whatever might have happened to Regina, however she looks, whatever state her mind is in, he knows he can heal her. And he will. Vincent knows that he was her strength, her strong foundation, and he can be that to her again.

He wanders the streets of Siruguppa, searching for a policeman or a police station.

When he finds one, he collects his breath and walks inside.

The officer at the front desk speaks perfect English.

He says there was only one women's prison in Goa back then, sixteen years ago. He writes down the name for Vincent. He says it is a ten-hour bus ride.

Vincent follows the policeman's directions to the bus station. A bus leaves for Fort Aguada in the morning. He counts and recounts his rupees. He has enough to get there, but not enough to come back.

But why come back?

He wanders through the streets, which are crowded, which stink of body odor and sewage going nowhere. He enters a food shop, pockets several items, pays for a liter of water with a sealed top.

This country roars, he thinks as he tries to tune out the racket all around him.

He spends the night in the bus station on a bench, wedged in with several other people. One woman offers him a samosa, which he accepts with gratitude. In the morning, he is the first one on the bus. He sits in the front seat.

He watches the road, every curve, as if he's driving.

"Y o, Rico," said Margaret as she stepped through the door into Garcia's Automotive.

"Yo, Margaret," he responded, warming already.

"The new day is upon us, for better or for worse," she said, as she dropped her bag on the floor and helped herself to some coffee.

Rico watched her, happy to be in the same room with her. "For better or for worse," she had said. Somehow, since she had shown up at his door, his life had gotten better and worse at the exact same time. Just a few hours ago, he had made love to his wife for the second time in two days, a fine thing after a four-year dry spell; but now he wanted to make love to Margaret, just pull the blinds and go at it on the cool concrete floor, though she had made it more than clear that that was not going to happen, and he supposed she meant what she said.

"Last night after we got home, I went to Fernando's grave," Rico blurted out, surprising himself. "First time I ever went."

Margaret had just seated herself on the folding chair. "You did? That's big." She was leaning slightly toward him and her green eyes, so intent upon his, made him feel for a moment that everything in the whole world had an emerald green tint. "How was it?"

"I got shook up," Rico said. "Started crying and everything." Why was it so easy to talk to this woman? To admit things to her that he would normally keep to himself?

"Crying is good," she said with conviction. "I'll bet you've both needed that for a long time."

"Both?"

"You and Fernando," she said. "Both." She was quiet for a few moments, and so was Rico. Then she added, "My grandfather used to say that when you cried for somebody, your tears found their way to them no matter where they were, and they suddenly thought of you and a little firecracker of love went off and the sparks found you, wherever you were. He said that's why you always feel better after you cry."

Rico considered this. He had a sudden image of a wise old white guy, somebody big like John Wayne, sitting in a rocking chair with a miniature Margaret on his knee. "And when did he tell you this?" he asked, with a smile just beginning to form.

"Oh . . ." Margaret hesitated for just a second and then said, "when my parents dumped me off with him when I was five and then disappeared. In the beginning, I cried all the time. He came up with a lot of stories about why crying was good, and I still remember them and I still believe them, every one."

Rico noticed that she had shifted in her chair and averted her eyes from his when she spoke. He knew instinctively that it wasn't the original event, but the telling of it that put her on the spot. Margaret has trouble opening up to me, he thought, and I have trouble closing down.

"Where did they go?" he asked.

"India. They never came back."

"Something happened to them. Something bad." He said this with authority.

Margaret turned her green gaze on him. "Donny—that's my grandfather—he tried to find them for a long time, a couple of years or more, but he never got anywhere. After a while, he gave up." She stood up suddenly. "It's okay, Rico. I'm over it. Let's weld." She turned and headed into the work bay before Rico had even gotten up out of his seat.

"What are we doing today?" Margaret asked as she pulled her hair back in a burgundy scrunchie and slipped a pair of goggles around her head like a hairband. "Another axle? Or the bodywork?"

"I got you set up over here," he said.

"You mean I'm going to start?" He could hear the excitement in her voice. "Wow!" she added, taking a protective leather apron off a hook and slipping it over her head. Then she began to dig through her big bag and came out with a few charts, obviously copied from one of her how-to books, that provided information on melting temperatures and the like. She had pasted them onto cardboard, and now she propped them up against the wall at the back of the workbench. She hooked a pen onto one. "In case I need to make notes," she said.

Rico found this all very amusing, her enthusiasm. Watching her get organized, he could see the little girl she had been, listening to her *abuelo*'s stories about how tears work, soaking them up. She was a person who soaked things up. All you had to do was watch her to see it happening. She had soaked up the story of Fernando, and somehow, by giving it to her, he had freed himself to visit his brother's grave. It was so mysterious, so unexpected.

It was not lost on him that he had now heard the first and only tidbit of truly personal information about her, this woman he felt he knew inside out for no good reason. She had been abandoned by her parents. As a father himself, Rico could not imagine such a thing. He had not been separated from his daughters for more than three days in their whole lives. Even on those three overnights—in Las Vegas, Nevada, to be specific—he suffered so much, missed them so thoroughly, that he was tempted to suggest to Rosalita that they pack up and go home. The neon lights of the Sin City were no match for the sparkle in his daughters' eyes. Even now he lived in dread that one of them would take it into her head to move out on her own. Rosalita said it was inevitable, while Rico stood in his backyard and imagined three more *casitas* on it.

Margaret had read enough and watched Rico enough to know the steps, and he had already told her, just last night, that the first order of business was to learn to control the temperature of the base metal. He had already set up his smallest oxyacetylene torch, bolted a steel plate to the edge of the workbench, and collected bits and pieces of mild steel, forged steel, cast brass, and cast iron for her to practice on. She used a clamp to secure her first piece of mild steel and then turned to Rico. "Should I just have at it?"

He nodded.

"What should I make?" she asked as she studied the array of small shapes stacked up on the workbench.

"Don't make anything. Just try to get the feel of it for a while," said Rico. "Y ten cuidado."

Margaret lowered her goggles over her eyes and slipped her hands into a pair of leather work gloves—size small—that she had bought for this purpose. "Bombs away," she said, and then she began to weld in earnest. She did not speak at all, as if silence were required of a welding apprentice. Rico stood by and watched, ready to step in to protect her, not to mention himself and his garage, if she was headed for something dangerous. But Margaret took it slowly, adjusting the oxygen, testing the flame, watching the metal puddle as she heated it. She tiptoed into her project like a guerrilla soldier and, before long, she had attached two pieces of mild steel together. She shut off the torch and held it up like a trophy.

"I know it's raggedy," she said, "but look, Rico! I actually welded something!" The rusty parts back in her yard were already crowding into the periphery of her vision, lining up, waiting to be welded, too.

"Not bad," Rico said. Her smile was so wide and he was so close to her that for the first time he noticed that she had a tiny chip off her right front tooth, just the tiniest chip, and he was consumed with a desire to know how it had happened. He realized in that instant, with Margaret holding up her welded piece of metal like a winning Bingo card, that, no matter what happened between them in the long run, he simply had to know everything there was to know about this woman.

It had occurred to him that he would not see her again after today until Monday, five days away. That was their deal: Monday, Tuesday, and Wednesday mornings. It was probably a good thing because, while she was a beautiful monkey wrench, she was still a monkey wrench that he personally had thrown into the day-to-day operations of his garage. He needed to keep his mind on his business, which was impossible when she was around. But he already missed her, even if she was standing just a few feet from him, her acetylene torch flaming steadily and her eyes barely blinking, so focused was she on what she was doing. Rico had a tall stool, and he went and got it for her.

"Try sitting down," he said. "Relax." He could see the cords in her neck and clenched jaw, as if she, personally, had to weld the whole universe back together in the next five minutes. Margaret rested her rear on the edge of the stool and kept right on working. Rico saw that she was lost to him for the moment, concentrating with such intensity that she had probably forgotten he was there. It was good to see a woman in that state. The women around his own house were easily distracted, particularly by the ringing of the phone. When the phone rang, a stampede started. This annoyed Rico, who had instituted a policy of no phone calls during dinner as a way of restoring balance.

Just thinking of his home, his three girls, his wife, and his mother, took Rico's breath away for a few seconds. Why? Because in increasingly bigger waves, it had occurred to him that he might chuck it all for a chance to be with Margaret. He had already imagined moving into her old adobe house, fixing it up bit by bit until it could hold up its head in the neighborhood. He'd already imagined big kettles of *posole* on the stove, which he would make for her, and a gravel driveway instead of a dirt one, which would cut down on the dust that blew around the yard in the wind. He'd already imagined a small bed, maybe just a single, in which they would sleep, so wrapped up in each other that it would take several seconds in the morning to figure out which arms and legs were whose.

At the same time, he felt sick at the possibility that any of it might actually happen, for if it did, it would mean personal wreckage beyond anything nature could serve up. How in the world could a simple man like Rico, for he thought of himself as a basic, nuts-and-bolts kind of *hombre,* reconcile such opposing desires? How could he walk away from everything and keep it, too? And if he did walk away, how long would it take for regret to consume him?

He glanced at Margaret, whose only interest as he did mental back flips all around her was the square of steel plate she was currently attempting to stitch via fire onto another one. It made him chuckle suddenly, his predicament. There was not a thing he could do about any of it. So he raised the Chevy Impala on the hydraulic lift and went to work. He kept half his mind on his job, while the other half noticed, with pleasure, the core of heat he experienced in his heart just having Margaret at work fifteen feet away.

Meanwhile, Margaret put each little bit of metal through its transformation from solid to liquefying, from cold to molten, from inflexible to hot putty. It was dizzying to her, the way everything could change, given the right circumstances, such as relentless heat, oxygen, and a determined welder. The idea that these little pieces of steel and iron and brass—so complete in themselves—were about to meld together forever, was somewhat shocking to her. It seemed so random.

She glanced up at Rico, who had his back to her as he used a monkey wrench to adjust something under the chassis of the Chevy on the lift. She knew he was falling in love with her, though she couldn't understand why. She could feel love in the air all around her, as if it seeped out of Rico's pores to form a little invisible cloud that made the dry desert air seem moist whenever he came near her. Today she had told him a family secret, a rare event for Margaret, who normally hoarded the story of her parents' disappearance, as if by sharing it she would be giving away the last of what she had of them.

She had to admit, he was sexy, with his beautiful teeth, his long dimples, and his arms that looked carved from something far sturdier than muscle and flesh. He had a way about him, a suggestion that he had endured and would endure, come what may. Margaret, who felt her whole life had been, until recently, one long endurance test, could not help but respond to that. She recognized it in Rico because she herself had so often had to carry on when she really would much rather have crawled away and hid.

So, despite her determination and her words, such as "I never get involved with married men—never," which left no room for interpretation, Margaret was not completely immune, and it bothered her. Even in this moment, as she rested on her stool preparing to fire up the torch once more, she could imagine Rico standing behind her, closing his arms around her to demonstrate how to handle the flames and the fire, teaching her how to weld in a risky hands-on way instead of the current hands-off one they had chosen. She could imagine his lips on the back of her neck, kissing her along the hairline, behind her ear, perhaps, until she couldn't stop herself from turning around, offering her mouth. It had been a long time since it had even occurred to her to imagine such things.

Margaret let out a breath that she didn't even know she had been holding and returned to work. And the moment she ignited the torch, all her ideas about Rico disappeared into the flames, and all she could think was, Be careful. Be careful when you play with fire.

By the end of the morning, Margaret had a lopsided cylinder to show for all her efforts. It was wider at the top, perhaps eighteen inches across, and narrower at the bottom, perhaps six inches. It suggested a conch shell, rolled and welded into a permanent spiral, or a cocoon. It took her hours, and she felt exhausted. When noon came, she carefully put the tools back in their assigned places.

Rico, in just three days, had begun to look forward to the moment when she released her hair, shook it out, and ran her fingers through it. Then she would carry her bag to the chair in the office, sit down, and dig through it until she found her wallet. She'd extract thirty or thirty-five dollars, depending on how long she stayed, and hand it to him.

"Thanks a lot, Rico," she would say, looking straight into his eyes. After she left, he would open the back of the frame and add it to the rest of the money she had given him. It was already a hundred dollars, no small amount for Rico. He still had no plan for what to do with it.

"So how'd it go?" he asked.

"Good, I think. I see what you mean about keeping the temperature even. I burned up five or six pieces before I began to get the feel of it."

He leaned back in the folding chair until the front feet were well off the ground. "What? Your charts didn't help?" he asked with a challenging little smile.

"Not really," she answered, and then laughed. "I didn't even look at them. But you knew I wouldn't, right?"

"I don't know anything," he said. "Everybody's different."

"You really think so?" Margaret asked, and Rico could feel them lifting off, when suddenly whatever they were talking about shifted shape and he felt he had to hang on to keep up.

"Are we still talking about welding?" he asked.

"We're talking about welders now," she informed him. "Do you really think they're all different?"

Rico thought about it for a few seconds. "Some are better and some are worse," he finally said.

"See?" she responded.

"See what?" He didn't feel there was anything to see.

"You could've told me I was wasting my time with the charts." For some reason, Margaret felt very irritated by this.

"You don't need me to tell you what to do every minute," he said.

"Look, I want you to tell me what to do."

Rico found this concept hilarious. If there was ever a woman who did what she wanted, it was Margaret. "That's what you want?" he asked, finding it difficult to keep a straight face.

"Yes, it is."

"Then come over here and kiss me," Rico said, feeling very far away from whatever they were originally talking about.

For just a fraction of a second, Margaret felt she was inside a giant prism. Shards of colored light were everywhere. She could disappear into them with just one simple movement. She was tempted, but instead she cocked her head and gave him a mock reprimanding look. "It ain't gonna happen, Rico."

He smiled as if he'd expected that would be her response. As if, Margaret thought, he had to make a joke about his desires in order to let some of the steam in his body blow off.

"There's nothing wrong with making a chart, Margaret," he said.

It was obvious to Rico, who, after all, lived with six females, that Margaret was revved up about something, though he didn't know what. At home, he quickly retreated from women in that state. Over the years he'd developed a coping mechanism that he called "doing a U-ey" away from a female of any age who had that particular aura of impatience about her. But today, instead, he wanted to move right into it so he said, "What's bothering you?"

"You want a list?" she responded testily.

"If you have one," Rico said.

She did not say, "I feel your lust and love, and I'm afraid it will get out of control and I will lose you as my welding teacher." She did not add, "I'm scared of the way I felt sprawled out with you on a rock by a busy little river. I'm terrified because I told you about my parents this morning, which is something I never do, and now I can't take the words back." Margaret had her own ways of doing a U-ey, so she said, or rather growled, "For one thing, I have to get a fucking job," and Rico started to laugh. Once he started, he couldn't stop.

"*Lo siento*," he said because he knew how women hated to be laughed at, even when they were being impossible. "It's just so funny."

"Why is it funny?" Margaret asked.

"Because everybody has to have a fucking job. Why fight it?"

Actually, she thought though she didn't say it, she wanted to stop fighting altogether. She wanted to stop struggling, too. Stop worrying and stop fretting and most of all stop doubting.

"I was thinking about what you said yesterday—about being a courier. That seems like a good job for me."

"Well, let's walk down the block and see if Benito's home. He's the guy I told you about."

"Really?" Margaret said, "okay."

She felt obligated to go since she had brought it up, but the truth was she didn't need a job at precisely this moment in her life. She still had enough money to get by for a few months if she was frugal, which she was. But she also knew that the welding equipment she wanted would cost at least two thousand dollars, maybe more; if a job, especially one that would put her and Magpie on the open desert road, fell into her lap, she would not say no.

So Rico locked up and they started down Barelas Road together, Margaret carrying her day's work in her arm like a grocery sack.

Rico saw Benito's pickup truck in the driveway. It was a ten-year-old Toyota that he kept in perfect shape. He opened the little chain-link gate to the narrow walkway and they went in. Margaret rested her cockeyed cylinder against the inside of the fence and followed Rico. When he knocked on the door, Benito answered, wearing nothing but a pair of boxer shorts. He had a big mug of coffee in his hand and he looked sleepy.

"*¿Qué pasa, ese?*"

"*Nada*," replied Rico. "We came by to find out what you have to do to become a courier."

When Benito heard the word "we," he widened his focus and noticed Margaret standing behind Rico on the narrow walkway. He glanced from her to Rico and then back to her again. Rico, who knew Benito for a long time, could see his mind working, putting pieces together.

"*Ándale*, come on in," said Benito. "I just got up. I made a run down to Roswell last night and didn't get home till three-thirty."

"This is Margaret. She needs a fucking job," Rico said, plastering himself against the wall so Margaret could step past him. As soon as she did, Benito gave Rico a little playful punch on the bicep.

"You got a car?" he asked.

"More or less," she replied.

"There's always work, especially if you can go at the last minute and don't mind the long hauls."

"What's long?"

"Couple hundred miles."

"That's do-able," she said.

They settled in Benito's living room, which was spotless. Somebody kept it that way, and one glance at Benito convinced Margaret it wasn't him. It looked as if he had a big family. There were pictures of kids everywhere.

"I got a business card around here somewhere." Benito got up and opened and closed a few drawers before he found it. He handed it to Margaret. It read "Roadrunner Courier Service." Then, in small print, "Running the road in New Mexico since 1974" with an address and phone number.

"Just stop by over there. Tell them Benito sent you."

"Thanks," said Margaret. "I will."

"You want some coffee?" Benito asked, as if he had suddenly remembered his manners.

"No, man. I gotta get back to work," Rico said, standing up. "*Gracias*, Benito."

Margaret got to her feet, too. "Yeah, thanks a lot, Benito," she said.

"You live in the neighborhood, Margaret?" he asked.

"Yeah. Around the block."

"*Bienvenida a Barelas,*" he said. "Stop in anytime," and she smiled.

Rico and Margaret let themselves out and proceeded down the walkway, where Margaret stopped for a second to hoist the welded metal into her arms. "I can't forget this wad of metal," she said, and Rico laughed. He pushed open the gate and she went through.

"You gonna check out the courier service?" Rico asked.

"I think so," Margaret answered. "I have to think about it a little more, though."

"Don't rush into anything." He smiled and she smiled back. But there, in the hot summer sun, it crossed her mind that she was rushing into everything, rushing into everything from the flames to the river, from the open road to the endless desert sky, from loneliness to, if she wasn't careful, love.

"Thanks, Rico. I'll see you Monday."

To Rico, her voice sounded light, as if saying goodbye to him for a five-day stretch was easy. It did not feel so easy for him, but he called, "*Hasta el lunes.*" Then he turned to the right and Margaret turned to the left, and they walked away from each other.

1990

*T*HERE IS no American prisoner named Regina Donnery in the Fort Aguada Jail for Women. The records go back ten years, and Vincent begs the officer, a young man with a fresh face and kind eyes, to check through all of them. He does, but finds nothing.

"Could I speak to the guards, perhaps?" Vincent asks. "Someone who has been here for sixteen years?"

"There is no such person," the officer says. He wears a name-tag which reads "Sandeep Singh."

Vincent feels dizzy. He reaches for the edge of the officer's desk to steady himself.

"What about . . . older records?" he finally asks.

"We don't have the personnel to do such a search."

Vincent feels a glimmer of hope. "But do you have records?" he asks. "Could I look through them myself?"

"I will ask my supervisor," says Sandeep Singh. "Come back in the morning."

"Please," Vincent responds. "Please. I beg you."

Vincent lets himself out of the office into the sharp sunlight. He starts walking. The town is six kilometers away. It is a tourist destination, and he heads there, hoping to find an American to listen to his story, to reach into his wallet. To help.

There is no one. He parcels out the last of his rupees. He buys small bits of food from street vendors. He steals what he can to eat. He finds an office building and enters it before dusk, hiding in a closet full of cleaning supplies until everyone leaves. He searches unlocked offices and desks for rupees or food. He rinses his clothes, hanging them to dry over the railing on the second floor. He drinks from the faucet in the bathroom. He sleeps on a short couch in the hallway. In the morning, he walks back to the prison.

He lives this way for three weeks, until finally Sandeep Singh leads him to a storage room on the edge of the prison grounds. Metal shelves are piled floor to ceiling with boxes. There are signs of rat infestation.

But Vincent goes through each one.

On the eleventh day, he finds a paper with Regina's name. It is written primarily in Hindi.

He carries it to Sandeep Singh.

Sandeep Singh reads it slowly.

He raises his eyes to Vincent's.

"She died of hepatitis in 1976, just two years after she arrived here. Her body was cremated." He touches Vincent's arm. "I give you my sympathy, Vincent," he says, as Vincent folds inward. He sits in the chair in Sandeep's office, which is full of people, and he cries like a baby.

Little by little, the noise in the room diminishes until there is silence.

Except for the sound of one old, broken man, sobbing.

WHEN MARGARET arrived at her house, she greeted Magpie in her usual affectionate manner, and then made a beeline to the cement pad where all her rusty parts were spread out. She carried her hunk of freshly welded metal to the pad, propped it up against the big elm tree, and stared at it for a long time. She had no idea how it happened, but somehow, between Benito's house and her own, she'd received an image of a finished product, and now she felt compelled to bring it into the world.

It had started with her spontaneous use of the word "wad." This was not a word she had much occasion to use, but it had had a place in her vocabulary, and in her mind, ever since the day Harold had given up on her. He had said, "Please. Let me help unravel the wad you use to get through life," and she had replied with a mean remark, one that—she thought as she lay paralyzed with grief in her bed for days afterward—had been formed completely from the pain in which she was and had always been entangled. It captured her imagination, this idea that she was wrapped in a protective sheath, one that made her safe from hurt though, paradoxically, was itself made of memories that hurt her, layered around her like a cocoon. As she had lain curled up like a baby in the womb on her foam mattress on Avenue B, she had drifted backward through the events that formed this mess—her deep loneliness and her hopelessness and her inability to trust that things could change, maybe get better. Her money struggles, formed in part by a compulsion to live below the radar, a cash-only lifestyle that made her feel like a scavenger, an eater-of-opportunity, a

New York City cockroach. Her losses: Harold, who had just walked away. Christina, her one true friend, who had died in the World Trade Center, when fire and melting metal ravaged the investment firm where she'd worked for just seven weeks. Donny, who collapsed behind the Bit O' Blarney bar and died in the arms of a regular who had nothing better to do but drink his afternoons away and stare out the window at the tugboats in the harbor. Vincent, her father, the love of her young life, and Regina, her mother, who had always been so elusive, the mother she barely remembered. And the word "derivative," which was carelessly applied to her artwork, the one port in the storm that was her life. Underneath all these layers was a terrified heart, one that had desperately needed to be wrapped in love to thrive, but had wadded itself in sorrow to survive in the meantime.

Now, all these years later, she'd been presented with an image. A woman breaking free. Margaret could see it in her mind: a tornado of metal parts, raggedy and welded together like armor. Below it, two ankles that perhaps seemed bound by the tight end, and two feet, too small to stand on. And from the top, a woman's head thrown back, her face looking skyward, and her two arms, lifted and free, emerging at last. She would call it, "Self-Portrait: Unraveling the Wad Used to Get Through Life." She would assemble her portrait from rusty engine parts, maybe hang it from the Chinese elm tree in her yard where it could remind her every day of what she was finally ready and able to do.

For all the years she'd painted, she had never, not once, made an overt self-reference, never created a painting that was even vaguely figurative. She had always stood before a blank canvas like a woman embarking on a journey from which she might not return. She loved that intensity. She loved moving into the paint as if it were a cave she had to find her way out of. Her impulse to weld was similar, but it felt more personal, bigger, and riskier.

She dumped a bucket of fresh parts onto the concrete pad and started to work. She chose gears for the head, and long railroad bolts for arms. She found screws for fingers and unidentifiable bits of machinery for ears and eyes. Feverishly, she worked her way into three dimensions, as if she knew her mental concepts had been flat for too long and needed to be multiplied by themselves, squared or cubed in her mind as well as her fingers, and now it was happening.

Creating artwork in three dimensions was far beyond her skill level for the moment, yet she could imagine a future self able to do it with ease, and she rushed toward her. By Monday, she would have all the parts figured out, and she would transport them intact to Garcia's Automotive and learn how to weld this unexpected self-portrait together permanently. She needed rusty nails. Pawing through her parts to no avail, she got in her car, Magpie in the backseat, and drove to Coronado Wrecking. She parked under a shade tree.

"Be right back," she said to Magpie, who was not allowed to get out of the car at the junkyard.

By this time they were used to seeing her. The woman at the desk, a middle-aged lady who looked far too put together to work in a junkyard—what with her decaled nails, pressed jeans, and print blouse—was on the phone, and just waved as Margaret signed in and let herself out the back door into the acres and acres of old sinks and bathtubs, massive wooden doors, assorted construction materials, cars, and machinery. Carrying her orange bucket from Home Depot and a pair of thick work gloves, she passed through the huge metal shed that contained thousands of doors and out the other side, into the realm of scrap metal.

Sometimes, when she entered Coronado Wrecking, Margaret felt that she was stepping into a post-modern cathedral. It took her breath away to see the dirt roads disappearing around the mountains of junk, a few pilgrims attempting to pillage, sack, and raid. It felt right for Margaret to be here, collecting what had been relegated to uselessness and reshaping it into something else. Within each section of the yard there was no particular order, and she had to poke around for a while before she found a pile of nails, small bolts, and nuts. She collected all there were, perhaps a quarter of her bucket, and headed back to the office to dump them on the scale.

"That was fast," said the woman with the decals on her nails as she weighed the parts. "Three dollars."

"I have my dog in the car," Margaret explained as she straightened out three crumpled bills from her pocket. "I don't want to leave her too long."

"No, you don't want to do that in this heat," said the woman as she tilted the scale back into Margaret's bucket, and then presented her with a receipt. "Well, see you next time."

"It'll be soon," Margaret said, and then, because she couldn't help it, she added, "I finally started welding today. My first time."

"Congratulations, honey," said the woman, smiling in such a way that Margaret knew she meant it.

When she got back in the car and turned on the radio to *Evening Edition*, she knew it was after five. That surprised her. Since she had been in New Mexico, time had changed, both shrunk and stretched. She had never inhabited time in this way, this no-job, no-classes, no-responsibilities way, and she liked it. Even if by the standards of the consumer world she was living a minimalist, if not a monastic life—where her major purchases were consistently made from a junkyard— it seemed luxurious to her, and she was grateful for it every single day.

But today she had told Rico she needed to get a job. She knew when she said it that it was a distraction, created in the moment to help her keep herself hidden, but something had backfired. It was as if the concept of "getting a job" was sitting in the back of the bus, and when he had asked her what was wrong, she had suddenly dragged it up to the driver's seat and forced it to sit down. Once she'd done that, it had taken the wheel, and now she was heading for the workplace. This was probably a good thing. She was all alone in the world, with no one to bail her out if she got in trouble, and could not afford to kid herself about her finances, though she had done well so far. Tomorrow, she thought, she would visit Roadrunner Courier Service and see what happened. If not tomorrow, then Friday.

She happened to be passing Fourth Street, the turn she would take to go to Garcia's Automotive, which naturally made her think of Rico. Rico of the acetylene torch. Rico of the TIG and MIG welding apparatus. Rico of the heat and flames and melting metal. Rico of the dragon tattoo and the dead brother. Rico of the "Come over here and kiss me."

It certainly wasn't as if Margaret had never heard that line before. Such comments were frequently fired like rockets into the air at the Stereophonic Lounge, where flirting with the bartender was a favorite sport. She had responded to Rico in exactly the way she would respond to any other guy: with a playful putdown and a change of subject. And, like the guys on the barstools, he had taken it in good humor and adapted immediately to the new conversational direction.

But that sentence kept ringing in her ears.

She wouldn't mind kissing him.

Margaret knew a thing or two about kissing. Some women didn't take it seriously. "It's just a kiss," she had heard them say, as if kisses were unimportant and therefore dismissable. Dismissable kisses, Margaret had noted, were usually illicit, conducted on the sly by married people or lovers whose part-ners would not think of a kiss with someone else as innocent. She had never seen it that way either. To her, to kiss was more like opening the door to a raging fire in the hallway. Everyone knows better than to do that. Everyone knows that when you open the door, the fire rushes in and consumes you. Once she was kissed, and, more importantly, once she kissed back, she was never the same again. A man had made his way inside her, and, once there, he could do damage. He could refuse to leave. He could fill her with hope and then walk out the door. He could disappear to India forever. Anyway, she barely knew

Rico. He was her teacher and perhaps her friend. He was also a married man.

She needed to erase "Then come over here and kiss me" from her mind and from her ears, too. "Change the fucking channel," she suddenly said out loud, as if her mind were a radio and she could adjust it at will. It was a phrase she had heard teenage girls in New York use, kids she'd sat next to on the subway, when their faces were lit with exasperation.

She made a right onto Eighth Street and headed home. The neighborhood was familiar to her now: the homeless woman, dressed in a raggedy trench coat with her short-haired dog on a leash, sat on a swing in a corner playground. Teenage boys with shaved heads worked on cars parked on the street. Young girls in revealing tops pushed strollers along sidewalks where weeds sprouted in the cracks. She had entered into nodding relationships with several neighbors, thanks to her walks around the block with Magpie. Little by little, Albuquerque was becoming home, even if she had only passed one short season here, just part of one summer, though in some ways it felt much longer. She parked her car in the driveway, locked up the gate for the night, and lost herself in rusty parts. It was already dark when she finally noticed that she was working in the dim glow of the one streetlight that lit the alley behind her house.

She went inside and turned on the bathwater. While it ran, Margaret washed her filthy hands in the bathroom sink. Brownish water, the color of dirt and rust, circled the drain, rinsing off her fingers in lighter and lighter shades until it ran clear. From the time she was little, she had always enjoyed the process of cleaning up. The idea that her body could be restored to its pristine state pleased her. Perhaps it was a reaction to Catholic school, where the nuns were always harping on the ways in which black marks were etched into a person's soul, possibly forever. It was unfair, she thought, especially the idea of Original Sin, which meant you arrived as a babe in arms with a soul already black with crimes you didn't even commit.

"Did Mommy and Daddy leave because of me?" she had asked Donny over and over for months after she'd first been deposited at his door.

"No, my darling," he had said. "They left because they're young and selfish and they want to see the world. Some people are restless like that, and your mother is one of them. They love you with all their hearts."

"Did I do something wrong?"

"No, Margaret. You're a wonderful little girl. You did everything right. Every single thing. Don't you be thinking it's your fault because it isn't."

But at night, in her bed, Margaret would make promises to God: If you bring them home, I promise I will never cry again. I promise I will not whine. I won't ever wake them up when they want to sleep, and I won't ever touch Daddy's paintings before they're dry. And . . ." Her litany went on and on though God never responded, and once it became obvious that her parents were gone for good, Margaret could actually feel her own black soul, right in her chest, heavy with the sins which drove her parents from her. Perhaps as compensation, she became the cleanest child in the whole world. She scrubbed and washed with such vigor that Donny sent his neighbor, Mrs. Sullivan, on a special mission to find the gentlest possible soap, and washcloths with next to no texture. He replaced his own fingernail brush, which had coarse bristles, with a soft nylon one, and he took to limiting the amount of time she could spend in the tub. Looking back, Margaret was amazed and touched by his sensitivity, by the small things he noticed about her and acted upon with love.

She glanced up from the sink and looked into her own eyes in the mirror. It was one of the things Donny had taught her to do when she was a child. "Look into your own eyes long enough, and you'll always know what to do," he had said. So there she was, staring into her green eyes in the bathroom mirror as the tub filled with water and steam collected on the edges of the mirror. She knew her eyes connected her to her own truth, just as Donny had said. She also knew that the truth she was looking for had to do with Rico, with his "Come over here and kiss me," and with the defenses she'd layered around her, just to get through life.

ALL AFTERNOON, Rico concentrated completely on the work he had to catch up on in the shop. He turned up the radio to cancel out any thoughts of Margaret, and he ignored the sense of emptiness that settled like dust in the shop the moment she walked out the door. He liked her ways, how she put his tools back in precisely the right places and even restacked the remaining pieces of metal and moved them to the back of the workbench so he'd have room to work there if he needed it. He liked the way she looked him in the eyes when she paid him. He wanted to do things for her—like tune up that old car of hers, especially if she ended up working for the courier service.

By five-thirty, he was exhausted and he shut everything down with a sense of relief. A look at his appointment book, though, warned him he'd be busting hump for the next three days. It wasn't until he climbed into his truck and pulled out of the parking lot that he thought of Rosalita. So far, he had not even told her about going to Jemez Springs with Margaret or visiting Fernando's grave. They had made love that very morning with all of that—where he had been until one in the morning and what he had been doing—hanging heavy in the air between them, and neither mentioned it. He found it very odd and somehow exciting.

Rico drove slowly over the speed humps on Riverside Drive. Wilfredo was out in the driveway shooting baskets. He waved and called out, "Rico, want to play?"

"Maybe later, Wilfredo," Rico answered. "I'm just getting home and I'm starved."

"Okay, maybe later," the boy responded.

Rico pulled into his driveway and parked. He hesitated for a few seconds, perhaps storing up some equilibrium before he headed inside. When he opened the front door, the smell of *arroz con pollo* enveloped him. It was so normal, so right, to enter his house full of women and smell the dinner cooking.

"Is that you, Rico?" Rosalita called. "Dinner's almost ready."

Her voice sounded natural, too. He moved to the kitchen door and looked in. Rosalita was fluttering around the stove. Elena was already at her place at the table, which was in the process of being set by Mirabel, and Jessica and Lucy were visible through the screen door, playing with a bright red kickball in the backyard.

"I'm going to take a quick shower," Rico said.

Rosalita looked up from the pots and pans. "*Cinco minutos*," she said, raising a wooden spatula in his direction like a saber.

"*Cinco minutos*," he repeated, already retreating from the kitchen doorway.

In the bathroom, which he had tiled himself in seafoam green, he stripped off his clothes and undid his long ponytail. His hair was as thick and straight as Margaret's, though not quite as long. Rosalita usually trimmed off a good four or five inches a year in the spring. Otherwise, all he did was wash it, comb it straight back, and gather it into a rubber band. He paused to examine himself in the mirror for a second while the shower water warmed up. He looked like a man ready for anything—muscular and trim and even a little bit wild, like an Indian from the old western movies, with his black hair loose and flowing over his shoulders.

He stepped into the shower, enjoying the beating of the hot water on his back, thinking how strange it was to come into his own house, to stand in the kitchen doorway where everything appeared to be quite normal, and know, clearly, that he and Rosalita were headed for a big scene and it would happen soon. Rico accepted and expected that, but he hoped, selfishly, that it could erupt in private. It was a wish that made him sad.

He hadn't even settled at his place at the table for one minute before Lucy asked, "Papi, where were you last night? You're always home for dinner."

Rico wasn't used to lying because he rarely had a reason to bother, but now he said, "I had to work, *mi hija*."

"So late?" she responded. "I heard you come in after midnight."

"Yeah, well, a good customer of mine, he needed his car this morning," Rico said, feeling worse with every word.

"You shouldn't have to stay so late," Lucy said.

"It almost never happens, thank God," Rosalita said as she placed a platter of *pollo* in the center of the table. As she leaned forward to do so, she temporarily blocked the visual line from Rico to Lucy, and he felt grateful. He tried to catch Rosalita's eye, but she didn't glance at him.

"So how was everybody's day?" Rico asked, realizing when he was halfway through the question that he had spoken the line Rosalita always said in this moment.

Ana had just slid into her chair. "I made an A on my psych test," she said, and everyone clapped. It was a little ritual that they always adhered to: good news from anybody got a round of applause.

"Tell us one of the questions, Ana," Maribel prompted. "Make it a hard one."

Ana thought for a moment and then said, "Okay. A serotonin reuptake inhibitor is most frequently prescribed in the treatment of a) color blindness, b) Alzheimer's disease, c) chronic depression, d) alcohol withdrawal, or e) obsessive compulsive disorder."

Everyone at the table was silent. Then Maribel said, in a matter of fact tone, "D. Alcohol withdrawal."

"Wrong!" said Ana, and she launched into the particulars of the serotonin reuptake inhibitor. The actual words soon faded for Rico, became like the pleasant hum of honeybees in the trumpet vines outside the window. He was happy here at dinner with his whole family, his harem, as Rosalita called it, gathered around, eating the food that he was able to put on the table for them. He loved the way Ana, with her interest in science, was always willing to dumb down complicated science concepts for them. Sometimes he would raise his hand in the midst of it all and she would call on him and he'd ask a question. "Professor Garcia," he would begin, "why does . . ." and she would look very serious and then continue on with more and more animation in her voice. She was the scholar in the group, and he had no idea where she got it. Lucy was the dreamer, and Maribel was the most like Rosalita—practical, down to earth, and calm.

Rico's eyes shifted to Rosalita. She sat opposite him, but her face was turned toward Ana, and he only saw her left profile. She had been a beautiful young girl, so fresh-faced and innocent that Rico had fallen for her at first sight. That had happened at her *quinceañera*, to which Rico had been invited because Elena and Rosalita's mother were church friends. He'd had nothing better to do so he tagged along, planning to feed his face, drink a few beers, and move into his evening. But when Rosalita had come out of the house, wearing high heels with a strap around the ankles and a low-cut flowered dress that left no doubt that she had achieved womanhood, he was smitten. He was almost twenty, a full-grown man, so he had respectfully asked her father for permission to dance with her. Once he took her in his arms, once she melted into him and gazed at him from underneath her eyelashes, thick with the mascara she was finally allowed to wear, his heart was already pounding under his shirt, and he had to fight the urge to lead her out of the backyard in front of everyone and disappear into the sunset in his truck.

He had been with several women by that time, but his heart had never acted up before, never felt inclined to open wide and welcome love. But he could barely refrain from whispering "*Te quiero mucho*, Rosalita" into her ear at the end of their first dance. It must have been clear that whatever had enveloped him had also descended on her because, even though it wasn't the politest thing to do at her *quinceañera*, she refused all the others—boys and men—and from then on, she was Rico's and that was that. After a month, Rosalita was riding her bicycle toward Garcia's Automotive at the same time Rico's father was leaving at the close of business. Within minutes of his exit, Rico would unlock the door to her, and they would climb into the backseat of whatever car was in the shop and not even come up for air until her curfew, which during the first year was eleven P.M. Rico wore condoms, colored ones that he bought in packages of fifty. Despite that precaution, Rosalita got pregnant before a year and a half had gone by. She gave birth to Lucy when she was just seventeen. Neither she nor Rico ever regretted it. Rico had already found his piece of land and, with his father's help, had purchased it on a twenty-year real estate contract. He and Rosalita moved in there together when only one room of the house was constructed—wheel barrowful of adobe by wheel barrowful—when there was no running water, an electrical panel consisting of two fuses, and an outhouse. They were deeply, completely happy.

Yet they never married, which was shameful, at least according to their families. It was Rosalita who said no, who had witnessed too much behind the closed doors of her own parents' marriage to believe in it. "I want to stay with you because of love," she insisted, "not because of a piece of paper." Here she would hold up her hand with her thumb and pointer finger touching as if there were a piece of paper between them. And sometimes she would add, "and if I have to leave, ever, I want to be free to go." To Rico, it didn't matter, though for many years every time they attended the wedding of a friend, he was filled with longing and proposed again, but Rosalita only smiled and said, "We don't need the piece of paper, Rico. We don't." Now he knew, though he hadn't until a few days ago, that a time had come when Rosalita had thought of leaving, but by then she did not feel free to go, paper or not.

Ana was wrapping up her psychology lecture when Rico finally tuned back in. The correct answer, he ascertained, to her multiple choice question was c) chronic depression. He nodded his head as if he finally understood, as if he had been listening intently with the others, but his eyes were on Rosalita. Had she been depressed for the past four years? Had she been living with regret, perhaps wishing she had run off with whatever man it was that arrived in her life and threw her off balance so completely that she had not been able to find her way back to Rico, whom she'd been with for close to two decades? Was he in the same predicament now? Heading for depression? Or had he just woken up from it?

Dinner progressed as it always did: with laughter and conversation and plenty of good food. Maribel, as always, had complaints about the manager at PetSmart, who, according to her, didn't know his ass from a hole in the ground. Lucy had a date coming up on Saturday night with a *Mexicano* who played the trumpet in a mariachi band. Ana would babysit for Jessica, provided Lucy swore to be home before Jessica started screaming to get up at five in the morning. Speaking of morning, Elena pleaded with Rico to sneak over and strangle the rooster who lived on the other side of the fence from her *casita*, the one who started crowing at four and never shut up until ten in the morning. Rosalita was quiet, but that was not new. Mainly, she asked who was ready for more *arroz con pollo* or who needed another drink. As always, she added food to Rico's plate without asking him. As always, she pretended to be surprised when the girls offered to do the clean up. "I wouldn't mind putting my feet up," she said, as she always did, and then she went into the living room and flicked on the television for the seven o'clock news.

Tonight, Rico followed her, leaving Maribel to walk Elena back to her *casita*.

"Rosalita, let's take a little drive," he said. "Or how about a walk by the river?"

She glanced up from the TV screen. "Why?" she said.

"So we can talk," Rico said.

"I don't feel like talking," she said. "I don't want to hear where you've been or what you've been doing."

Rico sat down at the opposite end of the couch. "It's not what you think," he said. "At least, not yet."

She looked at him now, and to Rico, she looked tired. "Were you with her last night?"

"For a while. We took a walk, that's all."

"It must have been a long walk."

"Afterward I went to Fernando's grave," Rico said. "I climbed over the wall of the cemetery."

Rosalita studied him. "Why?" she asked.

"I don't know. I was talking about him to Margaret, and later I just ended up there." Even saying the name Margaret out loud felt risky, and he realized with surprise that he was suddenly nervous about talking to Rosalita, the woman he had talked to every day for twenty-three years.

"What do you want from me, Rico?" she said.

He hesitated. "You could ask me if I'm okay," he finally said.

"Are you?"

"I don't know."

She moved toward him then. He put his arm around her shoulder the way he had always done, before those four years when it became clear that she didn't want him to touch her anymore.

"Well, look at this! Young love!" said Lucy as she came into the living room with Jessica on her hip. "Am I interrupting something?"

"No," said Rosalita.

"Good," replied Lucy, dropping her daughter into her mother's lap. "Sit with Grandma, *mi amor*, until Mommy finishes the dishes." Lucy turned around and vanished into the kitchen.

Rico had to laugh. Maybe that was family life in a nutshell. The walls could be collapsing, but until everyone was buried up to their necks in the rubble, life went on as usual. They had a granddaughter, a two-year-old who needed to be amused for a few minutes. Everything else was on the back burner. Jessica squirmed around and finally crawled onto Rico's lap.

"Up, up," she said, and Rico obliged, lifting her high above his head and pretending to drop her, which brought on great gales of laughter. Rosalita took the opportunity to move away from him, back to the other end of the sofa. She turned her attention to the evening news and seemed unreachable. Rico had expected fury from her, wrath, vicious words, and ultimatums, but her new silence felt full to the point of bursting, like a volcano or a pot of boiling water with its top on too tight.

Rico glanced at his wife again. Maybe she'd been waiting for this—a chance to get away without the guilt of having caused the breakup. But then he thought of the way she'd been in bed the last few nights, uninhibited and free in his arms, and a plot to escape seemed rather unlikely.

He did not know his own wife anymore, he thought to himself as he threw Jessica up in the air again and again. And to be truthful, he didn't know himself either.

1990

VINCENT HAS no idea there is enough left inside of him to feel so terrible. He thought he had bottomed out long ago, reached the point at which nothing really matters anymore. He is deeply shocked by this new wave of devastation. He has spent his whole life believing there is always something better, and now he knows that there is always something worse.

And this is it.

Regina dead.

Fourteen years.

Dead at twenty-six.

Vincent wanders the streets with no destination. He wishes he had money for alcohol or drugs, but there is nothing to dim the pain. No way to wipe it out except to feel it. Go through it.

He loses weight. More weight. One day he sees his reflection in a window and he thinks he looks like an old man. On that same day, he sees a beautiful young woman, a Hindu woman with long black hair that she has temporarily set free of its braid.

Her hair reminds him of Regina's.

It reminds him of Margaret's.

His daughter is twenty-two years old. Older than this Hindu woman whom he watches as she rebraids her hair and places a rubber band at the end.

It has not occurred to him that he could somehow get himself back to the United States, but now he decides to try. He still has a daughter.

He gets up from the steps of a statue in a local park that has become his home. He begins to walk.

He will walk all the way to Bombay if he has to. He will find the American embassy. He will manage it somehow.

He's going home.

ONCE L UCY had collected her daughter, taken her into the bathroom for a nice warm bath, Rico let himself out into the evening air, which had cooled considerably. The night was very dark, with just a tiny crescent of moon in the sky and his own outdoor lights turned off for the moment. He could vaguely hear the sound of the television set. He didn't want to compare Margaret and Rosalita. It did not seem productive or fair, and yet he could not help but recall Margaret's words when he told her about visiting his brother's grave. "That's big," she had said. Rosalita, on the other hand, had just asked a technical question: "Why?" Between the two, he found his comfort in Margaret's reaction, though he wasn't even sure why he needed a reaction or why he wanted to tell the story.

He walked back to his mother's *casita* and went in. "*Hola Elena, mi madre,*" he called as he always did.

"In here," she responded from the living room, as if he could not figure that out.

When he entered, Elena did a very uncharacteristic thing— she turned off the television. "I've already seen this one. It's a repeat," she said, as if she had to explain. She looked at him closely, though he knew she could not see his face. "How are you today, *mi hijo?*" she asked.

"Fine," he said, as if he was learning from Rosalita how to avoid a question.

"Fine?"

"Well . . ." He hesitated for a few seconds. "Not too bad."

Elena laughed. "That's more like it," she said. "Have some tea. There's hot water on the stove."

Rico got up and poured himself a cup. Tonight, he added two spoonfuls of honey instead of milk.

With all the family drama in the air, with Rosalita having taken Elena into her confidence just last night and Rico's anger because of it, with the dinner they'd all just sat through as if none of that had happened, Rico had no idea where to begin. But he knew he needed to talk to his mother about at least some parts of this whole complicated mess. But no words came, so he just sat there and sipped his tea, and so did Elena. It was easy to sit in silence with his mother.

After a while she asked, "Have you talked with Rosalita?"

"She doesn't want to talk," said Rico.

"How about yell?" Elena asked, and they both chuckled.

"No. I asked her to take a ride with me, and she said no. I don't know what else to do." He put his tea down on the tile table. "I can't figure her out. Maybe she wants it to end between us. Maybe this is her way of making sure that happens."

"Maybe," Elena agreed, thoughtfully, "but the way she was crying her heart out last night over here, I don't think so."

"She was crying her heart out?" It took him a few seconds to absorb this. "She's playing it cool with me."

"Maybe she's showing you how she feels in other ways."

Rico thought of Rosalita climbing on top of him that morning, of the way she flung her prim summer nightgown to the far corner of the room and began to slowly rock. He thought of the way she had slid across the couch just a half hour ago to press her body right next to his, how it took some pressure off him somehow.

"I guess so," he said, but his voice, even in his own ears, lacked certainty.

"This *gringa* woman—"

"Her name is Margaret," Rico cut in.

"Tell me what it is about Margaret that has you so captured," Elena said.

Rico looked at his mother. There was nothing in her tone that hinted to him of a setup, a seemingly innocent display of interest that would soon turn against the *gringa* home wrecker. And the simple truth was, he wanted to talk about Margaret in the way that people do when they are intoxicated with possibility. But where should he start? With the way the sunlight caught in her eyes so they seemed to spin like green pinwheels? With the fact that she was a bookworm, who had found him in a library book he had not even told her about? With the adorable way, he thought in retrospect, that she had hinted when they'd first met that she was an ex-NYPD policewoman out for a walk with an ex-NYPD police dog?

"She's an artist. She wants to learn to weld," he said instead. "She has all these pieces of crap lying around that she drags home from the junkyard, and she wants to weld them into sculptures. She asked me to teach her, and I said yes."

Elena lifted her tea cup to her lips and blew on it even though Rico was sure it was just lukewarm. One thing he liked about his mother was that she had the capacity to wait, to let things unfold in their own time.

"She was abandoned by her parents," he suddenly said. "They went to India and never came back. So she was raised by her grandfather in New York City. But he died, and now she doesn't have anybody. Nobody. Except her dog." Rico felt good talking about Margaret, and he wanted to construct a clear picture of her for his mother, one that would create the magic he felt when he was around her. So far, he was just providing the facts and that was not enough, so he added, "She makes me feel good, Elena. She asks me questions and before you know it, I'm doing something crazy like climbing over the cemetery wall to visit Fernando's grave and—"

Elena put her cup on the table. "What?" she said, "¿Qué dices, Rico?"

Rico realized then, in that moment when she was so startled, that he had not yet mentioned his visit to the cemetery to his mother.

"You never visit your brother's grave," Elena said.

"Well, I went," Rico said. "I told Margaret about him, and after I left here last night, I just drove around and ended up there."

Elena began to cry. Tears washed through her hazy blind eyes and ran down her cheeks. "At last," she said. "*Gracias a Dios.*"

Now Rico was startled. This was not a reaction he was prepared for. He hated to see any woman cry, most of all his mother.

"Now I can die in peace," she said, barely able to get the words out, "knowing you forgive Fernando."

"We were talking about Margaret," Rico said, his voice rising sharply. "We were talking about me for a change." It bothered him when his mother carried on about Fernando. It had gotten old, hearing the same story as they drove home from church week after week. "Besides, I didn't say I forgave him. I just went to his grave." He knew now that he would not tell her how he had fallen apart there, how he had remembered his boyhood hero with a strong feeling of love in his heart. And why not? Because here he was in a crisis of his own, a real one, and his mother was more concerned about Fernando, who was dead and gone for twenty-five years. That said it all. He stood up.

"Rico," Elena said, "please, wait, *mi hijo*, just for a second. You need to understand something. Nobody loved Fernando, nobody but me. Even your father gave up on him. Did you know I had to beg him to go to his own son's burial? I had to threaten to leave him if he wouldn't get in that car with me that day. I knew you were glad he was gone too, and I can't blame you, all the beatings you took. But all these years . . . all these years I've been waiting for some sign that somebody somewhere cared, and now you gave it to me."

Rico longed to walk out the door into the night where he could be alone, but he could not turn away from his mother.

"You don't understand, *mi Rico*, because everyone loves you—Rosalita, the girls, me, your father. Even this woman

Margaret, she probably loves you too, and maybe you love her. But Fernando never had that."

"He was a sick bastard, *mamacita*," Rico said. His voice was vicious, but he addressed her the way he had in the old days, long ago. "He was cruel."

"I know he was," Elena whispered. "I know." She raised her eyes to Rico's face. "But you visited his grave," she said. And seeing her like that, Rico moved to put his arms around her. He held her so closely he could feel her ribs beneath his hands through her old bathrobe, and he thought, *pobrecita,* she has suffered so much.

"I cried," Rico whispered into her ear. "I cried for him, *mamacita.*"

MARGARET CLIMBED into her bed that night and stretched her arms and legs. She felt calm and quiet, full and empty, like a five-pointed star resting comfortably on the blue-black nothingness of the universe. Moments like this one, in which she was relaxed and carefree and present, were rare for Margaret, though she noticed that they were arriving more frequently since she'd landed in her little adobe house by the Rio. Maybe in some mystical manner the coyote she saw on her morning walks was bringing them to her, she thought. Maybe she had found her place at last.

She was drowsy, a state she liked to linger in as long as possible. Falling slowly asleep was like falling apart, she thought. It took you somewhere new, into the big black void where, night by night, something replenished you enough to get you going again in the morning. Stretched out in that borderland of sleep, so comfortable in her bed with Magpie breathing loudly at her feet, Margaret began to dream of great chunks and rolls of metal, all waiting for her to come claim them.

Her whole art life had been about paper and pencils, canvas and oil paint; it had been about flat, portable, and indoors.

But now, mysteriously, she required industrial strength equipment, tanks of explosives, protective leather clothing, helmets, goggles, and temperatures so high that even the sound of the numbers scared her. Suddenly it was about outdoors and permanence, about standing still in the elements and slowly rusting.

Margaret awoke to the morning light and the sounds of the monkeys from the zoo. She loved the way their whoop-whoop-whoops permeated the neighborhood, made it seem, if you closed your eyes, like some jungle outpost. She had not set foot in a zoo since she'd gone to the big one in the Bronx on a class trip in the seventh grade. The caged animals there made her nervous and sad, and she refused to go back. Here, though, with the seals barking all day long and the monkeys calling out in their loud voices, the zoo seemed like it might be a friendly place, and she thought perhaps she should go for a visit instead of heading to Roadrunner Courier Service to ask about a job.

"It's obviously a classic case of avoidance, wouldn't you say?" she said to Magpie, who had raised her head from the bed when Margaret had first stirred. Magpie, as always, looked interested. She was an intelligent dog who understood English, Margaret was convinced, even difficult vocabulary words. "So what should I do, Mag? Fuck off all day at the zoo or try to get a job? Don't answer me yet. Let's think about it over coffee."

Margaret climbed out of bed and went into the kitchen, where she ground fresh coffee beans and filled her pot with water. Then she let Magpie out and watched her make her morning circuit to the four corners of the yard, like a conscientious security guard might. She was imagining replacing the chain-link fence with a wooden one, or better yet, an adobe wall—one with an old gate and vines with an abundance of colorful flowers spilling over the top. It was just a little house, and it needed work. Maybe the owners, a couple in their late fifties who had long since abandoned this neighborhood for what they called "the Heights," might be willing to sell it to her. Not that she had the money.

The thought of the word "money" propelled her toward her closet. She slid her fingers into the pockets of various cold weather coats and jackets that were pushed to the back, where she kept her cash. She should put it in the bank, she knew, but she had never in her life had a bank account. It simply felt better to have her money handy. Donny had kept cash all over the apartment, adding dollars here and there from his tips every night to one stash or the other, and she had carried on the tradition.

Margaret collected all of it, poured herself another big mug of coffee, and settled onto the futon couch in the living room to count up. She had $3,946 left, which could keep her—in the style she was accustomed to—for at least three more months.

But not if she bought welding equipment.

She sipped her coffee thoughtfully. Any normal person would look for a job immediately, but most normal people needed to feel secure, which was not something Margaret thought was possible in her own case. She'd had the rug pulled out from under her in too many big, important ways to believe in security. This gave her a kind of freedom that few people had, though she knew it was nothing to brag about.

She put her money back in its hiding place and went outside to stretch out in the hammock. The monkeys chattered like mad in the background, and Magpie paced the perimeter for the second time, while Margaret stared into the branches of the elm tree, imagining her self-portrait hanging there.

"I guess it can't hurt to check it out, right Mag?" Margaret said. Magpie didn't disagree, so after her breakfast of toast and coffee, Margaret took out the card Benito had given her and opened her Albuquerque Road Guide. She would present herself at Roadrunner Courier Service in person rather than call, a job-hunting strategy left over from her bartending days. She got dressed with slightly more care than usual, taking a crisp white blouse off a hangar and tucking it into her black jeans.

The office was on Louisiana just south of Central. Margaret was greatly amused by the way the streets were organized in

Albuquerque. For example, there was a section between her Barelas home and her day's destination known as the "presidents' streets," in which the north-south roads were named Washington, Adams, Jefferson, Madison, and so on, one street for each president, in chronological order. But the system petered out after Jackson, when it jumped to Truman and then disappeared completely, as if whoever had developed that street-naming strategy had grown bored with the concept or perhaps could not remember who came next after the founding fathers were laid to rest. The same thing applied to the state streets. They came in alphabetical order soon after the presidents, but quickly began to skip some states and totally ignore others. New York, for example, was miles away from the rest, in a different part of town not far from the river. On I-40, the exits jumped from Louisiana to Wyoming with no apology, and no New England states seemed to exist anywhere. It was all part of Albuquerque's crazy charm, she thought.

Pulling up in front of a small storefront where "Roadrunner Courier Service" was hand-stenciled in the window, she parked and went inside. A bald man in his sixties with a steel grey comb-over sat at a cluttered desk. He wore a telephone headset, into which he was speaking, and operated a complicated phone system that looked far more high tech than a guy in his age range could be expected to handle. He waved her toward a chair, of which there were four, all canvas director's chairs, lined up against the front window. The one she chose had "Steven Spielberg" scrolled across the back. Another desk, which looked neater, sat empty, obviously temporarily, since a large takeout cup from Starbucks was currently contributing white curls of steam to the stale air.

"I'll send Henry right over," the man behind the desk said into his headset. "I'll get him there within a half hour. No problem." He hung up and made a call to Henry, providing him with the name of a law firm and an address. The whole transaction took about two minutes. Maybe less.

"What can I do for you?" the man asked, speaking quickly, as if he were used to fitting in a few sentences between phone calls.

Margaret stood up. "I'm wondering if you're looking for any help," she said.

"That your car?" he asked with a shift of his head toward the front window.

"Yeah," she said, giving him a big bartender smile. "It might look bad, but it runs great. It only has sixty thousand miles on it."

He looked skeptical. "You got a valid New Mexico driver's license?"

"I'm planning to transfer it over today." She had not made it to the motor vehicle office yet, had put it off because it seemed daunting to officially kiss her former self goodbye. "My license is from New York."

"Is it clean?"

"Squeeky," said Margaret.

"Car insured?"

"Always."

The phone rang again, and the man made arrangements for the pickup of more legal paperwork, then pushed another button. "Henry, I got another stop for you," he said, barely pausing before he launched into the details. When he hung up, Margaret spoke fast. "I spoke to Benito, who lives in my neighborhood. He said you might need a driver to do long trips. I'd like to do that—as long as you've got. I just moved here, and I want to see the scenery."

Meanwhile, a toilet flushed nearby and an older woman, perhaps this man's mate as well as his business partner, let herself out of the restroom in the back and made her way through stacks of boxes and office supplies to her desk. "Pull up a chair," the woman said. "I'm Nancy."

"Margaret Shaw," replied Margaret, extending her hand.

"That's Leo," Nancy said with a little wave in her partner's direction. He was on the phone again, oblivious.

Nancy wore a track suit in pale green with darker green stripes down the sides. She was in good shape for a woman her age, too—enough to convince Margaret that the big latte on her desk was no doubt nonfat and probably decaf, too.

"Have you ever been out to the Navajo rez? Out by Gallup?" asked Nancy.

"Never been anywhere," Margaret replied, "which makes me more than happy to go."

"You want some coffee?" Nancy asked. "They just opened a Starbucks. It's really nice. Let's run over there." She was already collecting her purse from the bottom drawer of her desk. "I'll be right back," she called to Leo, and the two women walked out the door. Leo barely nodded. It was clear to Margaret that Nancy would use any excuse to take off from the Roadrunner office. The Starbucks was only half a block away, and as they walked, Nancy launched right into details about Margaret's potential job.

"We got a client forty, forty-five miles off I-40 northeast of Gallup. He lives at the end of about thirty miles of dirt road, and let me tell you, the roads are for shit once you get off the highway. Other drivers who've made the run tell me you can't go more than ten, fifteen miles an hour. That's why they don't want to go back. Takes too much time. Beats the hell out of their vehicles, too. You got four-wheel drive?"

"Yeah, but I've never used it," Margaret said.

"First time for everything, right?" Nancy replied. "Anyway, this client has a couple big boxes delivered to us every six months or so, and we run them out to him. You interested?"

"Is he Navajo?" Margaret asked.

"Who else would live out in the middle of nowhere? The last guy who went saw a bobcat sleeping on a rock by the side of this guy's driveway. Nobody wants the job, but if you're mostly interested in seeing the scenery . . ." Nancy let the question linger in the air.

"I want the job," Margaret said, "as long as I can bring my dog with me."

"You can bring three acrobatic midgets and a bearded lady for all I care," said Nancy, and they both laughed.

Margaret was already captivated with the idea of wandering along dirt roads on an Indian reservation, finding her way through lonely rock formations out of a John Wayne movie.

"I've got pretty good directions back at the office. This guy lives way up in the hills, but you leave the box with some old Indian lady. He leaves the money with her, too. Cash."

"Do I have to get officially hired?" Margaret asked.

"You're hired, honey, believe me," said Nancy.

They sat at a table outside Starbucks in an abbreviated patio on the west side, and Margaret stared out past the volcanoes at the horizon. From her New Mexico guide book, she knew Gallup was a few hours away, right near the Arizona state line. She smiled to herself.

She was heading into Indian country.

1991

*I*T TAKES him forty-one days to reach the American embassy in Bombay. Along the way, he begs. He steals. He approaches foreign tourists and tells them his long story. He can see the horror in their eyes. He is grateful for the rupees, and, in one case, the twenty dollar bill in U.S. currency pressed into his hand by a man in his fifties who has taken up yoga and is headed for a month-long retreat at an ashram in Mysore.

He tells his story once more to an administrative assistant in the embassy, an American man young enough to be his son. This man places a transatlantic phone call to Donny's apartment, but the number is disconnected. Vincent, whose parents died together in a freak chimney fire that destroyed their cabin three months before he met Regina, has no one else to call.

There is no one but Margaret left from his old life, and he has no idea where she is.

In the end, after several meetings and three months on the streets of Bombay, Vincent receives a passport and a stack of papers. By signing them, he promises to repay the cost of the one-way ticket to New York City. His passport will be deactivated until this debt is paid in full, they say, and Vincent nods and agrees to the terms.

He believes he will repay the debt, that he will somehow get on his feet again in his home country.

He believes that he will find his daughter, that she will welcome him into her life.

The administrative assistant, who has come to like Vincent and perhaps feel his pain a little bit, gives Vincent five crisp twenties in a sealed envelope. "That should last you about five minutes in New

York," he says, with a laugh. He shakes Vincent's hand and walks him to the door of his office.

As Vincent descends the stairs, he calls, "Vincent! Let me know if you find her."

"I will," Vincent promises, and he means it.

Even as Margaret sipped her expensive latte on the Starbucks patio, she had no illusions about the ease with which she'd become a Roadrunner employee. Nancy had made it clear: nobody else would take this job. That idea pleased Margaret—it made her feel like a nut, not a bad feeling. It made her feel unpredictable and adventurous.

But as she drove away from the office, headed to the Motor Vehicle Department to become an official New Mexican, a memory presented itself, a moment with Nick from long ago. He had shown up at her apartment, where she had retreated to lick her wounds in private after the rejection from the trendy SoHo art gallery owner. She had left Nick a message to that effect on his machine, which seemed the only polite thing to do since it was his connection that had sent her there in the first place. But she waited to call until she knew he would be in class. She did not want to speak to him—or anyone else, for that matter. She had wept nonstop, the kind of crying that wears a person out, the kind that made her ribs ache, her head so congested she could barely breathe.

Her buzzer was broken. Two hours later, when she heard him calling her from the street, she had no intention of letting him in, but after twenty minutes of hearing "Margaret! Margaret! Margaret!" from three floors down, she could not bear it anymore. She opened the window, throwing him the key to the downstairs door in an old change purse. She let him in, and that was when he had told her to shape up, get over it, get back on her feet. She had kept right on crying, and finally he grew exasperated and headed for the door. Turning around, he pointed an accusatory finger at her.

"You know the reason you won't make it as an artist?" he asked in a thin, cool voice. "Because you put being a nut first. You want to be a nut more than you want to be a success."

He stormed out, giving the door a good slam behind him. What he had said rang true in that moment, shone like a beacon of truth in the midst of her meltdown. She couldn't agree with the word "want." She didn't want to be a nut. She just was one. She could see that this simple fact could prevent her from becoming the somebody she wished to become. He hadn't said her nuttiness or self-destruction kept her from being a good, or maybe great, artist. He said it stopped her from being a success at it. There was a big difference, after all.

Sitting in her little studio apartment in the East Village, Margaret began to think about her parents: her mother, uncontrollable and wild and beautiful, a risk-junky who could not bear to sit still; and her father, a painter himself, whose black moods still colored her memory of him. She could vaguely recall images of him standing before a canvas, his hair a mess and his face contorted, as he furiously slapped paint onto it. She had a little mattress in the corner of their loft near Chinatown. She could actually remember sitting there, observing him, and wondering if he even remembered he had a little girl. And even Donny, her Rock of Gibraltar, had his dark phases. "It's just me Irish blood," he would say when she asked him what was wrong, why he seemed so deeply sad at times. "Me Irish melancholy coming home to roost." Given all that, what were her chances of ending up normal? She was actually surprised she'd done as well as she had.

But today, being designated by Nancy as the only nut willing to drive out to the middle of nowhere with a package from Roadrunner Courier Service, had made her feel happy. It might not contribute to her success as an artist, but it would add a few dollars to her fund for welding equipment, which was no small thing. Perhaps she would spend the night out there, parked by the side of a dirt road in total darkness, just she and Magpie. The backseat of the Colt Vista folded down, leaving plenty of room to stretch out. She decided to purchase an air mattress on her way home, just to keep in the car, along with the sleeping bag she already had. This could be an adventure if she treated it as one.

Margaret had already looked up the various locations of the Motor Vehicle Department, so she headed to the corner of Rio Bravo and Coors in the South Valley. Right next door, there was a smog inspection station featuring a wall mural of a buxom blonde babe in overalls, all tits and ass, under the name "JoyJoy's," and Margaret pulled in. Her car made it through the inspection process, though she politely declined the bumper sticker that read, "I passed gas at JoyJoy's." Then she crossed the lot, parked, and entered the MVD office.

She took a number from the dispenser just inside the door and settled into a molded plastic chair. All around her, little children attempted to get red gummy bears from a machine that took quarters, and outside, men in cowboy hats smoked in the parking lot. She heard only Spanish. There were twenty-eight numbers before hers, so she went next door to a coffee shop and had a chocolate-covered donut and an iced tea at the counter. When she returned, she dug into her bag for her sketchbook and began to draw. The images that came to her were of her self-portrait, waiting to be born from the fires at Garcia Automotive. She would not tell Rico that it was a portrait of her, though. "A feminine figure," she would say.

When her turn came, Margaret stepped forward, filled out forms, and had her photo taken. The license was good for ten years, and looking at it, it occurred to her that she'd be pushing fifty when the time came to renew. It seemed impossible, unacceptable. Forty-seven was too far in the future to be one driver's license away. It depressed her. Surprisingly, so did removing the New York plates from her car. Chapter closed, she thought. Turn the page.

Rico had remained at his mother's *casita* for a long time. Her dramatic comment—"Now I can die in peace"—had shocked him, and, holding her in his arms and feeling how fragile she was, he had suddenly been consumed with dread. Was Elena ready to depart this world? Was his visit to Fernando's grave the last nail in her coffin, as she seemed to imply? The act that set her free to die? He wanted to ask her to take those words back. This idea of life without her scared him that much.

But instead, they talked about Fernando. This time, when Elena started in with "He was a good boy until he was about twelve," Rico actually listened. He had heard it so many times that he had begun to hear that sentence as a signal to shut himself down, to become a man who nodded and grunted but set his mind elsewhere. Now he felt her confusion and pain, felt the way in which she searched for clues about what had gone wrong, and how she felt responsible and helpless and guilt-ridden, even now, after so many years.

"It was probably the testosterone," Rico said, echoing Margaret's words from just yesterday. "It was like poison to him for some reason."

"You think that was it?" Elena asked. "Can that happen?"

"We'll have to ask Ana," Rico said. He could just see the light in his daughter's eyes and hear her say, "Let me research it."

Elena segued into older memories, how handsome Fernando was as a baby, how proud she was to be a mother. He was one of those unusual babies who talked before he walked. He had a sweet tooth. No boy was ever happier to have a new brother than Fernando was when Rico came along. He liked arithmetic and music and hated English and history. He made his first Holy Communion wearing a little black suit that Elena had made on her old pedal sewing machine. On and on she went, up through the years, but when she arrived at twelve, Rico said, "It's late, Elena, let's call it a night," and she agreed.

"Lock up behind me," he said as he left. He heard the lock click into place as he walked along the path to his own house.

It was five to eleven, but Rosalita was still up, sitting in the same spot on the couch where she'd been when he left.

"Is everything okay with Elena?" she asked.

"I guess so," Rico responded.

"With you, everything is always a guess. Why is that, Rico?" Rosalita said, but she said it with a chuckle.

Rico did not take up her question. "She's on a Fernando jag," he said instead.

"What's new?" asked Rosalita, who had long ago grown tired of what she called Elena's hit tune, "What Happened to Fernando?"

Rico sat down in the middle of the sofa. "We're lucky, you know, Rosalita? That we never had any trouble like that with any of the girls."

"Well, there was that moment when Lucy got pregnant," Rosalita said.

Rico dismissed it with a wave of his hand. "It's not the same thing," he said.

"I know," Rosalita said. "I'm just saying we've had our hard times."

Perhaps because Rico had been listening to Elena in a new way, he felt calm, as if listening in that particular way soothed both mind and spirit. He turned to Rosalita, saying, "In case you're wondering, I haven't slept with Margaret. I haven't even kissed her."

"But you want to," she said in a matter of fact tone.

"I wouldn't mind," Rico said, "but that doesn't mean it's going to happen. She's said no, for one thing."

"So you asked her?"

"Not exactly, but it came up."

In this moment, late at night, calmly sitting on the sofa admitting feelings which are forbidden, which are rarely talked about calmly with one's own spouse, Rico felt unusually strong. It had to do with Elena, he thought, with her comment that she could now die in peace. She must have wanted to give up at times, and what she got in the end was so minimal—just a spontaneous visit to the cemetery by a brother who didn't even know why he was doing it. But it was enough to set her free. Even if Rico did not want her to be free enough to die on him, he was still inspired by her determination to claim some respect for her older son, no matter how long it took.

He reached toward Rosalita and covered her hand with his. She did not turn toward him, but she did not move her hand away from his either. "I'm so sorry about how lonely you've been for the last few years," he said.

Now she turned to face him. He could see tears in her eyes, silver crescents. "I'm sorry, too," she whispered. "I'm sorry you were lonely, Rico." And right then, as if the words "I'm sorry" had the power of a tidal wave, they were swept toward each other; and right there, in the living room where any of the girls could show up at any moment on their way to the bathroom, they made love.

When it was over, after they had collected their clothes from the floor, after they had moved into the bedroom and Rosalita had fallen asleep, Rico remained wide awake. He felt content and peaceful, lying there with his wife's head resting on his chest, and hearing the plaintive quality in the voices of the coyotes howling far away down the river.

A heightened awareness filled Rico with such awe that he kept his breathing as quiet as possible so as not to disturb the experience. He had his wife in his arms again, and suddenly their relationship seemed new. He had inadvertently given his mother the gift she had been waiting for. At the bottom of it all was Margaret, who had shown up in his shop and started an uproar.

He would not see her for several days, and that idea was unbearable. Rico already knew that he would concoct a reason to drop by her house. Did she feel the same way, he wondered. Was she over there in her little rented house dreaming of him? Perhaps plotting a way to see him long before Monday came? It did not seem at all contradictory to Rico that he was deeply happy that he and Rosalita were back on track, while he still had a desperate longing for Margaret.

That rooster that drove Elena mad had already started to crow before Rico finally drifted off. When he woke up, Rosalita was gone and he had just enough time to join Jessica and Lucy at the breakfast table and then head off to work himself. The events of the past few days, they were all good, he thought, but he was happy that he would be busy at the garage all day—too busy to think.

1991

*T*HE PLANE *approaches the city just before dawn. Vincent is tired. He has been on his way home for half his life, waiting to land. He peers out the window into the darkness, which ends at a wall of lights, even at this late hour.*

It is August.

Vincent wears sandals, and he is grateful that, however it happened, he is returning when the city is hot, when his clothing is suitable to the weather and he does not have to worry about freezing on the street.

He knows New York well, or at least he used to.

By the time he passes through Customs and Immigration, it is light outside. He steps through the revolving door, and it smells like pavement. There is a line of waiting taxis, but he finds his way to a local bus stop. The bus will take him to a subway station. The subway will take him into Manhattan. He will change trains as needed and finally emerge from underground on the corner of Eighth Avenue and Fiftieth Street.

He will walk to Donny's apartment.

Ring the bell.

Wait.

As HE opened the hood on a mint 1957 Thunderbird, one that he had personally kept alive against all odds for the past twenty years, it occurred to Rico that, while he had talked to Rosalita about Margaret, he had never talked to Margaret about Rosalita. He had admitted the truth about his infatuation to his wife as if she were a friend to whom he could say anything, rather than a spouse—and a jealous one, at least she had been in the past. She didn't show many signs of jealousy now. She seemed instead to have put on blinders and retreated into a more solid part of herself, as if hunkering down to wait out this tornado was the smart position to take. And maybe it was.

He wondered, as he tested the spark plugs and adjusted the carburetor, how he would have handled the news of Rosalita's big crush on whomever-it-was four years ago if she had admitted it when she was in its grip. Would he have flown into a rage? Clamped down on her, questioning where she was at all times, like most of the other Chicano guys he knew? Gone after the guy? He didn't know. He couldn't know, because Rosalita, unlike Rico, had never owned up to her secret yearning, her great temptation, her sudden desire for a new life that did not include him.

Of course, things were different, very different, four years ago when she had come to her fork in the road. He tried to think back. They had been together nineteen years at that point, no small amount of time. It was the year before Lucy got pregnant, a year after Ana's *quinceañera*, the year Maribel entered Rio Grande High. Rosalita was thirty-five, and he was thirty-nine. He didn't remember suspecting that there was another man anywhere on the horizon. He thought, as Rosalita withdrew, that it was a temporary state that lingered, brought on by the routine of so many years together coupled with the approach of middle age and all the adjustments women had to go through.

From that moment in the high school parking lot when Rosalita had finally told him the truth, Rico had fought the urge to press her for more information. He knew he was better off turning away from the details—both the identity of the man and knowing exactly how far it progressed. Knowledge of these things would eat at him. Because he was in the grip of his powerful lust for Margaret, because he had this idea in his mind that they shared a destiny, he had managed to remain somewhat detached, as if he were on a hilltop far away from this chaos.

But now, he realized that he wanted to talk to Rosalita about it. It seemed important, probably because they had started to fuck again, which was more or less the same thing as oiling the gears on this Thunderbird. It kept it going, and that was that. So when he arrived home that night, after dinner was done and Elena was safely delivered back to her *casita*, Rico stepped into the living room and said, "Come outside, Rosalita. It's a beautiful night. Come and see the stars." All the girls were there in the living room, and Rico knew instinctively that she would not want to reject such an invitation in front of them.

"Are there mosquitoes?" she asked halfheartedly, but before she even finished the question, she had gotten to her feet and slipped on her summer flats. She carried her glass of iced tea with her.

"No, not many," he answered. "Anyway, I'll light the citronella candles."

When she stepped out the door, he took her hand and led her to the back patio where, years ago, he had placed the flagstones, one by one, in the dirt, and then filled the cracks with fine sand that had set over time like cement. They had placed a round, glass-topped table with an umbrella in the middle of the patio, along with six chairs with waterproof cushions. Rico ignited the citronella, and soon the air was heavy with the scent of lemons. He lowered the umbrella, so they could have an unobstructed view of the sky, which was bursting with tiny white stars. It had cooled off to perhaps seventy degrees, and the night was unusually languid. Even the thousand South Valley dogs were quiet.

Rosalita took a long sip of her iced tea and then shook the glass so the ice cubes clinked against the sides. "I have the feeling that something bad is coming," she said with an attempt at a smile.

"Why did we stop talking to each other, Rosalita?" he asked with urgency. He could see that she was wary of him, and he wanted to reassure her. "I'm just looking back, trying to figure it out."

"I don't know if you can figure it out, Rico. Some things just happen."

"But we let it happen."

"We couldn't stop it."

Rico sat back in the chair and stared at the dark sky for a long moment. "I'm trying to talk to you, and I feel like I'm hitting a wall."

"I'm talking back," replied Rosalita. "You just don't like what I'm saying."

That was true. He wanted an opening, a place to slip inside and begin to explore, but he felt Rosalita was closing doors as fast as he pried them open.

"Whatever we would say, we'd probably only hurt each other," Rosalita said.

"You think so?" Rico paused to search for words. "We're so out of touch, Rosalita. I don't feel like I know you anymore."

Now Rosalita pushed back from the table. "Oh Rico, in fifteen minutes, you'll know me."

"What's that supposed to mean?"

"It means you're just in a mood."

"Okay," he said. "Forget I asked."

"That's predictable," said Rosalita with a sigh. "You might not know me, but I know you. I knew you would say that."

Rico felt trapped and helpless. Whatever he said, Rosalita reduced it, turned it into a dead end. He remembered this feeling, a cellular memory that surfaced strongly in this moment. Over those four years, there were suddenly dead ends everywhere, and after a while they stopped trying, both of them.

"Something has to change between us," Rico finally said.

"Everything is changing," Rosalita replied. "Haven't you noticed?"

"I mean for the better."

"Open your eyes, Rico," Rosalita said. "It's late. I have to get up early. *Que sueñes con los angelitos, mi amor.*" She kissed him quickly on the lips. "See you when you come in." Then she walked off toward the house.

Rico watched her go. She wore a loose dress, the kind she slopped around the house in after she had her bath, and Rico could see the shape of her body swaying a little from side to side under it as she walked along the path. Sitting there, paralyzed with frustration, he felt as if he'd suddenly been locked up in a coffin. It was easy to blame Rosalita, to see her as the one who'd slammed down the lid and bolted it shut. As a way of simply doing something new and different, Rico decided to sit there in the citronella glow and try very hard to see this conversation from her point of view.

She had reduced his quest for intimacy with her to a mood that would pass, and she had added that she could predict his "forget it" response. He had wanted an opening and had received a closing down, or so he felt. But staring into the black sky, knowing that it encompasses all the stars and planets of the universe, it hit him that it could be possible that a closing was really an opening, and that Rosalita's responses—while frustrating—might actually help him find his way if he looked at them in the right way. Despite everything, he trusted her, and he believed in her good will toward him.

He picked up two little pebbles from the ground and put them in front of him on the table. In the dim moonlight they looked like bone fragments because of their pale color. One could signify: "It means you're in a mood. In fifteen minutes you'll know me," a Rosalita idea; and his was "Forget it."

Rico was puzzled, but he had the crazy idea that he held the answer—or at least some clues—right in his hands. He had the sudden urge to phone Margaret for help, but since it was ten-thirty it seemed too late to call—especially since he'd also have to drive to the shop to find the slip of paper with her phone number. It occurred to him that he could swing by her house to see if the lights were on. It was, literally, one minute by car from her house to his shop, so maybe, just this once, if it looked like she was up, he would ignore the lateness of the hour and call.

Putting the two little stones in his pocket, he got up from the table, hopped into his truck, backed out of the driveway, and took off up Riverside Drive.

By THE time Margaret concluded her business at the Motor Vehicle Department and returned home, it was after two. The sun was high and intensely bright in the sky. Just feeling the rays on her shoulders as she walked from the car to her house made her instantly sleepy, and she made a beeline for the futon couch in the living room. Magpie came and settled on the floor next to her, and Margaret trailed her hand over the side of the couch to rest it on her best friend's head. Her last thought, just as she sank into sleep, was that she needed to bring plenty of fresh water on their trip farther into the wild west. She had a few plastic jugs, but, probably because she had seen so many western movies, she felt the need for a canteen, too. She remembered being in the movie theater with Donny, who loved westerns more than anything, and whispering, "He doesn't have enough water," as the lone cowboy, outlaw, or lawman scanned the empty desert that stretched way past the horizon. "It's just a movie," Donny would whisper back. "There's a catering truck filled with water parked nearby. Don't you worry." But for her own venture into the wilderness, she wanted to be extra sure.

Nancy had told her the boxes for the client were expected late the next afternoon, a Friday. There was no great rush on it, so Margaret planned to head out on Saturday or perhaps even Sunday. The directions Nancy had given her relied heavily on the odometer: Go west for 2.7 miles and take a right onto the dirt road. After 9.1 miles, you come to a Y. Bear right. Drive straight 28.6 miles and then start to look for a fence post on the left with an old Chock full o'Nuts coffee can nailed to it. There was a notation under that: "Bullet holes in coffee can make it hard to see." Reading that, Margaret had let out a little bleat of laughter.

"What's funny?" Nancy had asked.

Margaret read her the note.

"They got nothing better to do out there," she said. "They're living like a hundred years ago: no water, no electricity, no nothing."

"Really?" The idea of no simple home conveniences was hard to compute.

"Poverty's terrible, too," added Nancy.

"Doesn't it seem strange that somebody living like that has the money to pay a courier service to come out there once or twice a year," mused Margaret.

"Go figure," Nancy had said.

Margaret slept on the couch for two full hours and woke up wondering if she'd continue on straight through the evening and night if she just rolled over. She had slept more in her seven weeks in New Mexico than she ever had in New York. Maybe I'm really tired, she had thought when the daily naps began. Maybe she had years of stress to make up for. Later, she recalled a documentary she'd once seen on Death Row prisoners, in which the narrator mentioned that they often slept up to eighteen hours a day—about the same amount of time that Magpie probably logged. Maybe, in the temporary absence of pressure, Margaret was reverting to her own animal nature.

She made herself get up, though, and shuffle into the kitchen, open the fridge, and assemble the ingredients for a grilled cheese and tomato on whole wheat. When it was toasted to a golden brown on both sides, she poured herself a glass of sparkling water, added a dash of cranapple juice, and went outside. Drawn to the concrete pad under the elm tree, she stood amidst the rusty parts and simply studied them as she slowly ate her sandwich from one hand and sipped her drink from the other. The old engine parts, gears, screws, and everything else could fit together in a million ways; and no one, including Margaret, knew where they would end up until they were welded into place once and for all.

Perhaps that was what she liked the most about being an artist—that ability to stand, stare, and see things that weren't there just as clearly as the ones that were. Margaret felt at home on that edge between what was and what wasn't yet. In many ways, she felt she belonged there, suspended in those moments of pure potential. Yet, the drive was always toward form. She was thinking, as she stood there, about how a great actress can indicate the complexities of a character's personality by nothing more than a look that passes quickly over her face. She wanted her creation to have a face that could be read just as easily as a great actress', even if it was composed of rusty parts. The question was how to capture that hidden quality. Finally, she squatted down and began a new round of assembling. She had no plan. Furiously, she worked, part by part. Hours passed before she finally stood up again.

She went into the house to find Magpie's leash and started toward Eighth Street. Just one block north of her house was a ball field with a half-mile track circling it. Magpie liked to take a spin around it in the evening, pausing every few feet to sniff out whatever it is dogs seem so obsessed with. A Little League game was in progress and there, standing at the edge of it, was Benito. He saw Margaret, waved, and began to amble toward her.

"Hey, Benito," she said. "You got a kid in the game?"

"The umpire," he said, and Margaret's eyes followed his and came to rest behind home plate on a boy in a wheelchair. She turned slightly toward Benito, who added, "He got hit by a car. Drunk driver." Instantly, Margaret felt tears sting her eyes and was glad she had on sunglasses.

"I'm glad to see he's still in the game," she said, and Benito nodded. A few beats passed. "Hey, thanks for sending me to Roadrunner. I'm doing a job them," she said.

"Yeah? Where to?"

"Somewhere on the Navajo rez," she said.

"Sucker," he responded, and they both laughed.

"Did you ever make that run?"

"Once. Nobody does it twice. You lose money."

"How?"

"Keeps you from taking other jobs for that whole day, for one thing. You don't rack up very many miles considering the time it takes." Benito's eyes traveled back to the game for a few seconds. "Then there's the wear and tear on the vehicle. You ought to have Rico check out your car before you go. Road's pretty rough out there."

"That's a good idea. Maybe I'll see if he has any time tomorrow or Saturday," she said.

"Oh, he'll make time for you, trust me." Benito said as if there were another meaning underneath the words. Margaret chose to ignore that subtext, looking away, as if she needed to check on Magpie.

"Well," she said, "I'm on my way. Enjoy the game."

Benito smiled. "See you around the *barrio*."

Margaret and Magpie did the loop around the ball field and went home, where Margaret immersed herself in one of her library books on welding for over two hours. Then she opened her sketchbook and added details to the drawings she had done at motor vehicle. Just when she was about ready to get into bed, the phone rang. She glanced at the kitchen clock. It was quarter to eleven. She crossed to the phone but let the machine pick up.

"Margaret, it's Rico. Sorry to call you so late," he said.

She reached down and answered it. "Rico, hello. What's up?"

"I'm sorry to call you so late," he repeated. "I wouldn't normally do it, but I just drove by your house to see if your lights were still on and they were, so I figured you were still up."

"It's okay," she said. "Where are you?" He sounded breathless, as if he had just run in from outside.

"In my shop. I had to come over here to find your phone number." Rico was sitting in his office chair with his feet up on the desk. There was enough ambient light from outside to dial the phone, and now he relaxed in the semi-darkness. He hadn't been in the garage at this hour in years, and he was surprised by how quiet it was.

"Is something wrong?" she asked.

"No. I . . ." He reached into his pocket for the two little stones and rolled them between his fingers. "I just wanted to ask you something."

"Now?" Margaret said. She carried the phone to the living room and flopped down on the couch. "Shouldn't you be sleeping?"

"Probably, but . . ."

"Okay," said Margaret, "What is it?"

Rico could barely remember what had propelled him into his truck and ultimately into this late-night phone call. He had the two little stones in his hand, which were a reminder, but now words failed him. What could he do? Recount the conversation with Rosalita and ask Margaret for an opinion? Confer with her about what to do when the communication door got slammed in your face just as you were attempting to wedge it open?

"You're a good listener," he finally began. "I wanted to ask you how you do that."

Margaret laughed. "Really? That's why you called?"

"Sí, that's it," replied Rico.

"Okay, just let me think for a minute so I can give you a serious answer. Hold on." She placed the receiver on her chest and closed her eyes. To Rico, on the other end, it sounded like the waves of the sea were sloshing in the background. "Two things," she said, when she got back on in about half a minute. "One, you can't be planning what you're going to say the minute the other person shuts up. Two, you can't already have an idea of what you want to hear."

"I'm writing this down," Rico said, even though he wasn't. He knew he would not forget what she said.

"But remember," she added, "I hardly ever talk to anyone, so I like to savor what I hear. Other people probably hear too much and have to tune stuff out. Who knows how it works." She said nothing else for a few seconds.

"*Gracias*, Margaret," said Rico. "I knew you'd give me something to think about." It wasn't until right then, in this moment, that he realized he'd really called because he simply wanted to hear her voice. A whole day had gone by, and he felt thirsty for contact with her, parched.

"*De nada*, Rico," she responded. "Anything else?"

"No. *Buenas noches*," he said.

"G'night, Rico," she replied, and they hung up. No sooner had she replaced the phone in the cradle than she realized she'd forgotten to ask him if he could give her car the once-over in preparation for her trip to the rez. "I'll stop by and ask him tomorrow," she said out loud to Magpie.

Meanwhile, Rico sat in the dark for a few more minutes before he locked up and headed home. He slipped quietly into his bedroom, where Rosalita was sound asleep, undressed, and climbed into bed.

1991

HE WONDERS *if this is the same city. It is polished now, like a sapphire in the August sun, but all he remembers is grit. He arrives at Donny's building, which has a new front door, a new intercom system, and a new voice that answers from Apartment 4B. That person has never heard of Donny, never heard of Margaret. He says no, the Irish lady who Vincent remembers lived next door is no longer there. "She's not among the living," the voice says. She died two years ago.*

He backs away from the building as if it were on fire. He looks up at the windows of the fourth floor. All he sees in them are reflections of the other buildings, taller buildings that have gone up along the riverfront.

He walks to Fiftieth Street and turns the corner. Sacred Heart School is halfway down the block, and as he walks there, in a hurry, he prays that one of the nuns will remember a little girl who finished the eighth grade eleven years ago. That is not such a long time, he tells himself. But when he arrives at the place where the wrought-iron fencing should begin, the fence he remembers distinctly for its points and scrollwork is gone. There is no statue of Christ holding open his robe to show a heart pierced with a ring of thorns. There is a hotel instead. It has a two-story lobby with a doorman, and well-dressed guests are slipping in and out of taxis in the semicircular driveway.

He feels his heartbeat like a hammer in his chest.

How can things change so much in a city made of stone and concrete, he wonders. He gets on another subway train and takes it to lower Manhattan, even though he feels afraid of what will happen to him if his last landmark, the Bit O' Blarney bar, has disappeared, along with Donny and his apartment, along with Margaret and her school.

It has.

He stares into the glass front of the new highrise, and he sees himself reflected: an old man. He is dressed in clothes that are too big for him. Tears stream down his face. They stain his button-down collar shirt. They splash onto the pavement.

For most of the next day, Margaret obsessed about her sculpture. She spent so much time kneeling on the concrete pad in her work area that she finally made a quick run to the Home Depot to buy a thick doormat to protect her knees. The more she stared into the assortment of parts, the more complex her self-portrait became, and soon she was contending with issues related to the three dimensions, like visualizing how to keep the back of the head from flattening out when all the parts were resting on a flat surface as she laid them out. She collected her sketchbook from inside and made drawing after drawing, blueprints in a way, that she hoped would make sense when she finally began to weld.

At three in the afternoon, she collected Magpie and walked over to Garcia's Automotive. Rico was working on the rear brakes of a P.T. Cruiser that looked new compared to the classic cars he usually doctored. "Hey, Rico," she called, and he turned toward her, breaking into a big smile.

"Hey, girl," he said. "Hey, dog." He put down the wrench he was using and stepped away from the car.

"I forgot to tell you, I got a job at that courier service where Benito works. I'm going to deliver something way out on the Navajo rez over the weekend, and I was wondering if you had time tomorrow to check out my car before I go. Benito's been there before. He says I'd better make sure the car's in good shape for the ride."

"*No problema.* Bring it in tomorrow, say around two. I'll fit you in."

"Thanks, Rico. Everybody's acting like I'm taking my life in my hands to drive out there."

"Who's everybody?"

"Oh, the lady who runs the courier place, Benito, you know, everybody," she said with a little laugh.

"Got time for a coffee break?" he asked.

"Sure, if you do," she answered.

So Rico abandoned the job at hand, dumped out the remnants of his morning coffee, and made a fresh pot. While he tapped the coffee out of the can and into the paper filter, Margaret asked, "So, did you find anybody to listen to since I last talked to you?"

"Nope," he said.

"What brought that on anyway?"

"I was talking to Rosalita," Rico said. "I don't think I was listening to her."

"Well, if you were talking, guaranteed you weren't listening," Margaret said.

Rico was quite aware that he had said Rosalita's name, conjured up, perhaps, an image of him and his wife together in Margaret's mind. It felt risky to him to do that, though Margaret seemed unaffected.

"I think it's funny that you'd call me," she said. "I'm not the expert on the fine points of communication between spouses."

"I wanted a fresh point of view," Rico said.

Margaret nodded, but she looked somewhat perplexed. Then she added, "Hey, can I ask you something, Rico? And please say no if you feel like it."

"What?"

"Can I come over here and do some welding tomorrow? I know it's not our usual day, but I'm possessed. I have all the parts ready to be welded, and I want to move along with it. But I don't want to get in your way."

"You wouldn't be in the way," he said. "Saturdays, I just do oil changes and routine stuff. No welding."

"I'd pay you the same," she promised, "and try not to ask you any questions."

"*No problema*," he said, pouring her a mug of coffee and passing it to her.

"Really?"

"Really."

"That's so great. I have to get the basic structure welded before I can get into the challenging stuff, and even the basics are way beyond me and . . ." She talked and talked and Rico listened carefully, but even so it was quite a while before he figured out she was describing some kind of so-called feminine figure she meant to wrap up in that so-called wad she had made the other day. He did not laugh, though the whole picture made him want to, not out of disrespect for her, though. It was just so crazy, what artists did. What they thought was important to do. He could tell she was lost in another world, just telling him about it. So he stayed quiet and sipped his *café con leche* until she snapped out of the trance she was in and segued into, "Okay, break's over. I better get out of here. You have work to do, and I'm interrupting you." She got up and so did Magpie. Within a few seconds they were on their way down Barelas Road, and Rico was back under the Cruiser, replacing the worn-out brake pads.

The thought didn't arrive at once, but somehow, over the three hours between the time Margaret left and the moment when he cashed out the last customer of the day just after six, Rico realized that he was taking it for granted that he would be riding right along with Margaret on her adventure into the Navajo reservation. He didn't like the idea of her being all alone out there in an old car. She was a city girl, after all. A New Yorker, who probably couldn't tell east from west if her life depended on it. The possibility that she might not want him along for the ride crossed his mind, but he ignored it. The idea of accompanying her was perhaps a gesture in the right direction, a beginning attempt to tame his strong feelings into friendship. Of course, telling Rosalita what he intended to do with his Sunday presented its challenges, and he ignored that, too. It had been many years since he'd been out around Gallup, but one thing was certain: nothing would have changed much over there. Out on the rez, it remained timeless. Hawks, and sometimes eagles, drifted on air currents. Coyotes trotted along in search of a meal of prairie dog. Antelope and elk meandered in small herds along arid riverbeds. The sun bore down. That was it.

It was not the type of landscape Rico was drawn to. He preferred the greenbelt along the Rio, with the tangle of weeds ready to take over, the cactuses, the Spanish broom and stalky wildflowers in shades of orange and blue. He liked the New Mexican sunflowers that grew thick along the riverbank, and the low-lying *yerba del manso* with its cone-shaped white flowers, which could be collected and used to fight medical conditions from arthritis to asthma. He liked shade and Mexican birds of paradise and pampas grasses and river reeds that grew as tall as his house. Sometimes, like this very night, when he turned down Riverside Drive, with the *bosque* to the left and the adobe houses tucked in among the cottonwoods and the trumpet vines, he thought there was no place better to be than where he was. He was well aware, though, that half the people in the city of Albuquerque avoided the South Valley, which they equated with gangs and guns and drunken Mexicans. Those things were there, but they were in shorter supply than the horses, ponies, llamas in backyards, chickens and roosters scratching in the gravel, fruit trees, kids playing ball in the street, and garden patches where chile peppers grew.

He arrived home to see his whole family assembling on the patio for dinner. Rosalita liked to eat outside on the summer nights that weren't too hot. They had bought a small gas grill at a neighbor's yard sale, and Rosalita had taken to grilling vegetables and hunks of chicken or beef on wooden skewers.

"We're waiting for you, Papi," called Mirabel. "Hurry up!"

"I'll be right out," Rico called back. It was the same thing every night: six women of various ages all waiting for him to arrive, always telling him to hurry up or chanting "*Cinco minutos*" or "We're all starving, Papi!" He cleaned up quickly, as always, and put on a fresh button-up shirt with pictures of low riders on both the front and back, a gift from a satisfied customer who brought his car to Garcia's Automotive all the way from Flagstaff.

Food was already being dished out when he took his place at the table. They had to crowd in and barely had room to move their elbows. Tonight, they had Rosalita's shish kebabs with barbeque sauce, sliced avocados and tomatoes in oil and vinegar, corn tortillas, roasted *pappas*, and a cold corn and three-bean salad. "What a feast," Rico said as he filled his plate from bowl after bowl. And it felt like one, like a celebration of some sort, and Rico relaxed, enjoying himself and his family to such an extent that when Elena asked, "Does anybody want to go to the Breakfast Burrito Bash at the Holy Family church after mass on Sunday?" Rico simply replied, "I'm going to have to take you to church tomorrow night this week, *mi madre*, unless somebody else is willing to go on Sunday. On Sunday I'm taking a drive out to Gallup for the day."

"You are?" she said. Rico had never skipped a Sunday with her unless he was sick, which was rare.

"*Sí*, Elena," he said; and then, as an experiment in normalcy, he added, "I'm going to take a ride out there with my friend Margaret."

Suddenly silence descended on the table like a monsoon rain that came out of nowhere intent on spoiling the party—washing away the good feelings—and every single person turned to stare at Rico. But with his stomach full and his mind relaxed, Rico had to laugh at the scene that unfolded before him at the table. Each of his girls looked the most herself in this moment: Maribel's face was vaguely disgusted, as if she thought he, as she might put it, didn't know his ass from a hole in the ground; Ana's was curious and detached; Lucy looked like she might start to cry. Rosalita had turned her head slightly, as if she wanted to pretend she didn't hear anything. And Elena's hands fluttered to her chest, as if she wanted to make the sign of the cross but had temporarily forgotten how.

"Take it easy, everybody," Rico said, feeling very much like the man in control. "Margaret's somebody I'm teaching to weld. I want you all to meet her. Rosalita, maybe we could invite her over for dinner, no?" and then he said to the rest of the girls, "Mommy's already met her over at the shop."

Now their daughters looked back and forth from their mother to their father.

"Is that true?" asked Maribel with more than a little suspicion in her voice.

"Yes," said Rosalita in a voice that sounded lined with dynamite, "she seems like a very nice little *gringa*." Then she turned to her husband, her voice gathering wind and thunder, and she added, "Maybe she could just move in with us, Rico."

And that's when the cloud burst.

MEANWHILE, BACK in Barelas, Margaret noticed the neighborhood filling up with people and cars, which was certainly unusual. All along Santa Fe Avenue, where she lived, high-priced SUVs, Suburus, and Volvo coupes parallel-parked, spilling out families and lovers and friends who opened the trunks and took out folding chairs, picnic baskets, and blankets. They all marched like pilgrims down the block, and finally Margaret stopped a young couple and asked, "Where's everybody going?"

"Zoo Music," the man replied. He had light brown rasta hair in fat clumps that he had tied together like a cornstalk that sat on the top of his head. "Cadillac Bob and the Rhinestones. Ever heard of them?"

Margaret shook her head.

"It's a local band that's been playing together for twenty-five years. They got a great piano player—guy named Arnold Bodmer."

"They play the blues and oldies, mostly," added the woman, who looked more like a social worker than a rasta girl.

"Where?" asked Margaret.

"At the zoo. It's great. You should go," said the man, and they moved on. As an afterthought, he called back, "After the music's over, you can walk around the zoo for a while. Lots of the animals are active at night."

Margaret didn't have to think for very long. She had not heard live music since she'd left the Stereophonic Lounge, and she knew from her years there that music, especially the blues, would dislodge any discontent. Not that she felt discontent. She didn't. She felt good in her new life. She went inside, found her wallet, and, slipping a twenty and a ten into her pocket, she left the house.

"I'll be back in a little bit," she said to Magpie. "You take care of the house." Magpie settled on the other side of the gate as Margaret locked it and joined in the flow of people headed to the zoo. She did not hear any monkeys or seals, but she did hear the sounds of a band doing a sound check as she joined the line, paid her twelve dollars, and followed the group to a big, beautiful green lawn with a bandstand, where everyone was spreading their blankets and setting up camp chairs. Margaret found room on a wooden bench and sat down. She was happy to see that in front of the bandstand there was a paved section, a dance floor. She watched the musicians fill the stage, at least twelve of them, including three women singers who'd progressed into middle age but were still ready to rock out. One wore over-the-knee boots and a minidress. Another wore a white leather vest buttoned up with no shirt underneath.

They began their set with "Time," the Chambers Brothers rendition, and even before the first five bars had finished, people spilled from the crowd onto the dance floor. Margaret was one of them. Albuquerque dances, she thought. No waiting on the sidelines here for others to break the ice. And no worrying about having a partner, either. Margaret felt like an electrical current, a live wire. She danced until she was breathless and then kept right on dancing, weaving through the gyrating crowd as if she were a piece of thread sewing them all into one good time. Men caught her eye and smiled and she smiled quickly back, but she moved on and away, not interested in stopping to talk, not interested in what might happen, if anything. She wanted to feel the music, that's all. Just let it light her up.

There she was, all alone in a crowd of dancers, her black hair flying like the wind at night and her feet barely touching the ground. Margaret had once seen a photograph of horses in a big race, perhaps the Kentucky Derby or the Preakness, and she had noticed that all their feet were off the ground at once. She felt that way now, on this cool desert night in New Mexico, in this place between the volcanoes and the mountains. She was flying, and there was no such thing as time. And whatever had pulled her here—the image of coyotes trotting along the riverbank, the rusty parts waiting in the junkyard to be assembled, whatever—she was grateful she had opened herself and her life up wide, as wide as the desert sky.

When the band packed up and the revelers began to drift along the zoo paths, Margaret went home. She could not bear to see animals locked up, even if they were in what the informational signs identified as habitats instead of cages. If she could have, she would have taken them all with her, led them like the Pied Piper out of the zoo and down the city streets to her yard, where they could sleep in the hammock for all she cared. She walked home, back to her little house, where Magpie was still waiting by the gate, as if she hadn't even thought to move.

"Hey, big girl," Margaret said as she undid the gate and came inside. Magpie rose to her feet and led the way to the kitchen door. But before Margaret followed, she made a slight detour to the cement pad, where the rusty parts were silent and waiting.

"Tomorrow," she whispered to them, and they shimmered like burnished copper in the starlight.

1991

V INCENT BEGINS *a new life, the kind of life he had seen when he lived in New York before, lining up with men outside of shelters and soup kitchens. He waits in crowds of younger, stronger men for day jobs from Manpower. When he is not working, which is too much of the time, he walks the streets and looks into women's faces, searching for Margaret. He has never looked at so many women in his life.*

He finds a permanent job, washing dishes in a midtown restaurant. He works twelve hours days, seven days a week. His shift sets him free at midnight, and he goes home to a "Single Rooms Only" hotel, one of the few left on the Upper West Side, where he sleeps until six and then begins, day after day, to walk and walk, looking for Margaret. He calls it "pounding the beat." His beat becomes routine: on Mondays, he stands in the middle of Grand Central Station and scans the morning rush hour crowds. On Tuesdays, he covers Wall Street. On Wednesdays, he marches around the West Village and Chelsea, and so on.

It takes Vincent three years to save enough money to hire a private detective, a man named Snow who opened his own agency after being head of security at the Ritz-Carlton for fifteen years. Vincent pays him a two thousand dollar retainer in cash, ten and twenty dollar bills collected into a large wad and held secure with a blue rubber band. He fills out a form, feels devastated to notice that there is next to nothing on it when he's done: just her name, Margaret Donnery; her age, twenty-seven; her date of birth; her last known address; her last available photo, which Snow scans on his computer from the faded photo strip Vincent still carries in his wallet, and still looks at every morning before he takes the stairs down from the second floor of the hotel and begins to pound the beat.

It takes no time for Snow to burn through the retainer.

"I checked out every Margaret Donnery in the tristate area by phone," says Snow. "I did a search of the national databases. Nothing." He pauses. "On the plus side, I checked all the death registers, all the way back to when you left. There's nothing there for Margaret. And for the record, her grandfather died when she was eighteen, so she didn't end up a ward of the state, either." Snow stands up. "Sorry I couldn't help."

Vincent feels unable to get out of the chair. He grips its wooden arms like wreckage in the middle of the sea. "What if I got more money," he mumbles.

Snow shakes his head. "Save your money," he says. "Get on with your life."

"What if there's no life to get on with?" he asks as he gets up and, without waiting for an answer, makes his way to the door, takes the elevator down six floors, and steps out into the pouring rain.

He loses heart after that. With nothing left to live for, he feels himself dying.

He thinks about it for a long time.

Then he decides to fulfill Thomas Yazzie's last request. He does it so he can die knowing he did one thing right. Just one thing right. He stares at the map to Alice Yazzie's house, way out in the middle of nowhere, somewhere northeast of Gallup, New Mexico.

He quits his job and packs the sum total of his belongings into a knapsack.

He walks all the way to Port Authority.

He gets on a bus to New Mexico.

AT six in the morning, Margaret and Magpie left the house for a long, long walk by the Rio. They strolled past all of Margaret's spontaneous outdoor sculptures, some of which had been added to by strangers, some of which had been knocked down, some of which remained intact, waiting for the wind or rain or person that might alter their fate. Margaret actually called to each one. "Hello stones and sticks!" she would say, "Hello, branches and reeds!" But today, rather than stop and work, she wanted to press on, down the Rio. After perhaps two miles, the little footpath shrunk to half its already narrow width, and she and Magpie had to walk single file and often push shoulder-high weeds off to the side. Still, they kept going, on and on for another half-mile, until the path wound down right along the riverbank, and Margaret found herself in a field of sunflowers that grew so close together it was impossible to even consider passing between them.

"Look at this," she said to her dog. "We've hit the wall. A wall of sunflowers." The best way to see them was clearly from the middle of the Rio. Margaret walked to the edge of the bank and looked down. The water was shallow and she wasn't worried about being swept away by the gentle current, but it was brown, the color of chocolate milk, and she wondered what was in it besides mud. Anything could be in a river, particularly one that wound past national laboratories where such items as nuclear bombs were built. Sewage was probably dumped in this river too, and who knew what kind of algae and sludge might grow in the waters as they sat waiting for release in dam after dam upriver? Margaret was woefully uninformed about the state of nature, being a city person her whole life who took it for granted that a trip to the hospital for protective shots against disease was mandatory should anyone fall into the East River or the Hudson. She herself had been ordered off the beach at Rockaway when crates of medical debris had ridden the waves to shore. Routinely, she had seen the filth and junk collecting along the waterline around the whole of Manhattan when she'd taken walks along its shores long ago with Harold. Once they'd seen a family of tiny yellow ducks paddling at the river's edge around what Harold called a "Styrofoam iceberg," one of many that had washed up on the shore. It was sad, the filth and pollution.

But here, standing by her new river, when she thought in terms of toxic, it felt different. To step into what might be radioactive runoff was far worse than stepping on an old syringe, or was it? Margaret, ignoring the risks, took off her socks and sneakers, rolled her yoga pants halfway up her thighs, and stepped into the water. It was colder than she expected. Magpie was right behind her, and together they sloshed out to a sandbar. Several birds went airborne as they approached. Margaret had not even seen them. When she stepped out of the water and glanced down at her legs, she appeared to be wearing a pair of mud brown socks, which made her laugh. Turning around, she saw the sunflowers from this perspective, and the vision was so glorious, so unexpected, that she simply sat down where she was and stared. "A riot of color," she said to Magpie. Margaret was so moved by seeing so much beauty in this little hidden place that she felt inspired to contribute something immediately. She began to push the mud into a pile to make a shrine, a replica in miniature of the jagged ridges of the Sandia Mountains which she could see upriver. In front of it, she wrote "Home." It took a few hours, and the sun was burning a swatch down the river corridor when she finally felt ready to stop. They walked home, where Margaret took a shower and scrubbed her feet and legs with antibiotic soap in hopes of fending off whatever health disaster might have floated toward her.

There was a message on the phone machine from Nancy. The boxes had arrived at six the night before and she could pick them up any time today. So just after one, Margaret got in the car and drove to Roadrunner. The boxes were bigger than she expected. One was about the size of a very large air conditioner and the other was at least six feet long and a foot high. Leo packed them into the back of the Colt, and slid a hand truck in along the side so she could move them when she got there.

"There's not supposed to be anything breakable in either one," he said.

"No problem," said Margaret, who wanted to appear supremely capable. She was thinking, though, that Magpie would be a bit crowded for the drive out. She was used to having ample room to stretch out and sleep.

"What's all that junk on the front seat?" asked Leo, who happened to be standing near the passenger door.

"Some stuff I'm welding," Margaret responded. She had packed up her parts in two open boxes, figuring she'd go directly to Garcia's Automotive from Roadrunner.

"You a welder?"

"Not yet. Are you?"

"I did some in the navy," he said. "Long time ago."

"I might be asking you for some tips," Margaret said.

"Anything I can do to help," he said, actually looking at her for the first time. "Well, have a safe trip out there. Check in with us when you get back so we know you made it."

"Okay," said Margaret as she got into the car, started it up, and drove off.

Rico had a car up on the lift and two others in the parking area when she pulled in.

"You look busy," she said as she came into the garage. "Are you sure it's okay for me to be here."

Rico was obviously at a point in whatever he was doing where he could not stop because he barely glanced at her when he said, "It's fine, Margaret. Just get yourself set up."

It took her two trips to carry in the parts. She put the first box on the floor and slid it under the workbench so Rico would not trip over it. The second one, she placed on top of the bench, as far out of the way as possible. Then she collected the goggles and gloves, and set herself up to work. All this time, Rico had not said a word. Margaret, who was used to silence, did not find that strange; though after she had been working for perhaps twenty minutes, it occurred to her that he seemed turbulent as well as subdued, and she wondered if her presence there might be a problem for him. So she paid attention to what he was doing, and the next time he stepped away from the car, she turned off the torch and faced him.

"Rico, am I bothering you being here?" she asked.

"No. I got some shit on my mind is all," he said.

"Are you sure?"

"Sí, claro," he said.

So she turned around and went back to work. It was easy for Margaret to give Rico the privacy he needed. She focused on her work, and Rico had to interrupt her to ask for her car keys so he could move her car into the work bay. He actually laughed when she turned to him because she had the look of a mad scientist, and there on the workbench, right before his eyes, the female from hell was shaping up.

Margaret reached into her pocket. "Want me to drive it in?"

"No, I got it," Rico said. Then, with a nod in the direction of the workbench, he asked, "You got a name for it yet?"

"Yeah," she said. "It's called, 'Unraveling the Wad Used to Get Through Life.'"

Rico laughed. "Jesus, Margaret," he said.

Margaret threw him the car keys. He caught them and went outside for the Dodge. All day long, customers had come and gone from the shop. Some waited in the office; others disappeared and returned later. Their conversations were just a buzz in the background to Margaret, who felt as if her own blood was flowing out through the flames and the melting metal, and taking form before her eyes. She welded on each tiny piece with a breathless combination of precision and come-what-may, making mistakes and plowing right on anyway. So what if the female figure's ears were cockeyed and her right eyeball bulged out past the brow ridge? So what if the right shoulder and left were different lengths, and one hand seemed to be raised in a blessing while the other looked more like a rodeo rider waving to the crowd?

It was after four when she finally took a break, her shoulders and lower back aching. She poured herself some stale coffee and sat in Rico's office chair. He still had two more cars to work on before quitting time, though hers was obviously done, parked outside again in the spot usually reserved for customer pickup. She was about half finished with her coffee when Rico came into the office and sat down on the desk.

"So what time are we leaving for Gallup in the morning?" he asked.

Margaret absorbed the question for a few seconds before she said, "We?"

"Yeah. I don't want you taking that drive by yourself."

"Why? Is something fucked up with my car?"

"No, it looks good. I changed the oil, checked the fluids and tires, gave it a good going-over. It's not about the car."

Margaret sat forward in her chair. "You mean you just want to go? Like, for the ride?" This was not the picture she had of her adventure into the wilderness north of Gallup, and she needed a moment to see if her imagination could accommodate such a vast change.

"Just this once," Rico said.

"I'm really okay by myself," Margaret said. "You know, Rico, I'm always by myself."

"I know," he said, "But just this once I want to go with you."

So Margaret said, "Okay."

Last night, when Rosalita had said, "She seems like a very nice little *gringa*. Maybe she could just move in with us," for Rico everything froze in place. Even though it just lasted a second, it was long enough for the viewers of the scene, in this case his mother, daughters, and granddaughter too—though she was too little to understand anything except the sharp tone in her *abuela*'s voice—to acknowledge that something important had suddenly fallen apart and might never work again. If they had been watching a movie, somebody might move to the television to impatiently hit the "play" switch five or ten times. But there in the yard, with no possibility of that, there was the simple truth of their real life.

Maribel was the first to recover. "What's going on?" she demanded.

Rico wiped his mouth with his paper napkin and pushed back from the table.

"Papi? Mommy? What's going on?" Maribel repeated.

Rico might have expected to feel enraged in a moment like this, blindsided in the middle of a relaxed family dinner on the back patio by his own wife, the very woman he was trying so hard to understand. He felt speechless, though he fervently wanted to say the right words, the ones that would restore everything to what it had been just a few moments ago. He also felt defeated and sad, as if there were no room left for him at this table full of women. He wanted to give up, that was all. Just give up. Last night, Rosalita had accused him of being moody, and maybe she was right, because right now, as he sat with his paper napkin crumpled up in his hand, a wave of sadness so profound crashed over him that he felt his eyes fill with hot tears.

His daughters had never seen him cry before, except for a few tears he quickly brushed away at his father's funeral. He sat there, wearing one of his best shirts. He'd had a great dinner. It seemed impossible to have it all end like this. He felt so sapped of strength that he couldn't even get up and leave, so he just sat there as his daughters descended on Rosalita like a pack of wolves.

"Why are you making Papi cry?" Maribel yelled, while Lucy ran to his side and threw her arms around his neck. "Don't listen to her, Papi," she said. "She can be such a bitch; she really can," and Ana turned to her mother and said, "Happy now?" before she got up from the table, reached down to lift Jessica out of her high chair, and stalked off toward the house. Just before she got there, she turned around and fired off one more round at Rosalita. "Everyone has a right to have friends, whether you like it or not!" she yelled, a rare event for Ana; and then she opened the kitchen door and went in, slamming it behind her with such gusto that the whole house seemed to shake.

"I didn't mean it the way it sounded," Rosalita said in a low voice.

"Do you ever listen to yourself? The way you talk to us?" Maribel yelled back.

"That's enough, *mi hija*," he said, very quietly. Then he added, to nobody in particular, "I'm going to walk your *abuelita* back to her *casita* now." He got up and made his way around the table, where he helped Elena get to her feet. They started down the little path through the deadly nightshade to her house. Lucy and Maribel watched them go off toward the corner of the lot. Rosalita sat in her place with a blank look on her face as her daughters walked away from her, back to the house, and disappeared inside.

Rico did not want to talk once they got into Elena's kitchen, which she understood very well. She made him a cup of tea, and together they sat in front of the television for two shows. Then she said she was ready to go to bed. "Rico, *mi hijo*, you sleep right here on the couch if you want to," she said. "Give yourself a little time. Rosalita, too."

"*Gracias, mi madre*," he replied. "I think I will."

Elena found a fluffy pillow, some sheets, and a blanket in the closet, and brought them to her son. Then she kissed him on the cheek and went to bed.

Rico stripped off his nice shirt and hung it from the back of a kitchen chair. He stretched out on the couch in the dark as if he needed to recover from a bad beating. Why he felt that way, he was not sure.

In the morning, he went into the house to get dressed for work. Rosalita was sitting up in bed when he let himself in the bedroom door and hung up his shirt in the closet.

"Rico," she said. "I . . ."

"Not now, Rosalita," he responded. "I have to go to work."

She simply nodded once.

Rico left.

He could not remember a worse day in years, maybe in his whole life. He felt sick inside.

Sick of everything.

1994

WHEN HE gets off the bus three days later, Vincent steps into the bright blue sky. It seems to be everywhere. He hasn't seen the color blue so clearly since he was a young man, before all the trouble came to him. It feels like the perfect thing in which to disappear.

He buys himself a gallon of water and sets out.

He hitchhikes, and in the beginning he gets rides. He stretches out in the back of two different pickup trucks and watches the industrial sprawl of Gallup vanish, the garages and warehouses and cheap restaurant chains replaced by sand and rocks and silence.

He is deeply tired.

When he's dropped off at the corner of one dirt road, there is nothing in sight anywhere, except desert rocks like cathedrals in the distance and birds circling overhead. "Watch out for rattlesnakes," says the driver of the truck, a Navajo grandfather who wears a baseball cap with "ARMY" written across the front. "Don't let the bobcats see you." The man takes off, and, after the sounds of his truck dim and then disappear, Vincent is left in the total silence with nothing but the blue sky for company.

He finds it soothing.

He takes out Thomas' map and stares at it.

He still has about sixteen miles to go.

He starts walking, taking it slow because the sun is high in the sky, and there is nothing between him and it but air.

At times, he feels like giving up, just laying himself down by the side of the road and calling it the end of one long day. But he keeps on.

He reaches Alice Yazzie's door.

He knocks.

An old Indian lady answers. She has no fear in her eyes.

"I have a message from Thomas," he says, and he collapses.

WHEN MARGARET had shown up in his shop, Rico was so tied up in knots that he could barely acknowledge her, which, he noticed, she seemed to take in stride once he assured her she wasn't the cause of his bad mood. She simply went to work and left him alone. He focused on his work, too. It had always been a way to get his mind off things, a skill he had particularly perfected in the past four years. But today, even as he performed the routine garage tasks that comprised his Saturdays, he could not put what had happened last night completely out of his mind. Breaking down and crying like a baby in front of all his girls was not a proud moment for him.

What had bothered him about Rosalita's snide remark, which, he acknowledged, was not as bad as it could have been, was that he had been trying hard to come to terms with what to do about his feelings for Margaret. What better way, he had thought, than simply to treat her as someone who had a role with the Garcias: a family friend. He had considered it for a long while before his suggestion that they invite her for dinner. He had somehow not considered the possibility that such a suggestion would be met with bitter sarcasm.

It bothered him because his attempt to turn Margaret into a family friend as a way to neutralize his strong attraction was, in his mind, a creative solution. He imagined his whole family, whether they knew it or not, helping him to stay put. Letting go of the privacy between him and Margaret was a sacrifice. So when he suggested dinner, he felt as if he was giving something important away, something he wanted for himself yet knew he had to share. But Rosalita had thrown her napkin onto the table and made a comment which felt like a blow to him, one that he was too weak and too stunned to return.

That moment had gone by so fast and hit so hard that he still felt floored by it. At the table his frustration—to his dismay—had turned to tears. He knew right then that no matter what solution he tried, he simply could not win. His creative compromise was rejected without discussion, and he felt both helpless and misunderstood. He accepted finally that he would have to choose, that he could not have it all.

When his daughters—all of them—had risen to his defense, it both comforted and appalled him. Because what kind of man cries at the dinner table and then stands by while three young girls fight his battle? All mixed up in that was the shock he felt at the hostility they displayed toward their mother. All these years, as Rosalita had drifted around in her black cloud of regret or whatever it was, Rico had worked doubly hard to keep the family united for the benefit of the girls. But when he saw them turn on her, it became instantly clear that they had not been fooled for a moment, and Rosalita's distance, her impatience, her confusion, and her tension had affected them all, more than he knew or thought possible. So the moment of support from his daughters, which should have made him feel comforted, had just added to his sense of failure. He had not protected them. And they had turned on their mother, so he hadn't protected her, either.

Walking Elena back home, as she held onto his arm as she always did, he suddenly felt old and broken, like she was. Just before he had opened the door to her *casita* and stepped through, he had glanced back at the patio, and there was Rosalita, all alone at the table with nothing but the remnants of the family feast. His heart had gone out to her. But sometimes in life you turn away and let the person sink. He had gone inside with his mother, staring at those cop shows as if watching murders was a form of relief. He hadn't wanted to go home, back to his own bed, and he hadn't wanted to talk to Rosalita in the morning, though one glance at her made it clear she'd had an awful night. She looked ten years older.

Once, a long, long time ago, when the police had showed up at their house, Rico had seen them at the end of the driveway and he'd had a moment when he could have slipped into the room and removed the half-ounce of cocaine, as well as the handgun Fernando carried when he went out late at night. Rico could also have warned his brother so he would have been spared jail time. Fernando could have disappeared out the back door, passed through the missing board in the fence, and taken off down the alley. But Rico stood in the window instead and watched the cops close in on the house. It's time to face up to who you are, *mi hermano*, he had thought. Here come the cops to show you who you have become.

That moment had come back to him and he knew it had to do with Rosalita sitting there alone at the picnic table. She certainly was no Fernando, but she had been less than honest with her family, him, and maybe herself; and though he felt deeply sorry for her, he could not help her.

When he had gone to work, opened the shop and exchanged a few pleasantries with the first of his customers, he had felt locked up in a dark room. Later, the one thing he could see clearly was that he was going to Gallup with Margaret the next day. That is, if she would let him. He was doing that for complicated reasons that had nothing to do with Margaret or his feelings for her. It had to do with standing up as a man to Rosalita. He was working hard to manage himself and his feelings, and there she was, putting him down. He simply could not put up with that.

So when Margaret had shown up with her boxes of junk and gone to work, Rico had already known that he would invite himself along for the ride to the Indian rez. It was the only direction he could go if he wanted to retain any self-respect.

As soon as he saw her there, in her goggles and gloves, welding all those bolts and springs into that crazy-looking sculpture, he began to feel lighter, as if she were maybe welding his identity back into place.

Plus, the idea of being alone with her in a car for a whole day was appealing, because things he wanted to ask her and tell her were piling up inside him. Maybe he would tell her everything, all the things that had happened since he met her just one week ago. So when the moment was right, he simply said the word "we," and he felt better.

She had said, "I'm okay by myself, Rico. I'm always okay by myself," and he had replied, "Just this once."

They resonated in his ears, those words, after he said them. Just this once.

Just this once he was stepping outside the lines of his life.

Just this once he was turning his back on the rules.

Just this once he was doing what he wanted to do, and fuck the consequences.

Before Margaret's eyes, the self-portrait was born.

She fired up the torch and her fingers flew from part to part. Even the cumbersome gloves were not a hindrance. She moved into an altered space and time, and it simply began to happen.

It had taken her a long time to formulate a theory on her art. She had finally articulated it in a coffee-shop moment to Nick when she was already more than ten years into her painting life.

"Okay," she said, "it's like the painting is already done, so my hands know where to go, and all I have to do is stay out of the way and let them work. I have to keep the thinking out of it. And I can't look back."

"What do you mean—it's already done?"

"It's like it's mapped out already."

"Are you talking about in your subconscious mind or something?" Nick asked. "Because I'm not convinced there is one."

Margaret laughed. "Why don't you just forget about the labels for a few minutes, Nick." This was during the phase when Nick was married, when he and Margaret would meet and he would itemize his complaints about his wife and her middle-class expectations, her lack of understanding of the artist's path, and her slavery to social mores. Margaret would come away exhausted and vow not to see him for at least two months. She knew very well that he could not live in a world without labels. She also thought, privately, that he'd be a better painter if he could. She was a great admirer of his work, but she admired it in the way a person might admire a great suspension bridge or the tallest building in the world. His paintings were feats, achievements. They were architectural wonders, but Margaret wasn't captivated by them.

Two years later, after Nick's wife was history, Margaret had felt a strange compulsion to visit the Frick Collection on Seventieth Street to spend the afternoon silently before a particular painting by Titian called *Portrait of a Man in a Red Cap*. Lucky for her, there was a stone bench in front of it, and she had remained there staring so long that the edges of a male figure in the painting started to blur and all she saw was a web of color that he seemed to drop out of. It occurred to her that the whole painting had fallen from this web of color, just tumbled out of it like a raindrop that hesitates at the edge of the roof, collects itself into a shape, and then lets go. She felt as if paintings were hovering everywhere, waiting for a way in. She had called Nick and had run this idea by him.

"Margaret, are you stoned?" he had asked.

"Yeah," she said, even though she wasn't, at least, not technically. But she had spent the whole afternoon with an old master and then been catapulted ahead three centuries, out of the serenity of the Frick, into the razzle-dazzle of Fifth Avenue, and she felt as stoned as she ever had been.

"You sound it," he said. "Paintings hovering everywhere, waiting for a way in, huh?"

One thing Margaret knew: this sculpture of hers had been hovering, waiting for a way in, and she could barely keep up with it. With the hiss of the oxyacetylene torch in her ears and bits of rust riding like fish in miniscule puddles of melted iron, she attached piece after piece, watching the figure's hands take shape and her hair grow, her lips parting as if any minute they intended to start chanting, "Free at last!"

When she finally straightened up to rest for a few seconds, Margaret was convinced that she was born to weld. When her self-portrait had gone as far as she could take it in just one afternoon, when her arms and shoulders and lower back ached so much she knew she could not lift the torch one more time, she had finally moved to the office to sit down. The last thing she was thinking about was her trip the next day for Road-runner Courier Service. So when Rico had said, "What time are we leaving for Gallup in the morning?" it had taken her a few beats to figure out what he was talking about, and that he wanted to take the drive with her. No warning flares had suddenly lit up in her, so she had not protested.

Almost simultaneously, she'd had the idea of taking the sculpture along. Even though the two boxes she was hauling were quite large, there was still enough room to fit it in somewhere. An idea was forming: perhaps one day when she was finished, she would make a shrine of it in the middle of the desert and leave it there. This could be a reconnaissance mission. She felt without knowing why that she wanted the next, new round of rust to begin to form on it at the Navajo reservation.

They planned to start out around nine. Rico would drive to her house in his truck and park it in the yard. Then they would take off, with the sun at their back and the whole of I-40, which went clear to California, before them.

Margaret had worked another hour after her short break until Rico was ready to close. She tidied up, and paid Rico for the oil change, tune-up, and the use of his welding equipment. Then she placed her sculpture on the front seat of the car, and left. A few minutes later, she pulled into her driveway. She carried her self-portrait inside, resting it against the wall in the living room. My new patron saint, she thought. The patron saint of welders.

1994

ALICE PULLS Vincent inside the house. She leaves him on the cool dirt floor while she soaks a dishtowel in cold water and then places it over his forehead like a medicinal compress. She brings a bowl of water to his side and sprinkles it on his wrists and neck. She unties his hiking boots, soaks another towel, and places it like a tent over his feet. She prays over him, asking the Great Spirit for some special treatment for this white man who already looks like a ghost. She prays that he will stay alive long enough to deliver the message from her grandson who has been swallowed up by the world outside the reservation. When Vincent finally opens his eyes, she makes him sit up and she feeds him pinto beans and pours him a cup of tea that smells like dirt.

Vincent wishes he had a happy story to tell, and, perhaps because he dreads bringing such terrible news, he allows himself to fall asleep again, immediately after Alice has helped him get up off the floor and climb into her bed. She doesn't ask questions, doesn't push. She observes him, as if Thomas' story might seep out through his pores so she can absorb it.

It takes four days for Vincent to recover and one more after that before he summons the courage to deliver the truth.

He tells Alice the whole story while sitting next to her at her kitchen table, holding her hands. He notices that she is barely breathing. He gives her the map, turning it over so she can see the portrait he drew of Thomas at the moment of his passing. She presses it against her heart like a bandage.

Vincent feels the spirit of Thomas in him as he falls to his knees in front of Alice, wraps his arms around her, and holds her close. Her tears saturate his old denim shirt, which she has washed out for him every other day since he's been here. Alice asks him to walk with her, far out among the big rocks, where she wants to pray for Thomas' spirit.

She fills his backpack with items that she collects from both inside and outside the house. Feathers, stones, bits of string. A stack of what appear to Vincent to be old report cards. A white shirt. An oval-shaped piece of turquoise. Some water in a jar. Matches. Tobacco. The map.

They leave at sunrise. It is a long, long walk. The sun has climbed high in the sky when she says they have arrived.

Alice takes the backpack and asks him to wait for her. She disappears down a narrow path between boulders that barely allow sunbeams to slant through. He hears her voice, her singing, but it sounds far away. He sits with his back against the rocks, and spread out before him is the whole wide world.

She does not return until the sun is halfway to the horizon line.

They walk home in silence.

At the house, she makes a simple dinner, and while they are eating it, she asks him to tell her his own story, the whole thing. Vincent feels tongue-tied. He doesn't know where to start. And then suddenly he begins talking. He hears himself tell Alice about the fire that consumed his parents. About Regina and Margaret. About India, and prison, and the years he's spent trying and failing to find his daughter.

He barely looks up, but he feels Alice listening to him.

He knows he has never been listened to so intently, and it almost scares him.

When he finishes, he finally raises his eyes to hers. Her face is timeless and still, like the rocks they have visited, like the quiet here, broken only by the howls of the coyotes in the distance.

"You need a home," she says. "Stay here."

Vincent experiences a convulsion of sorrow, but the very next morning, he begins to build a shack just over the ridge. He builds it out of rocks and old boards which, Alice says, have been piled against the house since the last time Thomas visited, when he himself had thought of building a place.

Vincent takes care of Alice's flock of sheep and he watches over Alice, as Thomas would have.

MARGARET HAD arranged a blanket in the back, so Magpie had a little nest right behind the front passenger seat. She also stashed a five-pound bag of dog food and several gallon bottles of water in case they got stranded in the middle of nowhere. She had eight protein bars and hoped they would not totally melt in the heat.

Rico arrived at two minutes to nine. Margaret had never seen him out of his work clothes, and he looked vaguely dressed up to her, with a short-sleeve yellow shirt, beige jeans, and flip-flops. He reached into his truck for a pair of boots with socks stuffed inside. "In case we have to do any walking," he said as he put them in the car.

"Good idea. Let me get my sneakers," Margaret said. Next to the closet was a *nicho* and in it, among her rocks and shells, was the rusty old lock the sea had tossed onto the beach back in New York. Impulsively, she tucked it into her pocket. For good luck, she thought as she collected her shoes and went back outside.

"I want to stop at Java Joe's for a raspberry scone," she called to Rico as she locked up. "Did you eat?"

"Yeah, but I wouldn't mind some coffee for the road."

So they drove to the neighborhood diner and ordered large coffees to go and two scones, in case Rico changed his mind later. Then they got into the car to zigzag their way to the I-40 entrance on Rio Grande Boulevard. Margaret drove north along the river toward Central and then turned east, soon passing the Biopark. A week after she had arrived in Albuquerque, she had meandered through the lush botanical gardens until she found herself on a narrow path beside the tracks of a little old-fashioned train which ran between the zoo and the Biopark. As it chugged by, the engineer in the shiny black engine pulled the whistle and waved to Margaret and so did all the people on the train, both children and adults. She waved back. That moment, so filled with innocence and friendliness and good will, had brought tears into her eyes. Inexplicably, she felt that way now, misty-eyed, as she accelerated up the ramp to I-40. Time had been set aside, just for her and Rico to have some fun.

Perhaps Rico felt that time had been carved out for them too, but not in the same way. For him, it had been sledge-hammered out of granite. When he had arrived home last night after work, he had showered, then gone to collect Elena to take her to Saturday evening mass. She was dressed and ready, but even so they were a few minutes late, and had to crowd into one of the back pews where Elena had a hard time hearing the sermon. Rico was hungry but had no time to rustle up a meal until well after eight. Rosalita, sitting in the living room with the television on, had acknowledged him when he came in with a subdued "*Hola*, Rico," and the girls, one by one, had come into the kitchen, their eyes shaded with worry, to ask him if he was feeling any better today.

"I'm fine, *mi hija. No te preocupes.* It was just a bad moment for your papi. *Olvídalo.*"

"Do you want to talk about it?" asked Lucy.

"What's your new friend welding, anyway? I want to meet her," said Ana.

"Are you and Mama getting a divorce?" Maribel demanded to know.

While attempting to calm his daughters, he made himself some quesadillas. By the time he had planted himself at the table, all the girls were enthusiastically relating the small events of their days in an effort, he thought, to make everything seem normal. Rico had nodded as he chewed, making appropriate responses where required and asking obvious questions. He noticed the funny ways the girls had chosen to support him, such as scurrying to clean up after him instead of leaving him to do his own dishes, and avoiding all mention of what happened last night when he had put his head down on the table and wept.

Rosalita was absorbed in the television until he came out of the kitchen, and then she turned it off. "Rico," she said, "what's going on with you? Can we at least talk about it?"

"I'll tell you if you think you can listen." He felt tired just saying it.

"I can try," she said.

"Then let's go for a ride," he said, and this time she got up and followed him out to his truck. He headed toward the West Mesa and ended up at the volcanoes. Rosalita made no comment as they drove along the dirt road full of ruts and finally arrived at the base of the biggest volcano. The night was dark with not much of a moon, and no one else was anywhere in sight.

"Let's climb up there," Rico asked, pointing to a rock about a third of the way to the top.

"These aren't the best shoes for climbing, but I think I could get that far," Rosalita answered, and they got out of the truck and started toward the volcano, choosing their steps carefully in the darkness. Rico took his wife by the hand and guided her along. Once they reached the wide rock shelf, he helped her up onto it, and they both sat down. The night was still, with all the lights of Albuquerque twinkling in the distance and the craggy shapes of the East Mountains darker than the sky. Right down the center of the landscape, like a black snake, the river slithered. Neither spoke.

Finally, Rosalita began. "This is hard for me, but I want to say it." Rico nodded. Her features were not clear to him in the dark night. "What happened was, I did let myself fall a little bit in love with this other man. I didn't have the courage to leave you and the girls, probably because I didn't really want to, but at the time I thought I wanted to. I started to hate myself for not leaving and for wanting to leave. I think the hate I had toward myself spread out into my whole life and I couldn't face anyone, so I shut myself down and turned away from you. When I finally started to turn back—that was more than a year ago, Rico—you were gone. I kept waiting for a chance to get back in, and when one came, the first time we made love, I grabbed it. I know it's terrible, what I did. I know it's probably too late to fix it, too. That makes me sad because looking back, I know I was stupid. I didn't risk anything, and I lost it all, anyway."

Rico felt like a priest listening to a confession. It was a familiar role, one he'd perfected when he had begun to listen to Elena recount her litany of maternal sins, something that had gone on for twenty-six years. How many sins could a priest listen to before he simply didn't care anymore? What was his job, anyway? To give the blessing and say, "Go and sin no more," knowing full well the sinner would be back again next week with the same list. He said nothing. Rosalita, opening her heart to him was just one more person on the opposite side of the confessional screen waiting to receive penance and absolution.

"Here I am, doing all the talking," Rosalita suddenly said, "when I promised I would listen."

But Rico didn't feel like talking now. He couldn't. There was nowhere to start. "Come here, Rosalita," he said. She slid closer, and he put his arm around her. He pressed her head against his chest. "Listen to my heart," he said.

He could sense Rosalita's tension. She wanted to know who was staying or going, how they would manage from now on. He had no answers.

Rosalita whispered, "Are you going to Gallup tomorrow with Margaret?"

"Yes, I am," said Rico.

"I don't want you to go."

"I know you don't," Rico said, "but I'm going." He wondered if his heart had begun to beat faster, if she could hear how his blood was beginning to pump with more intensity.

"I'm afraid you'll never come back."

Rico said nothing.

"I'm afraid you won't be able to tear yourself away from her and come home."

Rico remained silent because he had no idea what to say.

"I'm afraid our whole life is crashing down around us," she said, and now Rico tightened his grip across her shoulders and said, "Shhhh, Rosalita. Be quiet."

Rosalita was afraid of everything, and Rico, sitting there in the dark night, noticed that he did not feel afraid of anything at all. It wasn't worth explaining because Rosalita would misinterpret any words he said, use them to soothe herself or to drive herself into some frenzy of fear, and he didn't want to be swept into her whirlwind either way. So he just kept a grip on her and stared into the endless sky, sprinkled with stars and planets.

By the time they turned into their driveway, it was a few minutes past eleven. They had not spoken much, and what they did say to each other was of no consequence, things like, "Are you tired?" and "Did you have enough for dinner?" They had both fallen right to sleep, though Rosalita had gotten up early enough to make a big breakfast for everyone. Rico could feel her watching him, feel her dread of the moment when he would get into his truck, back out of his parking place, and take off. The girls were quiet too, and when he finally left, everyone followed him out into the driveway, as if they were sending him off on a dangerous expedition to the North Pole rather than a day-trip down I-40. Witnessing their serious faces and whatever sense of impending doom that had driven them into the driveway to wave goodbye, Rico was tempted to just step on the brake and forget about this outing with Margaret, but he kept going.

When he pulled into Margaret's yard and saw her coming out the screen door with a couple of gallon bottles of water, the world became brighter and lighter; and when he placed his work boots onto the floor of the backseat and saw her sculpture tucked in on top of the long box they were about to deliver, he began to chuckle.

Before very long they were out on the open road. Rico gazed at the volcanoes as they sped by, trying to pick out the rock shelf he had sat on with his wife last night. Today, he was going in the opposite direction with a different woman. Rosalita was darkness and the moon, and Margaret was the bright sun, the morning breeze, and the empty road ahead.

"Feel free to identify any points of interest," Margaret remarked with a little grin.

Rico made a sweeping gesture and said, "Sand and rocks."

"Don't forget sky," Margaret added.

It was noisy in the car with all the windows open and the fan going full blast. The racket made it difficult to chat back and forth, which suited Rico fine. As for Margaret, she was entranced by the wide open space, and not far past Tohajiilee, which was just twenty miles into the trip, she pulled off the road and said, "Rico, would you drive? I would really love to just look out the window."

"*No problema*," he said, opening the passenger door while Margaret slid across the front seats and buckled up.

When he got back in the car, she said, "I've never seen anything so empty. I just have to look and look."

He flicked on the turn signal and pulled back out onto the highway. It felt good to take the wheel of her old car so she could drift where she wanted to. He would handle the forward motion and give her all the time she needed to look. He understood why she would want to. The sand and rocks and sky had stories, too. Margaret's eyes were dreamy as she followed the edges of white-topped mesas and the cliffs where rocks had crashed down and piled up below.

Following the directions, they exited at Thoreau about an hour later and began to meander quietly through the landscape, past wild horses and emaciated stray dogs, until Margaret said, "It's like being in a meditation, isn't it? I mean, not meditating, but being where you're supposed to get to," and Rico thought he knew what she meant.

After many more miles, Margaret said, "Let's stop for a minute and let Magpie out. If it's okay with you, I want to do a few sketches."

"Sure," Rico said, and he pulled to the side of the road. By this time, they had not passed another car or truck in perhaps twenty minutes, nor a house, though they did see a flock of sheep with a black-haired boy and two dogs, along with many circling hawks and one or two white-tailed rabbits. Margaret poured water for Magpie into the bowl she had brought, and Magpie slurped it up while Rico watched. She took a sketchbook and a pen from her bag and sat on the hood of the car, making sweeping movements across the empty pages and turning them more quickly than Rico could imagine a drawing being done. There was no sound except the crunch of his flip-flops on the dirt as he walked up the road a ways and back again, just to get his blood moving. It was hot and cloudless. It made Rico feel lazy, and when he returned to the car, and Margaret was still making those big gestures across page after page, he climbed up on the hood too and, leaning his back against the windshield, closed his eyes.

Was this the way it was supposed to be for a man and a woman, Rico wondered. Silent and empty and close and comfortable all at once? Were their bodies supposed to feel this lazy, like a big sombrero had covered their eyes and they had fallen into a deep sleep? Were men and women meant to search out unfamiliar landscapes? If so, what about the wives and daughters left behind, lined up in the driveway with fear in their eyes, their right hands lifted in unison to wave bye-bye? What about them?

Rico opened his eyes. Margaret was facing away from him, her feet on the hood of the car and her knees gathered up to provide a place to rest her sketchbook. He reached for her, his hand hovering just a few inches from the small of her back. Perhaps it was the hot desert sun that made the air between them seem to shimmer, as if it were made of silver and iridescence.

Margaret said, "Whew, it's hot as hell out here, isn't it?" and she snapped the sketchbook closed. "We need a shade tree." But there wasn't one, so they hustled Magpie back into the car, started it up, and continued on, another 13.5 miles before they took another turn, this time onto a narrow dirt road that had still not recovered from the spring melt, when ruts half as deep as the wheels were tall had formed.

"Shit," said Rico as he maneuvered the car along the edges of the ruts. It took a lot of concentration to drive safely. Meanwhile, Margaret paid no attention to the road. Rico could handle it, and all it would do—if she watched too hard—would cause her to grip the sides of her seat and take shallow breaths. Instead, she studied the scrubby growth, the silver threads in the green that made the sage look hand-painted, and the way the rocks rose up into the blue sky like prayers. On and on they went, inch by inch. It was easy to see why the other Roadrunners had made this trip once and then refused to go a second time, though Margaret herself could imagine coming again and again, driving over these same ruts until her hair turned as silver as the edges of the sagebrush.

1998

*I*T ISN'T *until four years have gone by, four years of blistering heat and freezing cold, four years of wind that mercilessly kicks the sand around and rain that pounds the dirt road into a sea of mud with ruts as deep as waves, that Vincent thinks of capturing some of this intense seasonal drama in paint. It has taken him that long to feel the rhythm of this place which changes, but never changes. He asks Alice, when she goes on her annual visit to her granddaughter, Thomas' sister Gracie and her three children in Phoenix for the month of July, to bring him some oil paints and some canvases. "Just a little starter kit," he says, "something to play with."*

He expects nothing, but as soon as he uncaps the bottle of linseed oil, he begins to swoon. He examines the tubes of paint, sixteen of them all laid out in a row, and he feels the colors in his blood. He begins to take long walks. He sets up a makeshift easel and loses himself in what he's finally doing again, after twenty-some years away from it.

It is Alice who suggests that they invest some of the money they live on, money that comes from the slaughter of the sheep each year, on some first-rate art supplies. "Sign Thomas' name to them," she says. She knows a fancy gallery near where her daughter lives in Phoenix that specializes in Native American art. She will take the paintings there herself, she says. She will dress in her long skirt and turquoise beads when she goes in for the first time.

Vincent feels neither shame nor pleasure as he agrees. They need the money, and he is used to scrabbling for it after a lifetime spent that way. He buys linen instead of canvas, buys pigments and mixes them himself. He has it all shipped to him from an art supply store in New York. When Gracie comes to pick up Alice, he has the paintings packed and ready to go.

He never leaves the home he has finally found.

Never wants to.

Aᴜᴛᴇʀ ᴀ while, Margaret placed her feet up against the dashboard. It was a position she liked to be in in a car, but she almost never had the opportunity, because how often was she a passenger? In New York, she was one of the only people she knew who even had a car, and aside from Rico, not one person in New Mexico had ever opened the door of the Dodge Colt Vista and gotten in. Having her feet off the floor made her feel she was floating in a bubble, moving along on an air current, disconnected and free. She found it soothing.

Rico, on the other hand, was working hard, maneuvering the car inches one way and inches the other along the edges of the deep ruts. He was so focused that he didn't even notice when Margaret stole a few private moments to study his pro-file. *El rey*, she thought, as she noticed the color of his lips, a shade somewhere between salmon and burnt sienna, and his long black ponytail, gathered into a rubber band. He looked so strong, his hands gripping the wheel as if it were trying to get away from him. He seemed permanent and big, bigger than just a man, though perhaps that had to do with the rock formations in the distance which made everything seem mag-nificent. She wanted to reach out, touch him, place her fingers on his forearm where the veins rose like rivers leading every-where. She felt it in her hands, this desire to make contact, to feel his warmth like sunlight as she touched him, but she knew better.

"How far have we gone since we made the turn?" she asked.

Rico glanced down at the odometer. "7.6 miles."

"Keep your eye peeled for the coffee can," Margaret said. "It says here it's 8.1 miles."

"Good," said Rico. "This is some fucking crazy road we're on."

"That it is," Margaret responded.

It took eight minutes to travel the last half mile, and then they saw it: the bullet-ridden Chock full o'Nuts coffee can and the long driveway off to the left. Rico made the turn. An adobe building, low to the ground and almost invisible, sat in the distance, perhaps two hundred feet. The hard-packed driveway was actually in better shape than the road, and Rico drove to the door and shut off the car. The cloud of dust they had raised took its time to settle down.

"Made it," Rico announced.

Neither made a move to get out of the car.

"There doesn't seem to be a welcoming committee," Margaret remarked, staring at the door, which had not opened. "Let me go knock."

"I'll come with you," Rico said, as if he did not want her out in all this emptiness on her own. They both stepped out of the car, and Rico came around to her side. "Let's pretend to be Jehovah's Witnesses," he said, and Margaret laughed. It rang out in the stunning silence like a rifle shot.

Together they approached the house, which showed no sign of life whatsoever. When they got closer, they saw a note, written on an old brown paper bag, tacked to the door. It read, "Please put boxes inside. Door is open. Money is on the table. Thank you."

Margaret knocked anyway and called, "Hello, anybody here?"

There was no answer, so Rico turned the doorknob and the door swung inward. It was dark inside, and when Rico pushed the door wider, a patch of sunlight appeared on the dirt floor like a painting of a white triangle.

"Hello?" Margaret called again, but no one answered.

The house was just one tidy room with a wood stove in the middle, an old couch and armchair, and a wooden table with four mismatched chairs. An iron bed was pushed into the corner with a Navajo blanket in muted colors folded across the bottom. Kerosene lanterns were placed here and there, and gallon jars filled with beans and rice and dried herbs lined several homemade shelves along one wall. A five-gallon water bottle was upended on a ceramic base with a spigot, and six more water bottles were lined up against the wall behind it in the little kitchen area, which included a small stove and a sink basin with no faucets and a pail under the drain. Two framed portraits of children in Indian boarding school uniforms, decades old, hung on the wall, but nothing else. Narrow windows kept out the sun in the summer and the cold in the winter. "It's a *National Geographic* moment," Margaret whispered as she stepped inside, where it was ten degrees cooler.

On the table was a smooth round rock, and peeking from underneath it was a stack of twenty-dollar bills. Margaret crossed the room and picked them up. She counted it out: $220. "All here," she said. It was time to unload the car, muscle the two big boxes into the house and back the car out of the driveway, but she was captivated by this strange place. "I didn't know people still lived like this," she said to Rico. "No electricity, no water. Wow."

"Pretty basic," Rico replied. "Propane stove, though. At least they can cook. And a good wood stove for heat."

Margaret crossed to a window in the back and peered out. "Look, there's an outhouse," she said. "I've never seen a real one before."

"You'll have to make a visit," Rico said, not adding that he himself had one in his backyard.

"Rico, could you let Magpie out and give her a drink?" asked Margaret. "I want to sit here for a minute. It's so interesting."

Rico nodded and stepped back into the burning heat. He opened the door for Magpie, filled her water bowl, and then unlocked the back of the Colt and surveyed the thirty feet from the end of the driveway to the door. He pulled out the hand truck and set it aside, realizing instantly that it would never work in the sand. It would take both of them to carry the heavy boxes inside. He was just about to ease the first one out of the car when he remembered Margaret's sculpture resting on top of it. He slid it out and held it up. How odd it seemed, this nuts and bolts and rusty parts vestige of the industrialized world out here in the empty desert. He knew she wasn't done with it, for he had seen her second box of parts tucked beneath his workbench. But already this female form, as she called it, had taken on a life. She seemed to be rising up, her arms held high. He lifted it closer and studied the joints where she had welded one piece to the next. It was amazing work for a beginner.

Not too far from the back of the car was a big rock, and Rico leaned the sculpture against it. The figure, with her arms lifted and her hair spiraling off her head at crazy angles, made him chuckle. Delightful, he thought—not a word he ever remembered using. But that's what he felt looking at that sculpture. Delighted.

Margaret came out and joined him.

"This looks good," Rico said. "Well done."

"It's not actually done," Margaret said, "but thanks, Rico. For teaching me."

He nodded. He felt good inside, special. Together, they studied Margaret's work, and it felt to Rico as if the woman rising was blessing them, personally, right then and there, in the middle of nowhere on the Indian rez.

"Let's drag these boxes in," he said. "We'll start with the long one. Can you get inside the car and push it out?"

"Okay," Margaret said, moving to the driver's door, getting in, and then leaning over the seat to give the long box a mighty shove as Rico pulled. When it had moved a few feet, Margaret came outside and around the car again.

"Do you think you can carry that end?" Rico asked. "It's pretty fucking heavy."

"Sure," Margaret said, but when it dropped off the tailgate it weighed more than she expected, and before they got to the house she began to lose her grip.

"Just let it drop," Rico said, and she did.

Rico swung his side up so the box rested on its end in the dirt. With it upright, the shipping label, which had been face down in the car, was suddenly visible. "Wow, look at that!" Margaret said, out loud but mostly to herself. "Pearl Paint."

"What is it?"

"It's an art supply store in New York. I went there all the time. It has a great selection. Five floors." Her voice trailed off. "On Canal Street," she added for no real reason. "How weird is that?"

Rico looked around, a grand sweep of the silent landscape. "Yeah," he said. "Not the first thing you'd expect to deliver out here."

While he was saying those words, as they hovered in the air between them, that was the precise moment when Margaret's eyes moved to the rest of the words on the shipping label. Black letters and bar codes. Right above the second line which read "c/o Roadrunner Courier Service," there was a name, and that was where her eyes stopped. She read it again, closed her eyes, opened them, and read it again. And each time it said the same thing: Vincent Donnery. She fell to her knees.

"Margaret," Rico cried out, and his voice sounded very far away to her. "Margaret, what's the matter."

She looked up at him. Her sunglasses were black squares matching her hair, but her face was white, whiter than clouds, and when she spoke, her words were like an echo wafting through the canyon.

"It's my father's name, Rico," she said. "Vincent Donnery."

Rico laid the box down carefully in the dirt and came to her.

What happens in a moment that makes no sense is that everything blurs. Edges become liquid and pour like lava over the landscape until everything glows red with heat and fire. As

Margaret sinks into the sand, her knees burn from the heat. Rico wraps his arms around her. He is on his knees too.

"We'll find him," he whispers.

And in the end, it's easy. As easy as walking to the car and leaning on the horn, the sounds ripping through the landscape like a knife. It takes less than two minutes, just a few staggered heartbeats, until over the hill there comes a man, an old and broken man. He wears a straw hat, like Claude Monet. He is skin and bones. His face has a thousand rivers in it. His eyes are green.

Margaret stands perfectly still, as still as the rocks around her.

Rico waits, off to the side.

The man approaches. He seems dizzy. He whispers, "Regina?"

"I'm Margaret," she responds in a voice as clear as water.

1998

ALICE HAS *taught him the parts she knows of the Blessing Way.*

It is all he can do: pray each morning for the well-being of his daughter, wherever she is and whoever she has become.

It is the first thing he does every morning. Before he mixes paint. Before he waters the sheep. Before he joins Alice for tea.

He has blessed Margaret every day.

For years.

Rico is alone in the Dodge Colt Vista, heading east toward Albuquerque. The sun is setting behind him, throwing ribbons of light that turn the sand of the desert temporarily crimson. His heart is full, and he thinks what it's full of is love, though love is an imprecise word which might not cover tremors of awe and ache and aftershock. He drives along at sixty-five miles per hour, slow for him, but it is as fast as he can make himself go, knowing that every mile separates him a little more from the middle of nowhere, which is where everything happens, or so he now thinks.

He had stood off to the side where he belonged as Vincent approached and then abruptly stopped. Margaret was standing alone, and Rico had noticed her posture—strange for such a moment—how straight and tall she was for such a small person, and the idea flashed that she was very brave, meeting her fate head on. Margaret and Vincent had faced each other from perhaps thirty feet, and Rico had felt both invisible and important, the third point in a mysterious triangle, perhaps. Magpie had moved to Margaret, her protector—like a real police dog—and kept her eyes on Vincent. In that second, paradoxically, what presented itself as an image in his mind was that windshield long ago, the one that shattered in the accident after Fernando's death, and the way it hesitated before it fell apart; and Rico wondered exactly what was breaking now, when all he cared about was Margaret.

They began running toward each other. Vincent's arms circled his daughter, pulling her close to him. Rico could hear his words: "Margaret, my little girl, I searched for you, I searched and searched for you, and I couldn't find you," and Rico was relieved to hear them, because what kind of a reunion could this be if Vincent hadn't done at least that? Margaret did not seem to need those words, though. She had one of her own— "Daddy"—which she repeated over and over into her father's bony chest. Rico could feel their hearts beating, pounding like Indian drums in the still air. And then tears—Margaret's and Vincent's and, if the whole truth be told, Rico's too—flew through the air like comets and disappeared.

"You look just like your mother, just like Regina," Vincent said when he peeled himself away from Margaret for a second, but, as if he couldn't bear to look at her from even a foot away, he pulled her to him again and buried his face in her hair, which he wound around his hand. A long time passed before they stepped apart, and even then she kept a grip on his scrawny upper arm as if she were afraid he might suddenly disappear again. "Is this your husband?" Vincent had asked, when he had finally collected himself enough to acknowledge Rico.

"No, this is my friend Rico," she answered. Her eyes, as she turned to Rico, glistened like a thousand stars, but she managed to say, "Rico, I'd like you to meet my father, Vincent."

Rico wished, deeply wished in that moment, that he was her husband. He wanted to be the one, the man who saw her more clearly than anyone else, who stood by her and hoped and waited no matter what happened, which is what he knew very well a husband does. It takes everything a man has and more to be a good husband, and he knew that he had not earned that title with Margaret, and he never would. But a friend was an honorable thing too, an important thing. He stepped forward and shook hands with Vincent Donnery, whose green eyes had joy in them and pain too. Rico had seen eyes full of pain his whole life—Elena's most of all, and his father's. Rosalita's, for the past four years. And his daughters' as they watched him back away from them this very morning, back out of the driveway and leave. But he had never seen pain like this.

"Let's go in the house," Vincent said as he reached for his daughter's hand. "Come in, come in."

They all entered, including Magpie, who promptly stretched out on the cool dirt floor and dozed off. Vincent made tea on the old stove while Margaret and Rico settled at the table. Rico noticed that Margaret could not take her eyes off her father, even when he turned from them to reach for a jar of dried herbs, to grab a good handful which he dumped into an old porcelain teapot.

"Is this your house?" she suddenly asked, because now that she was inside again she recalled Nancy from Roadrunner saying that an old Indian lady lived in the house where the boxes were to be delivered.

"It belongs to the grandmother of an old friend. Let me make some tea, and then I'll tell you the story. A long, long story."

Driving home now, along I-40, which is primarily a straight line from California all the way to Nashville and therefore doesn't take supreme concentration, Rico marvels at the idea that he never, not once from beginning to end, thought he should get up and leave, go for a walk or sit in the car or do something so the two of them could be alone together. He belonged, and he stayed right where he was. Perhaps it was the house, or the setting, so isolated in the great empty space of the desert, or maybe the idea that Indians always tell stories and there they were, in an Indian's home on an Indian rez.

Vincent sat down and closed his hand over Margaret's on the table. His appeared to be twice the size of hers. His finger-nails were dirty, and age spots had spread like shadows across his knuckles. Rico was thinking, and he wondered if Margaret was, that the last time Vincent had covered her hand with his own she had been five years old. Five. And now she was thirty-seven. So much time had vanished.

The story began: how, as Donny suspected, Vincent and Regina had run out of money in Goa and had seen a chance for easy cash, just putting a hashish seller and buyer together. But everything went bad, and right about the time they thought they'd be returning home, back to their little girl for whom they both ached, they were arrested. He spoke about the years in prison, stopping now and then for a few seconds to sip his tea. He began to sob when he described how he had searched for Regina after his release, how he discovered she was dead, had been dead for fourteen years.

Rico watched Margaret receive this news. She barely breathed, but she placed her other hand on top of Vincent's, creating a little stack of father-daughter hands on the table; and Rico choked up because he remembered, powerfully, exactly who he was: the father of three daughters. Husband to Rosalita.

Vincent had paused for a few seconds and then added, "I'm so sorry, Margaret. I'm so sorry." She got up, moved behind him, leaned over, and kissed the top of his head. She smoothed his scraggly hair out of his eyes and tucked it behind his ear as if he were a little boy.

Rico stared down at his own hands on the tabletop. He felt sucked into a black hole by Vincent's story. So much tragedy made his heart convulse with sorrow, and he wondered if it would help Margaret to know all this. But he already knew the answer was yes. For just a second, he was swept back into the parking lot of Albuquerque High School where Rosalita had said, "I hope you feel better, knowing," and he realized that he did. There were lost years for Rico and Rosalita, but many more than that for Vincent and Margaret.

"Everything is okay now, Daddy," Margaret whispered, her voice as soft as morning light, and Rico knew that it was true.

Vincent continued his story, describing how he had arrived in New York and searched and searched for his little girl. "I even hired a detective and he came up with nothing. Nothing. He said he checked out every Margaret Donnery in the country."

Margaret took a little breath and said, "Donny was worried about keeping custody when . . . when you and Mommy disappeared. So he just . . . well, we just used his last name from then on." And then she added, in an Irish brogue, "To beat the bureaucracy."

"You sound just like him," Vincent said, and he laughed heartily. "It's okay, honey. It's all okay."

The part of the story that tied them to the present moment was the story of Thomas Yazzie, who had died with a strong love for his grandmother, died blessing her. Thomas had given him a map, Vincent said, which he followed to this door, where he had remained for the last ten years and where he expected to die.

Alice was the only person in his world, he said.

Until today.

He was sixty-one years old now. Several of his teeth had fallen out. He had some kind of stomach trouble which he avoided by eating next to nothing. Four years ago, he said, he had started to paint again, nothing too taxing or innovative, just realistic desert landscapes. Alice had taught him how to pray for the well-being of a loved one, the Blessing Way, and he had prayed for Margaret every single day. But he had never imagined, even once, that his prayers would bring her to him. He was not a lucky person, had never been one. But now he was.

"I used to think I could control things," Vincent said, as his story drew to a close. "My big lesson in life was learning I can't."

Rico wondered if Vincent expected an equally long story from Margaret. Rico would have liked to hear one too, but she was not inclined toward storytelling. "I never thought for one minute I was in control," was what she said; and then added, "Tell me about my mother." She only had Donny's version to go by, and now she had the chance to hear more. To Rico, she seemed to be in a trance, which was probably a normal thing for a person in her circumstance, as she listened to Vincent's love stories about her mother.

It was close to six-thirty when Rico's thoughts returned to the mother of his own daughters, his mother and his granddaughter back in Albuquerque. "It's getting late," he reluctantly observed, which caused Margaret to turn to Vincent and ask, "Do you think I could stay here for a while?"

"Oh, yes," he said. "Please. I can't possibly let you go. And Alice wouldn't have it any other way."

So Rico and Vincent carried the two boxes from Pearl Paint inside, while Margaret unloaded the bag of dog food and searched around under the front seat of the car for the protein bars. She left two on the seat for Rico. A few minutes later, when Rico was ready to leave, they all stepped outside together.

"Should I come back for you?" he asked.

"How about in a week?" Margaret answered, and then she had turned to Vincent. "Would that be okay?"

"It'll be a start," Vincent said, "and Alice will be back in a few days, so you'll have a chance to meet each other."

Vincent shook Rico's hand and, for no reason Rico could discern, said, "Thank you, thank you." He stepped back inside while Margaret walked with Rico toward the car. At the driver's door, they stopped and stood facing each other in the great silence.

"I don't have the right words, Rico," Margaret whispered, and tears filled the green of her eyes like spring rain.

"We don't need any, Margaret," Rico replied, his eyes brown and accepting, like fertile earth.

When she moved toward him he felt the kiss he had been waiting for, and dreaming of, about to happen at long last, and he leaned down to receive it. She pressed against him, her hand wrapping around the nape of his neck. She lifted her face to him. He closed his eyes and waited for their lips to touch.

Perhaps it was the afterglow of Vincent's story, or the magical nature of deserts when the relentless summer sun begins its descent, but Rico felt suspended in a timeless place. In this place of altered time, he remembered the first moment he saw Margaret, when she had stood in the halo of light in the door of his shop, and he thought for one crazy second that she was the Virgin of Guadalupe. He felt, strongly, in that moment that she was his destiny, but now he understands that destiny is not singular, like a star falling through the night sky, but complex, a kaleidoscope with all the parts shifting, tearing apart fathers and daughters and husbands and wives, and shifting again to fling them back together.

He felt Margaret's breath sweet on his skin, like light, and in that moment he admitted the truth: he loved her. He loved her like an ache that demands to be experienced, one that has to get better or worse over time. But he belonged with Rosalita, with Lucy and Ana and Maribel and Jessica. Margaret belonged here with her father, whom she never would have found without his help, and that was what Rico would choose to remember.

He had never experienced a more tender kiss, one that had so much not-said in it. They held each other, breathless, while the words they didn't say swirled around them.

Rico goes over and over this story as he drives east, as tractor trailer trucks speed past him on the interstate. He feels as if he has survived a flood. He feels both sad and deeply grateful. Somewhere between Grants and Tohajiilee, he realizes that he, too, has a long story to tell when he sits down to dinner at home, where he belongs, surrounded by all his girls.

MARGARET RESTS in Alice Yazzie's iron bed. It is too late to be wide-eyed in the extreme darkness, but Margaret cannot even think of sleep. There is no sound anywhere except, every now and then, the howls of a coyote pack far away. She wonders if there is a message for her in their voices, a story she needs to hear but cannot quite decipher. She knows she would never be here, in Alice Yazzie's home with her long lost father just over the ridge in his, if, back in New York, she had not read in a travel magazine that coyotes run along the river, right in the middle of Albuquerque, and felt compelled to see this with her own eyes. But she realizes, as she muses, that she always imagined a lone coyote when the truth is they often come in packs. She listens more carefully to the coyotes' call.

Did they summon her here to New Mexico, she wonders. Because there are only three possible explanations for why she has come, and that is what Margaret is thinking about as she lies in Alice Yazzie's bed in the cool night—cool enough now for Margaret to unfold the Navajo blanket that Alice herself has woven, and draw it up until it covers her heart. If not the coyotes, she reasons, then her father's blessings, which he learned from Alice and threw into the sky every morning at dawn. Option number three has to do with the nature of randomness—perhaps understanding that everything is random, or perhaps that nothing is. Margaret isn't sure which.

Over and over, she re-experiences the moment when she saw her father's name on the shipping label of the box from Pearl Paint. It knocked her to her knees, and yet, in some small way, she expected it, though not perhaps in that precise moment. She understands now, looking back, that she reserved a little hope that she would see her parents again and buried it deep inside her. When she saw her father's name, she felt yes, finally, and she knew hope had always been there.

He had come over the ridge, blinded in the glare of the sun, until he was almost upon her, and then he had abruptly stopped and whispered, "Regina?" Margaret wonders if he thought he was dying in that moment, and that his great love, dead for thirty years, stood ready to greet him. He had looked so old and beaten, so vulnerable. She remembered a father as big as the world, a father whose arms could sweep her up to the sky.

"I searched for you," he had said into her ear. "I searched and searched for you and I couldn't find you." Remembering that, Margaret begins to think about what she has searched for, and the answer is not much—not love, not money, not fame. Not really her parents, either. But then Margaret remembers her paintings, and she knows she has searched and searched for something there. Perhaps it was belief. Perhaps the will to go on.

She imagines the three years Vincent spent in New York, looking for her. Had they missed each other by seconds? Had he followed a whim and ridden the A-train to the end of the line at Rockaway Beach when, a few blocks away, Margaret was walking Magpie in that same direction? They would never know. And Vincent could not have expected or even hoped, as he approached Alice Yazzie's door, the autumn light dimming and the shadows of the rocks disappearing into darkness, that she was the person who would save him.

Margaret wonders if it is Rico who has saved her.

True, she did not arrive at the doorway of Garcia's Automotive half-dead. She did not appear in his doorway with a hand-drawn map and a story to tell a grandmother filled with sadness. She had just wanted to learn to weld. But now, in Alice's iron bed, she entertains the notion that perhaps there was something beyond metal that she was destined to forge through heat and fire. She wonders if it was something basic: connection.

In her mind, she watches her days with Rico flicker by like an old-fashioned home movie. She can even imagine narrating it: here's the moment where I first saw Rico. He held the torch above his head as he worked, and I saw sparks flying onto the concrete floor of the garage. I could see the heat in him, the way he took one thing and radically changed it into another.

Here is the moment he showed up at my house later that evening. He felt my desire strongly and thought it was for him, the welding lessons just a subterfuge.

And here is how his face froze and then contorted with shame when I set him straight.

On through the images she could go, certain now that each moment, each conversation, each secret they exchanged, and each step they took toward each other, was another scrap welded into a mystery that would both solidify and unravel the instant Vincent appeared over the ridge in the sharp glare of the afternoon sun.

She does not allow herself to linger on their one kiss, on the way her hand so naturally wound itself around his neck and pulled him to her. She will not admit that even now, hours later, she still feels the aftershock of his lips on hers. She knows she will never experience his lips again, but she will, once in a while, perhaps allow herself to recall the current, the way it arced between them, a memory that will last forever.

Forever is a long time, and Margaret feels better contemplating it while on her feet under the night sky, so she slips from Alice's bed. She wears a nightgown that Vincent has found for her in Alice's tiny chest of drawers, and she pulls on her sneakers because her father has warned her against the ants, spiders, and snakes. She opens the door and steps out. She notices a shimmering edge against the big rock by the driveway, a crescent that reiterates the shape of the waxing moon, and she moves toward it.

It is her self-portrait, her arms raised like streaks of dark lightning in the night, and her unblinking eyes warm on Margaret. Each small square of metal, each patch, shimmers like a mystery. Margaret squats down for a better look. She reaches out, her fingers tracing the edges of the rust that ride the metal. It seems to have splintered into a thousand parts, and she raises her head to look at the sky searching for the source of light.

She sees a billion stars, star paths leading everywhere, and it suddenly occurs to her that perhaps each one has a story to tell. Perhaps each person's story gathers force, collects details like particles of dust, and assembles a meaning. She scans the sky all the way to the horizon. Which one is her mother's, she wonders. Which one is Donny's? Which one is Vincent's, and Rico's, and Fernando's, and Thomas Yazzie's?

Which one is hers?

She imagines the stories swirling together, wrapping themselves around each other as they tumble silently to earth.

"Tell me," Margaret whispers into the night. She raises her arms up, like her self-portrait, to receive them.

She listens carefully.